Baptists
at Our
Barbecue

Baptists at Our Barbecue

Robert Farrell Smith

BOOKCRAFT

Salt Lake City, Utah

Bookcraft is a registered trademark of Deseret Book Company.

Visit us at www.deseretbook.com

Library of Congress Cataloging-in-Publication Data

Smith, Robert F., 1970–
    Baptists at our barbeque / Robert Farrell Smith.
        p.   cm.
    ISBN 1-57008-822-5 (pbk.)
    1. Baptists–Fiction. 2. Mormons—Fiction. I. Title.
    PS3569.M537928 B3 2002
    813'.54—dc21   2002001345

Printed in the United States of America   21239-6949
Edwards Brothers Incorporated, Ann Arbor, MI

10   9   8   7   6   5   4   3   2   1

To my

brothers and sisters

to my

father and mother,

whose lives have been

selflessly devoted to their

seven children

and to Krista,

the most worthwhile and gorgeous

person I know

ACKNOWLEDGMENTS

The list of who I would like to thank grows each time I sit down to write it. I find myself wanting to mention everyone from my third-grade teacher who praised my poem about gum to the last kind customer who just read one of my books and found it to be more than a half-rate doorstop. But for the sake of time and paper I hope that it is sufficient to simply say "thank you" to everyone who has ever been kind, supportive, and patient with me. My life is that much better because of each and every one of you.

CHAPTER ONE

THE FINAL STRAW

It's not as if I didn't like Utah; I mean geographically it is one of the most magnificent places on earth. But truth be known there are just too many Mormons—more specifically, too many Mormons trying to set me up with their daughters, cousins, nieces, or friend of a friend of a neighbor of a relative that only lengthy pedigree charts could connect.

In my opinion, there are few things more painful than turning twenty-nine and still being single. The moment that happens, it's as if everyone you know suddenly turns crazy, flying around in a frenzy, trying to help you correct your spiritual fate.

If well-meaning ward members are not actively trying to pair you up with a chosen member of the opposite sex whom they believe to be "just perfect" for you, then they are spreading rumors. The kind of rumors about you not liking women, or . . .

"He's just too picky. There are plenty of available women out there. Take my daughter Heidi for example . . . "

Yes, let's take Heidi for example. I took Heidi out once. Not having any background on her, I agreed to a blind date. Had the gods been merciful I would have been struck by a large cement truck well before the date actually came to pass. Apparently, mercy doesn't apply to dating.

The date went like this: Heidi picked me up, she dropped me off, and my back still doesn't work correctly. The in-between details are inconsequential, except I looked at her sort of funny when I first saw her. But in all fairness, I think most people would find a twenty-five-year-old wearing a bonnet odd.

My twenty-ninth birthday was a joke. I received more cakes than I would care to count. They were all given to me by women in the ward who had daughters who were slipping from the temporary status of unwed to the permanent station of old maid.

"Felicity made it herself—the frosting matches your eyes."

"Thanks," I said, eyeing my third angel food cake frosted with blue icing.

"She's in the car if you would like to talk to her."

"That's all right. Just tell her thanks for me."

"Honestly, Tartan, you would think that a proper thanks would follow the delivery of such a cake."

So I spent the afternoon of my twenty-ninth birthday leaning into the car windows of girls who had made me cakes, thanking them for the trouble, and thinking of ways to get out of this crazy town.

It's not that I didn't like women, no not at all. In fact I would have liked nothing more than to find a wife and settle down, but somehow I fell behind in the dating game. I am one of those sibling-deprived, one-parent-disabled, only-child types. My father, Jake, left my mom a couple of months after I was born. He had some sort of problem with responsibility. So that, and a list of other reasons I was never told, prompted him to leave my mom and me.

But we survived.

My mom changed my name from Jake to Tartan after my father left us. She was particularly fond of the Scottish and of the fabric they wore around their waist. And even though it is a unique name, I'm happy she gave it to me instead of her second choice—"Plaid."

Dad did return once when I was five, but Mom refused to let him see me, and so he left without incident. I received a card from him when I was fourteen. I guess he was trying to patch things up. The five bucks he sent did little for the reconstruction of our once family, and I was mad that he thought me to have such a low payoff price.

I didn't need his money. Mom and I were just fine.

There were sacrifices, however.

I had to get a job the moment I met age approval from the child labor laws. So my adolescent years were spent working much more than dating. In fact I did just about everything more than I dated. Which, according to my bishop, was a shame, seeing how I was such a "strapping lad." Are bishops supposed to say things like that?

I went on a mission late because I needed to earn the money myself. When I finally returned I was twenty-seven and counting. I dated a few nice girls, but never the right one.

I finished school and began working for the forest service. It was what I had always wanted to do. It held the promise of exciting, rugged, and dangerous times in the wild outdoors. But in reality it turned out to be a lot of tree watching and form completion. True, there was that one time when a small sapling fell on a dog and I had to pull it off, and that thrilling day when a campfire broke free from its ring of rocks and ignited a garbage receptacle.

But that was about it in the adventure department.

I did enjoy giving lectures to school kids and working to instill a love for the great outdoors in others. But these opportunities seemed to come my way less and less these days. Provo was flooded with forest rangers who fought constantly for the best positions. I knew that if I were going to go anywhere with my job I would have to move on. I also knew that I wasn't exactly making forward leaps and bounds in my personal and spiritual life here, either.

All these things were brewing in my mind when my mother produced the straw that broke this single's back and made it perfectly clear that change was needed—and now! We were eating corn, still frozen and right from the bag. There was also a lot of grape soda consumed that night.

"Tartan, can I ask you something?" Mom said, suddenly very serious.

"Sure, Mom. What is it?" I asked.

"Well, I'm not sure how to say this," she hedged, "but I think as your mom I should know." Mom put some corn in her mouth and crunched loudly.

I took a swig of soda before responding. "What is it, Mom?"

"The women in my book circle have been talking, and they are sort of saying that you ... Well, that you are ... You know ... "

"What?" I asked.

"Gail says that you are too attractive not to be married."

"What is that supposed to mean?" I questioned.

"I was reading in *People* magazine about a makeup artist who had chosen an alternative lifestyle."

I couldn't believe it! What was Mom saying? My mind instantly began packing my bags and thinking of places I could move to get away from all of this. I wanted a wife, and I didn't want to have to sift through the selection that Provo had to offer anymore. I wanted to be somewhere where twenty-nine was still young and people didn't feel inspired to run my love life for me. I had felt compelled in the past to stay around for Mom, but she had her book circle friends to keep her company. She didn't need me around anymore, and I needed to get out.

"Mom!"

"Well?" she said.

I got up from the table and kissed her on the forehead. I could feel her jaws clicking as she ground her corn. I could also feel my inner compass shifting from north to south as my life slipped from complacent to something well outside my comfort zone. I was going to move.

I took the very next transfer that came through at work.

CHAPTER TWO

LONGFELLOW, U.S.A.

My first thought was that I should have waited for the second transfer. Longfellow was the laziest town I had ever set eyes on. Situated deep in the mountains it sat comfortably isolated from the outside world. The nearest big city was about two hours away, and between here and there was almost nothing. It did have a paved road that started all of two miles before town. There was a bar with a packaged liquor sign that looked like it was installed in the early sixties, a post office, a library, and a grocery store the size of most big-town convenience stores. There were two gas stations, but only one that sold gas. The other one had a large particleboard sign leaning out front that read:

SLUSH SHOP
NO GAS!
SLUSHES AND BAIT ONLY

There was a video store larger than the Baptist church and a small shed with the words "Longfellow Police Department" above the door. Houses were scattered around like loose change in a kitchen utility drawer, and the surrounding area was impressively lush. Trees taller than the ones I was accustomed to stood everywhere, looking stiff, rigid, and slightly majestic. It was as if they were upset to be rooted where they were but still had to perform their duty with some honor. The giant mountains that surrounded the town all wore what looked to be white, snow toupees. Only a couple of the smaller ones had enough self-esteem to sit there bald, their rocky foreheads shining in the afternoon sun.

I couldn't seem to find the road I needed, or the map I had been given, so I pulled up to the police shed to ask for directions. Inside I found a short man with large eyes sitting at a tiny desk completely free of papers. In fact the only thing on top of it was a small red notebook that was lying open and appeared to be filled with doodles. There was a large industrial-size trash can in the corner and a big, square, cork bulletin board on the wall. The bulletin board was crumbling from too many pins having been pushed into it over the years. A large piece of canary yellow paper was the only thing pinned to it now. It said, "When in doubt—Don't!" There was a big, bulky radio in the corner that had two sets of rabbit ears on top and a microphone dangling from its metal belly.

I had to duck as I went through the door. It was obvious there were not many cops who were 6'2" around here. I nodded hello, stepping all the way inside and shutting the door softly behind me.

"Can I help you?" the short man asked, sounding slightly stand-offish.

"I hope so. The name's Tartan Jones."

I paused, hoping that my name might mean something to him. Obviously it didn't.

"Yeah, and?"

"I'm going to be hosting the lookout station up on Flint's Peak."

"Oh, you're Clark Stucki's replacement," he said, finally coming to life. "Too bad about him. Nice guy, just a little too curious I guess. He left so suddenly that none of us got a chance to find out who would replace him. I've been trying to get ahold of your supervisor for days. I just can't stand not knowing; it drives me absolutely batty."

That didn't appear to be too long a drive.

"I'm Bob Evans and I'm the law around here. You got a problem, come to Bob." He stuck a finger in his ear and twisted it violently.

"I've been helping folks for over thirty years and plan to keep doing it for at least another two." Bob pondered what he had just said as he chewed on the end of his thick mustache and looked towards the ceiling.

"Actually I could use some help finding Flint's Peak. I can't seem to find my map," I said.

"No problem," Bob chirped, "let me get you one from my office." He jumped up from his chair and pounced through a back door that appeared to lead outside. I heard a car door shut and then he came back in. "Here you go," he said, handing me a Xeroxed map of the area. "That spot there is Flint's," he pointed. "This X here is us."

"Thanks," I said.

"You're welcome. I hope you like it here."

"I'm sure I will," I said, lying. "Looks like a nice town."

"It is, and you'll do well as long as you ain't a Baptist or a Mormon."

My countenance quivered.

"Why do you say that?" I asked.

"Bad blood between the two."

"Over what?"

"Well, since you're interested . . . "

Had I indicated that?

"Our town was settled by a Mormon named Wally Longfellow. Old Brigham Young himself sent the poor stooge out to settle this place, but crazy Wally never really did too well. He did build a few things, but he eventually drowned while swimming up in the Beaver. Stories say it was a full stomach that killed him—you know, cramps after eating. I, like a lot of other folks, believe it was a couple of his polygamous wives that did him in. They got a little fed up with old Wally and held him under longer than his lungs would allow.

"After he died the town just sort of fell apart. A couple of his wives went back to Utah, a couple stayed here. Then a few years later a fire destroyed just about everything Wally had built up." Bob made a little crackling fire sound for effect. "That's when the trouble began. A Baptist preacher by the name of John Boot stumbled upon this place and took it upon himself to rebuild our town, to breathe life into its wheezing lungs.

"John worked hard, got the numbers up to where there were only ten more Mormons than Baptists; then he made his fatal mistake. He wanted to change the name of the town to Boot instead of Longfellow. Well, even the Baptists didn't like that. Can you blame them? I mean who wants to live in 'Boot'?

"The Mormons started preaching against pride and claiming that John was vain by wanting to name the town after himself." Bob stopped, waiting for me to say something.

"What happened?" I obliged.

"Well, John did get the 'boot,' just not the way he wanted." Bob laughed to himself. "He left town one night with the Baptist custodian. Word is they wed and had two kids.

"To this day the Mormons and the Baptists still can't stand each other. Too many differences in doctrine for them to be compatible. The population of our town is exactly 558. Two hundred and sixty-two Mormons, two hundred and sixty-two Baptists, ten Catholics, eleven Presbyterians, nine Methodists, three atheists, and Fern."

"What religion is she?" I asked innocently.

Bob looked around nervously as if someone could possibly be hiding within the 150 square feet of the police department. "If I were you I would never say that again."

"Say what?" I asked confused.

"Fern is a *he*, not a *she*, and he don't like anybody to say different. A little touchy about the name thing."

"I can see why," I said. "What parents in their right mind would name a boy Fern?"

"Yeah, me, too. I like a good solid name like Bob, or John . . . What did you say your name was?"

"Tartan."

"Or Tartan," Bob said, trying to be kind.

"So what religion is he?" I asked.

"Who?"

"Fern," I replied.

"Fern's got no religion; he's just easily swayed. He owns the bait and slush shop and holds the honor of possessing more Books of Mormon than any other town member. I think every single Mormon has given him at least one. He committed to baptism once. Then

Loni, the Baptist organist, made him a couple of apple pies and a pair of felt trousers, which convinced him that just maybe the Mormons weren't right. The Baptists blew it, though. They threw a swimming party up at Beaver Lake and invited Fern. Well, while Fern was underwater the parson said a prayer and baptized Fern into the faith without Fern knowing. Fern was pretty upset. The Baptists act like Fern is one of theirs now. The Mormons say it ain't so 'cause of Fern not giving his consent. I think right now Fern is leaning toward the Mormons, but that will change with the next home-cooked meal someone puts in front of him.

"Things are kind of calm around here now that Clark's gone. He was the Baptists' most recent accomplishment. About four months back he became one of them and threw off the balance of things, but he's gone now, and I think that's good. 'Course Betty Ann is expecting, but then Sister Reese has a niece coming to stay for a while, so things will still be balanced."

"Bob, do you mind if I ask what religion you are?"

"No, not at all. I'm atheist."

I sort of snickered.

"What's so funny?" Bob asked.

"I don't know, I guess you don't strike me as an atheist."

"Haven't always been. I was born a meat-eating, potato-mashing, religiously red-blooded American, but with all this feuding going on, my stomach is sort of turned off to the idea of religion and all. Heck, I was a Mormon once, then a Baptist. I helped with the Catholics live nativity scene and even donated money to the Presbyterians for their new pews. In the end I discovered that I really can't even begin to understand God, let alone the people he has pulling for him down here, so I just decided to unbelieve in him."

I nodded, as if what he had just said made sense.

Bob paused.

"What religion are you?" he asked.

"Mormon," I said matter-of-factly.

Bob laughed in hopes that I was joking.

"You're not kidding?"

"Nope."

"Any chance of keeping it a secret?"

"Don't think so."

Bob checked his gun as if he might be needing it sometime in the next few minutes.

"I should be going," I said.

Bob pulled out a fresh toothpick and stuck it in his mouth. He appeared to be carefully contemplating the words we had exchanged. "I'd never want to be known as unfriendly, so welcome, despite the fact that you're a Mormon. Just watch yourself, and don't go acting like you were sent here to give the Mormons some sort of advantage. Understand?"

"I have a few Baptist friends," I said in defense of myself.

"Now you have a few Baptist enemies."

I left the police shed more confused than I had been when I had entered it. I had transferred to get away from all the religious complications, and now here I was in the middle of some sort of Jed Clampett feud. What were the Mormons doing here?

I tried to console myself. Surely it couldn't be that bad! Most of the townsfolk were probably unaware of any feud. I mean, Longfellow was not *that* far from a big city, and I was sure people here had too much to do to be concerned about just who was who and what was what, religiously speaking.

I stopped at the working filling station, filled up with ten dollars worth of gas, and washed my windshield while the clerk talked on the phone inside. He hung up as I entered.

"That gonna do it?" he asked.

"And this," I said, picking up a bag of Corn Nuts and setting it on the counter.

"Heard you're Mormon," the attendant said.

"How'd you hear that?" I asked.

"Bob."

I rubbed my temples with my hand and contemplated the life that lay ahead of me. What would it be like living outside a town where the cop's major function was to act as town crier and official gossip?

"What else did Bob tell you?" I asked.

"Said you had a funny name. Tart or something."

"Tartan."

"That's what he said, Tart or something."

"Anything else?"

"Probably, but I had to hang up 'cause you came in. Didn't think it would be right, you know, talking about someone when they're right there in the room with you."

How ethical, I thought.

"What about you . . . Roy," I said, reading the stitched name off the label of his grease-monkey jumpsuit and running my frustrated fingers through my brown hair. "What religion are you?"

"Baptist," he said proudly, "and I'm Willie. Roy's my older brother."

"Well, Willie, is it all right if a Mormon buys gas from a Baptist? Or does that go against one of your rules?"

"Heck, that's all right, business is business. Besides, it would be mighty unchristian of me to refuse you service—it's almost an hour drive to the next station."

"Mighty Christian of you, Willie."

Willie smiled as if God himself had just heaped affirmation upon him.

I paid Willie what I owed him and crossed the road to the Slush Shop to see if Fern might have any idea where and what time the Mormon church services started.

Fern's shop was a haven of junk and things that looked remotely valuable. There was a large cooler in the middle of the shop with the word "Worms" painted in bright red letters on it. Next to it stood a slush machine that looked as old as the man sitting near it. I stuck out my hand in an attempt to shake his hand. He sprang from his rocker with the agility of a young kid and started trying to sell me things.

"I'm Fern."

"I'm—"

"Worms?"

"No, thanks."

"Fish eggs?"

"No, really."

"Cold slush? Both cherry and raspberry are working today."

"Actually—" I tried to say.

"We don't have gas, but if things go well this summer we might start pumping it again. Think we should?"

"Sure, I—"

"Used to have gas, used to be the only station in the city."

"You mean town?" I corrected.

"No, in the whole city. Then old Willie gets himself a little inheritance from his father and decides to open up his own station. *Youth*," Fern said bitterly.

"Willie doesn't serve slushes," I said, pointing out Fern's strong point and trying to calm him down.

"He doesn't, does he? I like you, boy. What did you say your name was?"

"Tartan, Tartan Jones."

"Bob said you had a weird name."

"Bob talked to you, too?"

"Bob talks to everybody. There ain't been no real police business here for years. So Bob spends most of his time taking care of other people's business. Weeded the flower pots in front of the Stop & Shop last week, and did a fine job of it. I think the last real crime we had in this city was when Martha's fool boy Joey stole her pie off her windowsill. It took Bob four hours to track him down, and by then Joey had eaten it. Bob had a hard time making a case out of that one."

"I can imagine."

Fern looked me up and down, stopping at my hair.

"Red?" he asked.

"No, brown," I corrected.

"Looks red."

"Must be the light," I offered.

"Come here," Fern said, leading me behind the counter and out into what used to be a garage but now was some sort of living quarters. By the look of things Fern lived quite humbly. Everything except his giant screen TV looked at least his age or older. He led me to a bookshelf whose shelves were bending under the weight of what looked to be a hundred various copies of the Book of Mormon.

"See these?" he asked.

"I sure do."

"People give them to me all the time," Fern said proudly. "I'm partial to the Mormons," he whispered. "Good people, a little funny at times, but good people. Might even become one myself someday. I was this close," he said indicating his near miss with his wrinkled fingers. "This close to being baptized and then . . . well, Bob already told you all about that."

Bob was an amazing man, and to say that I wasn't beginning to fear him would be a lie. Anyone who could communicate with so many so quickly obviously deserved to be watched.

"Actually, Fern, that's sort of why I stopped by. I was wondering if you might know where the Mormons meet on Sunday."

"Sure do. They meet at President Wingate's house." He walked me back out into his shop and up to the windows so we could see out.

"All right," he said, "you go to where the pavement ends, then drive for about a half-mile more. You'll see a large tarp tied down over a tractor—turn left there, and it's the only house on the right. Church starts at eleven something."

Oh, the accuracy of it all.

"Thanks, Fern."

"Slush?" he asked.

I left Fern's place with a cherry slush and an even bigger concern about the length of time I would last in Longfellow. I decided to stop off at the library to see if they had anything worth reading. It was a small library by big-city standards, but it appeared well-stocked and nicely organized. A large lady offered me assistance, but I declined, feeling confident that I could find what I needed on my own. I brought my few books to the large lady and inquired about getting a library card. She pulled out a small slip of paper, which I then filled out and pushed back to her.

"What is your occupation?" she asked.

"I work with the forest service. I'm going to be hosting Flint's Peak for the next little while."

"Oh, Clark's replacement. Curiosity killed the cat you know."

That was the second reference to Clark's curiosity. I decided to find out more.

"What was Clark curious about?" I asked.

"You don't know?" she questioned.

"I don't," I answered honestly.

"Clark joined up with the Baptists a few months back and right off started bad-mouthing the Mormons like few before him had dared. The Mormons didn't mind much—they had been called filthy names before," she leaned in closer, and lowered her voice to a whisper—"but then Clark started to bring up things about the Mormon temples, asking questions that a decent person just shouldn't have been asking. The Baptists had always been respectful of the things the Mormons do in the temple, but not Clark. He even ordered—through the mail—a book telling all about the Mormon temples. He went around blabbing things and making fun of sacred stuff. The Mormons finally had enough," she raised her voice. "They harassed him until he left. The coward slinked away in the dead of night, and good riddance to him too. Things have been much better without him." She spit a small hair out of her mouth and onto the counter.

I couldn't believe I was about to ask her this, but it seemed so normal to be interested in each person's religion here in this town. So, as if it were actually my business, I asked, "Are you Mormon?"

"Yes, I am. I've got one of the strongest testimonies around," she said, as if boasting about her garden or stamp collection.

"I'm sure you do," I responded.

"Longwinded is a funny little town," she said. "Since the main highway was put in we don't get many people passing through, except of course in the summertime. City folk just love to come up here and steal our fish and litter our rich mountain tapestry. Anyhow, as I was saying," she continued, "there's been two major influxes into our town." She held up one finger. "One was the faithful Mormons." She held up another. "And two was the Baptists; hard to stay strong when those Baptists run around confusing everyone."

In my opinion it didn't seem like any citizen in this town needed any help becoming confused. I'd never met a more secluded, out-of-touch bunch. And major influxes? There could be no major influx in a town of 558. This was some sort of Shangri-la gone horribly wrong. Provo seemed like a sophisticated, avant-garde metropolis next to this place.

The librarian handed me my temporary card.

"Welcome to Longwinded, Mr. Jones," she said, once again refer-ring to Longfellow as Longwinded.

"The name of the town is Long*fellow* isn't it?" I asked.

"On the record it is," she said.

"But . . . " I coaxed.

"But, years ago Buddy Haymosses made his boy Ricky read the complete works of Henry Longfellow. Ricky didn't much like read-ing in the first place, and he found Longfellow to be particularly bor-ing. So out of protest he spray painted "winded" between Long and Fellow on the sign coming into town. No one really disagreed with his opinion, so it sort of stuck. Even I, as one of the staunchest opponents of vandalism, had to chuckle at the deed. None of the locals refer to this place as Longfellow anymore. We're Longwinded, through and through."

I'd say.

I gathered up my books and turned to walk away.

"Wait a minute, Mr. Jones . . . you didn't say what religion you were."

"Mormon," I grimaced.

"That's what I had heard. I guess it's 'Brother' then."

Oh, Brother.

"I guess so," I said.

"Well, I'm Sister Wingate. I run the public library during the week and the church library on Sunday. I also teach homemaking to those sisters that can't get out anymore."

"Huh." I could think of nothing else to say.

"See you Sunday?" she asked.

"I should be there," I said, remaining as uncommitted as possible.

"Oh, and, Brother, don't be afraid to let others know your reli-gion. Wear it like a proud badge," she added.

I could feel the pin pricking me even as we spoke.

I stopped at the Stop & Shop convenience store and picked up a few groceries. The woman working there watched me like a hawk and then started in on how they now carried two brands of tooth-paste.

I got into my truck and drove as fast as I could to the place where I'd be living until I could find a way out of here. Longwinded was supposed to be an answer. Instead it was turning out to be a whole new set of problems. How stupid I had been to think that geography was my problem. Mountains and valleys I could move with faith, but these people?

I had serious doubts.

CHAPTER THREE

CHARITY SUFFERETH LONG

Charity tossed the phone down and fell back limply into the small, pink chair she had been given when she was only twelve. Giant sobs rocked her as if she were riding one of the quarter rides out in front of the local K-mart. The reality of what Howard had just done was settling in fast.

Words she had never even thought before filled her mind. She kept them inside her head, letting them make her feel even worse.

It wasn't like her to cry, but it was a full day later before her tears finally dried out.

CHAPTER FOUR

A PLACE TO HANG MY . . .

Had my living accommodations been anything less wonderful I might have turned around and headed back right then, but the station up on Flint's was even better than I had hoped. Apparently some money had been sunk into the place, and for that I was grateful. The equipment was new and not as bulky as the stuff we had at the Provo station, and my living quarters were comfortable and clean. All in all it was a surpassingly nice setup for such an unimportant outpost.

The cabin itself sat on a knoll on the top of Flint's Peak, and the view was one even God must have gawked at. Short trees cloaked the cabin and made it almost invisible from two sides. Long grass and gravel lay loosely on the other two. Mount Taylor sat next to Flint's to the east, its massive height and bulk too great for the eyes to take in with a single glance.

I put my belongings away and cooked up a dinner of grilled cheese sandwiches and frozen peas. I ate my food out on the large wood deck, where the mountain air made the cheap cheese taste exotic and flavored the peas in the most wonderful of ways.

After dinner I called Mom and told her how I was situated. She seemed to be all right with my being gone. I could hear one of her friends screaming something like, "Check this one out," in the background. I skipped any sort of prayer that night, vowing to pray longer the following day.

≈   ≈   ≈   ≈   ≈

My spirits were in decent shape the next morning. The sun warmed the air up to a sensible degree, and the clouds thinned themselves out, allowing the blue sky some much needed elbow room.

The top of Flint's Peak wasn't much larger than a football field, and at each edge it dropped down and spilled into the surrounding forest. It was the perfect place to watch for fire and to keep an eye on all things. The only real blemish was the knowledge that somewhere down below sat Longwinded. God had the most complicated sense of humor. Here nature had created a spot like few others in this world, and almost as if to keep the earth humble he allowed Longwinded to find footing in its soil.

I discovered a small trail at the back of the peak that appeared to wind deep into the forest. I was contemplating hiking it when I heard a vehicle coming up the road below. I returned to my station just in time to see a Jeep pull up. It was a beat-up old thing, lime green, with the Forest Service emblem painted on the door. A couple of red lights poked up out of the roof and a large winch sat awkwardly on the front bumper.

A man who looked to be in his late forties climbed out and headed my way.

"Tartan?"

"Yes," I answered.

"I'm Fred from up on Mt. Taylor. Just came down to see if you made it all right. Looks like you did," he said, sizing me up.

"I'm here," I said enthusiastically. Fred wasn't a particularly attractive man. In fact, at first glance you could see why he might have chosen a life hidden among the trees. His forehead was enormous, despite the fact that he had a rather full head of hair, and his legs came up to his neck, leaving nature to grant him one of the smallest bodies I had ever seen. Gangly was far too mild a description. No, Fred had passed gangly, limbs ago.

Fred explained a few things I already knew how to do, went over what my duties would be, and then commented negatively on the fact that I was a Mormon (Bob had told him). Apparently Fred couldn't see any real purpose for religion. His God was the trees and lakes my God had created.

Fred gave me a list of appointments and meetings I would be attending, forced out a "Glad you are here," and then left.

I chastised myself for not telling him exactly how I felt. Flint's was fine, but I couldn't just hang out on my knoll like some sort of discontented hermit. I needed to meet people. I needed to mix. How was this possible in a place like Longwinded? I would never find a girl here.

I would never be happy here.

I would never get out of here.

I could feel it.

Like the cold hand of your first grade teacher pulling you by the ear, I was being dragged down to the principal's office where an old man with no hair and bad breath would rule that because of my misdeeds I would be sentenced to sit in the corner of Longwinded until hell froze over. Me, with my pointed dunce hat, my back turned to a town that prided itself on having a Stop & Shop that now sold two different brands of toothpaste.

I decided that before I threw in the towel I would check out church this Sunday. I felt confident the ward here would be full of Longwinded irregulars, but in the context of a ward, odd just might come across as normal. And certainly God wouldn't leave me completely alone. There would have to be one reasonably sane person, and just maybe that person could be a girl, and an attractive single one at that.

I prayed long and hard that day. I'm sure world peace and global harmony were among my petitions, but overwhelmingly my pleas were, "Please don't let me turn thirty here!" I added a small clause that provided for me staying past thirty as long as I was married. There was an even smaller clause that asked for her to be a person of intellect and beauty. I felt that I was really giving God a good chance to help me be strong.

I wouldn't start doubting him until after Sunday.

CHAPTER FIVE

CHARITY ENVIETH NOT

Charity closed her book, tired of having to read each line twice just to understand it. Normally a book like the one she was reading would be devoured within a couple of hours, but tonight her mind was too busy sorting out feelings to be able to think clearly.

She was particularly mad about what one of her friends had asked earlier in the day.

"Are you jealous of Annie?"

Jealous of Annie?

Annie could have Howard for all Charity cared. As sad as his choice had made her, she could think of nothing less appealing than getting Howard back.

Charity picked her book up again, read two more pages, and then went to bed.

CHAPTER SIX

MARTIN

The next morning I spent some time personalizing my place and then calling some friends in Provo to fill them in on my life. I tried to make them envious by describing Longwinded as a quaint mountain wonderland. It wasn't easy to do. Later that afternoon I decided to check out the path I had seen the day before.

After a short dip and a steep climb, the path leveled out and became so overgrown that you almost couldn't see it any longer. I followed the trail until I came to an old hut that looked abandoned; like Goldilocks, my curiosity got the best of me. After knocking, I pushed open the squeaky wood door to find a room about the size of most garages. There was a worn leather couch against the far wall and a huge iron stove in the center of the room. It was clear from the pictures on the wall and the objects scattered around that someone did live here. I backed quickly out of the room and into the open air of the forest. A voice startled me.

"You didn't take anything, did you?" it questioned.

I turned to find a man in his early thirties carrying an armload of wood. His face was home to a thin beard that even if grown out for years wouldn't amount to much more than heavy peach fuzz. His clothes looked clean and he spoke with no drawl or bumpkin slur.

I tried to apologize for trespassing. "I wasn't sure if anyone lived here. Sorry about walking in."

"No big deal. Not much to steal in there."

"Can I help?" I asked, nodding at the logs in his arms.

He handed them to me and then led me around the cabin to an area where other logs were already stacked. He took the logs from me one by one and stacked them neatly upon the already established pile.

"Do you live alone here?" I asked.

"Yep, all alone."

"Been here long?"

He paused and thought for a moment. "Let's see," he said to himself. "My ex-wife, Kim, left me eighteen months, two weeks, and four days ago. Took me around five weeks to move out here, so . . . " he looked straight at me, "I guess I've been here about a year and a half." He pulled out a linen handkerchief and wiped his beard and brow. "You Clark's replacement?" he asked.

"I am," I said sticking out my hand. "My name's Tartan Jones."

"I'm Martin."

Martin shook my hand as if he were accustomed to shaking hands. He then invited me in to sit for a while and sample some sweet sap pie he had made earlier in the day. I wanted to decline but felt compelled to go in and get to know my neighbor better.

I sat on the leather couch and watched him cut up a piece of the stickiest looking pie I had ever seen. He handed me my slice and then started in on his. I prodded mine a bit, and then, like I was running and jumping into a frozen lake, I dove in.

Let me make this perfectly clear.

NEVER IN MY LIFE HAD I TASTED ANYTHING SO SWEET!

I could feel new cavities forming and old cavities opening as the sugary substance shellacked my teeth and coated my mouth. I was afraid to swallow for fear that what was in my mouth wouldn't make it down my throat.

Martin looked at me and smiled. I was scared that the stuff was going to seal my mouth shut. I did my best charade of a person drinking water, hoping that he would get me a glass.

"Water?" he asked.

I violently nodded yes.

"I don't have running water, but I do have a canteen full of . . . ."

I frantically waved my hands, indicating that I didn't care and would he please just hurry.

Martin picked up his canteen and slowly undid the top. He then put his mouth over the opening and drank deeply.

Gulp.

Gulp.

Ahhhh!

He removed the canteen from his sticky mouth and used the sleeve of his shirt to wipe his lips. He then took the end of his shirt and tried to wipe off the wreckage his mouth had left behind.

"Good as new," he said, handing it over to me.

Choices.

I could breathe out of my nose until I managed to make it home, or I could pretend that I hadn't seen what I saw and just take a drink. But I didn't even know this man. He could have some debilitating disease that required you to live away from society so there would be no way that others could catch it. A disease transferred only through the grooves of a canteen nozzle. Of course no disease could be as life threatening as me suffocating to death in the next two minutes.

I grabbed the canteen and drank deeply. I could feel the sap running down my throat and coating my stomach like some sort of industrial-strength Pepto-Bismol. After three or four big gulps I realized that the water didn't taste right and my throat was beginning to burn.

"Your water tastes rotten," I said, handing the canteen back to Martin.

"It isn't water," Martin explained. "It's vodka."

My virgin stomach trembled.

"Have another bite," Martin said, referring to the piece of pie I was neglecting on my plate.

"Do you have any water?" I asked weakly.

"Sorry," Martin said. "One day a week I fill my canteen up with liquor just to make things interesting for myself.

Things were about to get interesting.

I had a weak stomach. My whole life I had been plagued by it. I remember seeing the movie *Bambi* as a child. While all my friends cried when Bambi's mom was shot, I was throwing up Whoppers and Raisinets.

I had a weak stomach and I was about due. This whole Longwinded thing had given me enough stress to permanently turn my stomach inside out. And now I had just poured about a gallon of vodka on top of it all.

My stomach rumbled.

I took a couple more bites of pie. I was hoping to seal off my throat and prevent what nature was telling me was now inevitable.

"Are you all right?" Martin asked. "You don't look too hot."

Poor Martin. He was struggling to get over a woman and turning himself into a hermit by living miles away from civilization. His home was older than both of our lifetimes combined. No roads, no electricity, and no running water. Sure he had fire, but even that was dated. Poor lonely Martin.

And here I was, his first visitor in probably months, about to insult both his cooking and his hospitality with an undignified display of intestinal weakness. I jumped to my feet in hopes of getting outside before it happened. No such luck.

I threw up all over his couch.

We both just stood there staring at the mess for a few moments.

"Sorry," I said, embarrassed, but feeling much better.

"Wish I had a dog," was Martin's only reply.

Martin and I cleaned up the couch and spent the rest of the afternoon talking about women, the evils of liquor, and the value of a good dog.

I liked my closest neighbor. I'm not sure exactly how he felt about me.

CHAPTER SEVEN

CHARITY IS NOT PUFFED UP

Charity looked out over the yard and toward the wide setting sun. She looked around the porch she was sitting on and wondered how things could appear so normal when everything had changed. Her discouraged thoughts were disrupted by the whine of the screen door as her mother stepped out onto the porch.

"Dinner's ready," her mother said.

"I'm not really hungry," Charity smiled.

In light of what had happened, eating seemed like such a chore.

"You have to eat, Charity," her mother insisted.

"Maybe later."

Charity's mother stepped back inside, leaving Charity to herself.

The sun had long since disappeared when Charity finally stood up and called it a night. By then, she had resolved some things, and her mood had brightened a bit.

In her room, she looked closely in the mirror. She pulled her belt tight and turned sideways to study her reflection. She had lost three pounds since Howard had changed his mind. Her long blond hair looked a little limp, but her teeth looked whiter than ever. Never one to brag, she had to admit to herself that Howard had lost something better than he deserved. Life would go on.

CHAPTER EIGHT

THE BEAVER, SOME BEAGLES, AND A BOTHER

Thursday after I gave a brief presentation to some school kids in a neighboring town, I drove up to Beaver Lake. It was larger than it appeared on the map and probably the most beautiful lake I had ever seen. Mountains stood as if holding hands in a circle around it. The water was crystal clear and filled you with the desire to run and jump in. The lake reminded me of all the positive reasons why I worked for the Forest Service. It made me a more complete person just to look at it.

After checking out the lake and helping some campers locate their spot, I headed into town to find Martin a dog. He seemed so lonely up in that cabin by himself. I was hoping a dog might make his life a little better.

Sherry at the Stop & Shop informed me that while Longwinded had no animal shelter (stray animals were usually hunted down and shot by the Smith boys), Loni Butler's beagle was frequently pregnant. I got directions to Loni's house and drove over to see her, hopeful that she had pups for sale.

It was my lucky day. Loni had two beagle and mutt puppies that she was just itching to give away. Loni turned out to be the same Loni whom Bob had told me played the organ for the Baptists. The fact that I was a Mormon didn't stop her from giving me the dogs. She was so anxious for two less mouths to feed that I could have been a "New Ager" and still received the pups.

So far, Loni was the most attractive person I had met in the area. She was a little bit older than I, addicted to daytime talk shows, and had previously been married to a man she described as "vulgar." I didn't have to guess any of this because she was incredibly forthcoming about her life. So any mystery that might have surrounded her was gone thanks to her knack for telling strangers everything.

I put both dogs in the cab of my truck and got in.

"Thanks for the dogs," I said, trying to pull away.

"No problem, glad to have them off my hands. My ex-husband, Troy, hated dogs, but me, I love them. He would go into some sort of sneezing fit every time he got near one. Almost sent him to the hospital once. Troy hates the hospital—bad prostate. The thing would swell up to the size of a cantaloupe whenever he sat for more than a couple of hours. He wasn't a bad man, just had a tough time staying away from the liquor. He was always real sorry in the morning."

"I'm sure he was," I said quickly before she started back up again. "See you around."

"O.K. If you ever need more dogs just let me know. Regina, my female beagle, has got a cyst on her ovary so she might not have too many more litters. Of course she had all that bleeding a couple of litters ago, but then there was only some light mucus with this last batch."

"Bye," I said, pressing hard on the gas.

Loni turned and walked back inside. Any attraction I might have felt for her was gone the moment she said *mucus.*

Sherry at the Stop & Shop helped me choose between the three types of dog food they had. The choice was one I could have made on my own, but she seemed so excited to have something to do.

The Stop & Shop was a micro Wal-Mart minus the low prices and large selection. Sherry, the owner, did have a little bit of everything. There were even a couple of blouses for women and a nice selection of jeans if your size fell somewhere between 40 and 52. The ten pounds of dog food I bought cost about the same as a large brick of gold. No competition drove Sherry's prices sky high. I left the Stop & Shop and decided to check out the town bar. It was a decision that I made with little or no thought. I wasn't going to get any liquor or start swapping filthy stories, I was just interested in seeing everything Longwinded had to offer. I left both dogs in the truck and walked in.

A fat man with a tiny head stood behind the counter and greeted me.

There was one other person in there, and he was playing pool at a pool table that looked at least two hundred years old. It leaned to one side and was so worn in places on the surface that the balls rolled down worn felt tracks directly into the pockets. The walls were covered with neon beer signs and paneling as dark as tar. I sat down at the bar and ordered a Sprite.

"You the new Mormon?" the bartender asked.

"I think so."

"I'm Scott," he said, wiping off his hands with the towel tucked into his apron and shaking my hand.

"Tartan."

"We serve food here as well," he informed me as I drank my drink.

I picked up the card-sized menu and read my options. All six items on the menu revolved around eggs. It was obvious that Scott kept chickens out back.

I sipped my drink and looked over at the pool player. He made a particularly poor shot and swore after he missed it. I nodded at him when he glanced over my way.

"What are you staring at?" he asked rudely.

"Just looking around."

"Well I don't like no pretty Mormon watching over my shoulder."

"Thanks," I said, referring to his calling me pretty.

He threw his pool cue down against the table and it flipped up and hit him in the head. Scott started laughing first.

The pool player picked up a pool ball and threw it in our direction. It missed both of us and bounced off one of the bar stools.

"Take it easy, Rich," Scott said, suddenly sober.

This Rich guy picked up another ball and threw it. Scott caught it. Rich picked up two more, and threw one with each hand, throwing like a girl with his left. One almost hit me this time; the other one broke a glass from off the bar. I ducked behind a nearby table and pulled a chair in front of my face.

"Mormon, Mormon, Mormon," Rich yelled, apparently unaware of any really clever names to call me.

"Cut it out, Rich!" Scott demanded.

I picked up my chair and ran towards Rich. He was too slow to grab any more balls, and with my chair I easily pushed him up against the wall.

"Sissy boy," he said, as I twisted his arm behind his back and pushed him out of the bar.

"Hey!" he screamed. "I thought Mormons were supposed to be nice."

"We are, normally," I answered.

"You ain't supposed to be in a bar, anyhow," he argued. "Mormons only drink water."

I threw Rich down just outside of the bar. He landed on his belly, face in the grass.

"I owe you," he said, turning over and pointing his dirty hand at me. "My father hated Mormons, my grandfather hated Mormons, and I hate Mormons."

What a fine legacy, I thought.

Scott pulled the door shut as I walked back in and sat down. He then got out a dustpan and swept up the broken glass as I finished my drink.

I thanked Scott for the drink and then stepped out into the early afternoon. Rich was sitting in his beat-up truck guzzling a beer and waiting for me to come out. I smiled in his direction and then walked toward my vehicle. Rich flashed his headlights at me as if he were making some sort of threat. I knew someone like Rich would never come out of the safety of his truck to actually face me. I was bigger than he, stronger, and even though I had no proof of it at the time, I felt pretty confident I was smarter.

Rich rolled down his window and started calling me names.

"Stupid Mormon water drinker!" he yelled.

There was my proof. I knew now that I was smarter, too.

"Dumb Joseph Smith lover!"

I raised my head high and started walking toward him.

Rich quickly started to roll up his window. His arm was flying like crazy as he pumped that sheet of glass into the up position. I had called his bluff—exactly what he hadn't wanted. With his window closed Rich hung his head and tried to look as though he were sleeping.

I was a lot smarter.

I turned and walked away from him. I could hear Rich now, telling his friends about how he faked me out by acting like he was asleep. I didn't care, and more importantly I didn't want to do anything that would rip this town even further apart.

I was reaching for my truck door when something hit me in the back of the head. I turned around just as Rich's empty beer can rattled to a stop against the asphalt. I had been assaulted by an empty container of Bud.

This was war.

Before I could join the battle, however, Bob pulled up behind Rich's truck. The lights on Bob's patrol car were blinking wildly, and he stepped out of his car with such an exaggerated air of authority that I almost laughed.

"I'll take care of this, Tartan," Bob said, holding his hand up to signal me to stop.

Bob pulled out his ticket book and riffled through it, flipping to the right page.

"We have laws against littering," he said sternly to Rich.

Rich slumped down in his seat.

"I'll tell you what, though, if you promise to stop throwing your beer cans around, I'll write you up for loitering instead. The fine's less." Bob started to scratch away in his book.

Good old Bob. I would come to find out that he didn't ever have the heart to give people the punishment they truly deserved. Heck, he probably knew that Rich had been out of work for a while and couldn't afford too many monetary surprises such as tickets. So, as usual, he cut him some slack and ticketed him for a cheaper infraction of the law. I heard from Fred later that it was the same with everyone else. No one in Longwinded ever got a ticket for the crime they had actually committed. Bob was just too soft.

"Thanks, Bob," I said, waving at him and getting into my truck. The two dogs wagged their tails, happy I had returned.

"No problem," Bob said.

I watched Bob pull out a box of freezer strength Ziplock bags from his patrol car. He ripped out a single bag and stretched it open. He then picked up the discarded beer can and dropped it in the bag.

Bob sealed the bag and then started to wave it in Rich's face. "See this? See this?! This is Longwinded's greatest foe—trash."

How true, I thought cynically

As I pulled away I could hear Rich trying to tell Bob about how Mormons, not trash, were Longwinded's greatest foe. I had made an enemy in Longwinded. And Rich Paddlefin was not one to forgive and forget. He had more of a tendency to vaguely remember and attempt to repay.

≁   ≁   ≁   ≁   ≁

Martin loved the dog. He named him Rex, after some heroic grandfather of his. I named mine Albert, confident that there had to be some heroic Alberts out there somewhere.

Later that night as I was lying in bed I got a call over my radio from Rich.

"This is Forty-nine, over," I answered.

"You stinking Mormon," a male voice slurred at the other end.

"Is that you, Rich?" I asked.

He seemed thrown off by my question. I could almost hear him trying to think something up.

"Maybe," he said, confused.

"Rich, go to bed," I said authoritatively.

"Mormons are deceived," I heard him say as I clicked off.

Rich made me uneasy for some reason—he seemed just dumb enough to worry about. Who knows what a person with his intellect was capable of by virtue of never thinking a thing through first.

I crawled into bed, thinking back fondly of Provo and the people I knew there. The closest thing to Rich we had there was Mr. Scarp. He was a neighbor who lived a couple of houses down who was convinced that all Mormons had at least three hidden wives. His theory was that we Mormons used food storage as a front for building big pantries in which to keep our secret wives. I almost missed Mr. Scarp.

I rolled over, letting sleep cloud my mind and lift me above the mentally inbred shackles of my new home.

CHAPTER NINE

CHARITY DOTH NOT BEHAVE HERSELF

There wasn't much time. Charity moved as quickly as she could. Howard would be here any second now and for what she had in mind, timing was everything. She threw the silver framed pictures and countless mementos into the large box. If Howard wanted his things back she would give him everything. Charity tore through the closet, picking out shirts that he had let her borrow, or given her, at some point past and threw them in. This felt right. She dug through her CDs, pulling out his as well as those with anything that had any memory or song attached to him. She found letters he had sent and cards he had given. Charity stopped for a second to let the emotions of the past wash over her. She hated the feeling. She rummaged wildly through her drawers, spotting the bracelet Howard had given her on her last birthday. She took great pleasure in tossing it into the mix. The box was now piled high with tokens and trinkets of a once great love. Charity stared at it for a moment, allowing the thoughts in her head to push her further. The box lacked something.

Charity ran to the bathroom and brought back two huge bottles of shampoo and a full tube of toothpaste. She took great care in emptying their contents over everything. She then stared at the mess. Something was still lacking. A car door slammed outside and she knew that Howard had arrived. She suddenly realized what was missing. She pulled her engagement ring out from her desk and flung it into the goo-filled box. Perfect. She then picked up the entire thing and walked to her bedroom window. With the second story window open she called out Howard's name and saw him look up and wander over.

He called up toward her, "Charity, I hope you won't make—"

Howard never finished his sentence—unless, you consider screaming a proper way of signing off.

Charity's aim had been true.

It was the last time she saw Howard for quite some time.

CHAPTER TEN

"WELCOME, WELCOME, SABBATH MORNING"

I put on the only nice shirt I owned and wrapped a tie around my neck. I attempted to wipe off my shoes, to give them the appearance of being clean. My pants were now highwaters thanks to washing them in water that had been a tad too hot. For some reason I imagined that floods might make me fit in a little better at church.

Fern's directions were adequate, and I found the house the Mormons held church in with no problem. It was a nice, large log home, most likely one of those premade houses that arrived like a giant set of Lincoln Logs, requiring only that you stack them correctly. They had been stacked beautifully. Small flower gardens dotted the entrance, and a brass sign that read "God's Bungalow" hung above the huge front door.

For some reason, people were coming out of the large log home and getting back into their cars.

People looked at me funny as I jumped out of my truck and walked up to the door. I stopped a young mother who was holding two children.

"Is church over?" I asked.

"You could say that. It's been canceled."

"Canceled?" I asked, confused.

"President Wingate wants nothing to do with the Church anymore. He's finally had his fill." She said this as if it were something everyone had expected.

"What?" I asked, even though I understood every word she had said.

"We'll have to hold church somewhere else."

The young mother took her two kids and hiked off to her dusty station wagon. I stood there in the doorway unsure of what to do next.

"You best be going," a lady's voice told me.

I turned to find the librarian, Sister Wingate.

"Sister Wingate."

"Maybe not for long," she said coldly.

"You're the branch president's wife?" I asked.

"*Former* branch president."

"I had no idea," I said. "You didn't tell me that your husband was—"

"Unlike so many these days," she said, cutting me off, "I have enough spiritual modesty to not run around bragging about my husband's position."

Spiritual modesty?

"No, I—" I started to say.

"Mister Jones, I am in no mood to stand around talking to you or any of the hypocritical, so-called Saints in this town. So if you could please just leave us alone."

"Well, where should I go?" I asked. "Will they be holding church someplace else?"

"No structure big enough. Now be on your way," she said, shooing me as if I were a stray dog with mange.

"Sister Wingate," I reasoned.

"Mister Jones," she said with an air of finality.

I turned to walk away.

"Books are due back at the library a week from Monday," she added.

"Excuse me?" I said.

"Business, Mr. Jones, business." She then slammed the door on any further conversation.

I stood by my truck for a few minutes trying to sort things out. All the cars that had been here earlier were now gone, and I stood alone beside the gravel road.

"This stinks," I said aloud.

A small car turned onto the road and approached me fast. It slowed down and stopped next to me. A young man about my age with freckled skin and thinning hair rolled down the window.

"Who are you?" he asked.

"Tartan Jones."

"The forest ranger?"

"That's me."

"Where is everybody, Mr. Tartan Jones?"

"They all took off. I guess President Wingate threw them out."

"The old boy finally did it," he said with a slight smile. "Been threatening to, you know. When they made him branch president everyone knew that it was just because he had a house big enough to hold us. Heck, President Wingate said no at first. Don't know why he finally accepted. Lot of rumors as to the reason."

"I can imagine."

"Not a bad guy, just sort of confused. Not a bad president either, just too proud to conform."

"Conform to what?" I asked.

"We Mormons haven't sung hymns in our meetings for years, since singing is sort of a Baptist thing."

"No hymns?" I asked.

"Not a one. Sister Moore was caught humming 'Love One Another' a few months back, and the Booth family almost lynched her. Wasn't pretty."

"Tough branch."

"We've gotten better. In fact a couple of weeks ago Church head-quarters sent a letter calling us to repentance and asking us to please start singing hymns again. So we voted on it. I don't know if we all had soft hearts that day or if it was our anticipation of the potluck lunch after church. Either way we voted for hymns again. President Wingate wasn't happy about our decision.

"But we stuck with it, realizing just how stupid we had been and looking forward to singing once again. 'Course we didn't have any hymn books—burned them all at the Pinewood Derby a few years back. So Sister Lynn made photocopies of 'I Heard the Bells on Christmas Day.' She found a copy of it in the public library in the complete works of Longfellow. So we all had copies of that one song, the original version with all seven stanzas. We didn't care, it just felt so great to sing again. We've sung that song twice each meeting for the last couple of weeks. We tried to come up with some other songs, but then people would argue over the words or the tune. So we stuck to 'I Heard the Bells.' No one minded except President Wingate. Blew up a week ago at the beginning of our meeting. Swore that if he ever heard that song again he would leave the Church. Problem was that at the end of the meeting we had nothing else to sing. So . . . "

"He's leaving the Church because of a song?"

"Because of a song sung over and over. He said he was done, but none of us believed him."

"What will happen?"

"I'm sure Sister Lynn will know what to do. Everyone's probably gone over there."

✑   ✑   ✑   ✑   ✑

I followed the tiny car to a small stucco home that was about five miles out of town. There were twelve or thirteen cars parked outside and people spilling out of the windows and doors of the house.

I parked and strode up to the door, somewhat uncertain of what to do. The guy with the freckles cut me off before I got to the house.

"Did I tell you I was Chad?"

"No."

"Well, I'm Chad."

"And whose house is this?"

"Sister Lynn's. She's great."

I walked into the house and all eyes focused on me. I adjusted my tie out of nervousness and waved a shy "Hi." A tall lady with really big hair approached me. She was in her late forties and looked to me like a "Sister Lynn."

"You must be the tiebreaker."

"I think I am."

"Well, normally we Mormons aren't so disheveled. But we've had a little situation today."

"I heard."

Attention was quickly diverted from me.

"What do we do?" an unknown voice spoke up. "We've got nowhere to go."

Sister Lynn turned from me and held up her hands. "Think of the pioneers," she offered.

There was a small pause while everyone conjured up their idea of pioneers in their heads.

"Let's call Salt Lake," someone offered.

"Yeah, they've been promising us a building for years, and I say this is the perfect time to finally get it," someone suggested.

"What if they won't?" asked the young mother I had talked to earlier.

"Do you think President Wingate might change his mind?" I asked.

They all stared at me as if I were crazy.

"Call Salt Lake," someone yelled.

Sister Lynn picked up her portable phone and set it in the lap of a rather old gentleman who had up to this point remained silent.

"Who's he?" I whispered to Chad.

"That's Heber. He used to be quite chummy with the prophet. Still has some pull with the Church leaders."

Heber looked old enough to have personally known every latter-day prophet since Joseph Smith. He had an oxygen tank by his side and was breathing shallowly through the plastic tubes that connected him to it.

"Heber, will you?" Sister Lynn asked.

Heber's head shook and then sort of fell to the side—I guess it was a yes.

Sister Lynn wheeled him into her bedroom and shut the door behind him. I suppose he needed some privacy. Everyone huddled into small cliques to discuss what they thought the outcome would be. Then we all gathered and compared ideas. I tried to be as involved as possible but felt for some reason that this wasn't really my fight. I mean, I was the new kid in the area. I was also occupied with checking out every person there.

The members were surprisingly normal looking. There were a lot more women then men in attendance, I figured the branch was home to a lot of inactive husbands. An older lady kept looking at me and eventually slid up behind me. She tugged on my sleeve to get my attention. I leaned closer to hear her whisper.

"Is it true that you're single?"

"Guilty," I said nervously.

"Well I'm Sister Christianson, and even though I'm certain fate would throw you two together sooner or later, I feel a need to help it along. See my daughter over there, blue dress, red hair?" she asked pointing.

Heaven help me.

"That's Wendy. Pretty as a jewel," she said reflectively. "Not many people to date here in Longwinded; in fact Wendy has only been out two times. She's eighteen, but could easily pass for twenty wouldn't you say?"

I nodded.

"And this small town has helped her keep her virtue intact. Priceless bonus, wouldn't you agree?"

I started looking around the room for a way out.

"Wouldn't you agree?" she asked again.

"Oh, yes. Too bad I'm so old," I said. "I'm sure she'll make someone a good wife."

"How old are you?"

"Twenty-nine."

"That's nothing. Her great grandfather was sixty-two when he married a seventeen-year-old." She said as if this settled things.

"I think it would be best—" I started to say. Before I could finish my sentence, Sister Lynn started calling everyone together for a prayer.

Chad offered a nice prayer asking for a new building and listing all the many sacrifices they had made on their journey to get one. When the prayer was finished, Heber was still in the other room on the phone—things looked good.

I had pulled away from Sister Christianson and was now trying very hard to keep us separated by at least half the room. Most of the members avoided making eye contact with me. But I discovered that as soon as I introduced myself to them, they would warm up and start chattering away. They were nice people—peculiar, just like all other Mormons, but still characteristically nice. I found out that the lady with the two kids was Sister Phoebe North. Her husband drove truck and was gone a majority of the time. Her twins, Daniel and Zeke, were the limpest looking things I had ever seen. They lay on her like wilted lettuce.

I walked around Sister Lynn's house by myself, looking at all the pictures on the wall. There was a great sense of anticipation in the air. Heber had been on the phone for a long time now. Every minute longer was like another confirmation of the building we all constructed in our minds. A couple of people had even drawn pictures of what they envisioned the new building was going to look like. Their renditions were now being passed around.

I was looking at a photograph of Sister Lynn on a horse, when she came up behind me.

"You know when Bob first told me Clark's replacement was a Mormon I almost flipped," she said. "It will be nice to be in the majority again. Although I must say that I personally hold no grudges against the Baptists here. What an odd town, don't you think?"

"It has its eccentricities."

"Well, Tartan, I hope you stay around for a while. Longwinded could use more people like you."

I liked Sister Lynn. She seemed so normal.

"Heber's been in there a long time," she commented.

I nodded in agreement.

An hour later Heber was still on the phone, and the natives were restless. Sister Lynn for the first time began to worry about her phone bill.

"Maybe we should have waited until a cheaper rate time," she said.

The two Young Women in the branch made some cookies in Sister Lynn's kitchen and then forgot to turn off the oven. A young kid by the name of Lehi attempted to climb into it while playing hide-and-seek. Sister North came running into the living room screaming, "Lehi's climbed into the oven and burned himself!"

It was at that moment I first felt pangs of comfort here in Longwinded. Surrounded by Saints, I found the familiarity of home. I could see Father Lehi hiking up his robes to climb into the Kenmore range oven, his white beard melting from the heat.

Little Lehi turned out to be all right. Heber, however, was a different story. Lehi's father, out of necessity, had to go into Sister Lynn's bathroom to get some salve to put on Lehi's burns. In the process he discovered that Heber was no longer talking on the phone. Instead he lay slumped over in prayer. But after half an hour we all began to worry.

"No one prays that long," Sister North said.

So Sister Lynn went in to check on him. It was then we discovered that poor Heber was as dead as some of the prophets he must have known. The disconnected phone lay on the pillow next to him, silent. Someone suggested we give him a blessing and try to bring him back to life.

"Like the Savior did to Lazarus."

But even the Savior must have seen that Heber's earthly stay was over. The concern then shifted to our new church. In the eyes of many, Heber had blown it.

"Couldn't he have held on until we got the building?" someone asked.

A prayer was offered by Sister North on Heber's behalf. When we all opened our eyes we could almost see Heber's spirit slip away from the room. Unfortunately the peaceful feeling in the room didn't last long.

Some of the younger kids got mad at Sister Lynn for not letting them have Heber's oxygen tank. They could see quite clearly that he would never need it again.

"She's just being difficult," one of the mothers said, in reference to the tank and Sister Lynn.

I couldn't believe anyone could be so insensitive about Heber's death. Then Chad explained to me that Heber had been itching for some time to go be with his wife on the other side.

"His fondest wish was to leave this earth and be with her again," Chad explained.

"How old was he?" I asked.

"Ninety-one, I think."

"He must have had a nice long life," I said.

"That's nothing," Chad contended. "Orvil's father lived to be one hundred and seven.

"Who's Orvil?" I asked.

Chad looked around the room searching for Orvil. "I guess he's not here," he said. "I'm sure he'll be here soon. Poor Heber," he mumbled.

I concurred, while at the same time thinking about how great it must be to turn in a ninety-one-year-old body for one of those after-life models that floats and can travel at the speed of thought. Heber was probably loving it.

I was one of the lucky ones chosen to help carry Heber out into Sister Lynn's truck. I thought we should have left the body right where it had expired. But Bob showed up and instructed us to haul it off to the police shed.

Bob and I were carrying the body. Bob had the arms and I had the feet. Bob didn't want Heber staring at us, so we were carrying him face down. We were about halfway to the truck when our progress was suddenly stopped by a man on a horse. I wouldn't normally describe a man as beautiful, but this guy could have invented the word. He was Native American and sat proudly in the saddle, his long black hair blowing in the wind. He wore regular clothes, but somehow he made a flannel shirt look like an important piece of clothing. He held his hand up as if to gesture us to stop. We did. I could see he was going to speak, and I wondered what profound wisdom he was going to utter.

"What's up, Bob?" he asked.

"Not much, Orvil. What have you been doing?"

"Went to the Wingate's and got an earful from Wynona."

"I'm sure you did."

"Figured something would be going on here."

"Figured right," Bob said. "Have you met Tartan here?" Bob asked.

"Nope."

I tried to extend my hand, but I was still holding onto Heber's feet.

"You the one manning Flint's?" he asked.

"I am."

"I've meant to stop by; I have a couple areas I want to tell you about. I also wanted to show you a few trails that might help you find your way around the mountain. There is one that winds all the . . . "

Now perhaps it was nothing out of the ordinary for a cop, a ranger, and a horse-riding Native American to have a nice chat over the corpse of an elderly man here in Longwinded. But me being so new and all, I found it rather awkward. And whereas Heber at this very moment might have been up in heaven floating around light as the wind, he had left his earthly shell here with us—and it was beginning to feel quite heavy.

I was about to say something when Orvil finally caught on.

"Hey, what are you doing with Heber?" he asked.

"He's dead," Bob said dryly.

"No kidding?" Orvil said, amazed.

"Yep," Bob said nostalgically. "Hard to imagine life around these parts without Heber."

"I'll say," Orvil added. "I guess membership with the Baptists is even again."

"Hadn't thought about it," Bob said, "but I guess you're right."

I was getting tired.

"Bob, shouldn't we get Heber over to the truck before he decomposes?" I asked.

"Oh, it takes a body a ripe long time to decompose," Bob explained.

"I was joking," I tried to explain.

Orvil and Bob exchanged glances. I could almost hear them thinking—city boy.

We laid Heber right side up in Sister Lynn's truck and covered him with a ground tarp. Orvil hopped off his horse to help us. Bob sat down on the tailgate of the truck and wiped off his forehead and mustache.

"It's hot this year," he said.

"Sure is," Orvil said, taking a seat next to him.

I was getting a little upset. There was a dead man behind them and they were just carrying on like it didn't matter.

"It would be a good day to make sun tea," Bob said to Orvil.

I had finally had enough.

"There is a dead person behind you," I argued.

They both stared at me for a few moments and then broke out in a courtesy laugh.

"You got some sense of humor, Tartan," Bob said.

I hung my head in defeat and walked away. Their casual attitude toward Heber's death made my stomach uneasy.

As I got into my truck and drove away, I noticed Sister Lynn chasing after Lehi, who had made off with Heber's oxygen tank.

One Sunday down. Fate had shown me no possibilities. I needed possibilities.

CHAPTER ELEVEN

CHARITY BELIEVETH ALL THINGS

Charity's face remained calm, showing no sign of upheaval within. She was perfectly aware of how lucky she was to have found out what Howard was like before she married him. It sounded cliché, but it was true—her future was hers now. Finding out at a later date would have been much worse.

Howard was gone, and with a little time she would be better because of it. There was no reason for her to dwell on it any longer.

Charity lay back on her bed and started to figure out her future. The invitation to stay with her aunt seemed like the best thing at the time. It would give her a chance to pull away from everything and start over. Charity worried that it might look as if she were running away from it all, but she was at the point where that just didn't matter.

Charity picked the letter back up and read it again. It was a very real possibility.

CHAPTER TWELVE

DIM

The funeral was held two days later at the home of Sister Lynn. Heber's casket was too large to fit through any of her doors, and it was raining like crazy. So they backed the hearse up to Sister Lynn's front patio and everyone crawled inside it to take a look. It was quite a sight to see some of those sisters climbing into the confined space of that hearse to take a look at a man who had died two days before.

"He wasn't pretty in life," Sister Lynn would say to somewhat prepare them before they climbed inside.

"He was prettier than he is now" was the response from most of those who quickly crawled back out.

I had talked Martin into coming along. He had a fascination with death and so found the whole funeral rather uplifting. He spent a lot of time in the passenger seat of the hearse asking the driver if he had ever had a coffin fall out and what the top speed of a hearse was.

Heber had been the oldest man in the whole town, so even some of the Baptists liked him. A few showed up to pay their respects, but they left as soon as socially possible.

I had a chance to speak with Loni, or rather a chance for her to talk to me. I found out her father had died when she was four from some strange parasite and that her mother had lost four fingers in some sort of garage door accident. She did have a somewhat tragic past, but I selfishly felt I was suffering more than she had by having to listen to it. She invited me over for dinner sometime in the future. I thought about telling her I was allergic to dinner or that forest fires were most likely to erupt between the hours of five and eight. But I didn't, and instead I agreed to come over sometime in the next couple of weeks.

We Mormons had brought treats and side dishes in an effort to turn the funeral into more of a buffet than an occasion for mourning. We all ate and talked respectfully of the deceased.

With Heber now dead, the title of "Oldest Living Longwinded Man" went to Fern, and he wore the title like a badge of honor. Being the oldest man seemed to give him some sort of right to complain and reminisce more than usual. He also had begun walking with a limp. It was almost as though the title alone called for an increase in physical ailments and a desire to act ten years older.

Fern was chosen to give a speech in Heber's behalf. He sat in Sister Lynn's La-Z-Boy, leaning to the right, and eulogized as best he could.

"Heber and I grew up together," he started out.

This was going to be insightful.

"We used to take Lou Anne Dixon and Mary Shelf up to the Beaver and in between stealing kisses we would scheme about getting out of this town. Never happened." Fern paused to look reflective. "I remember my first horse, Daisy. My sister gave it one of those sissy names, but I still liked it. That thing could jump like a frog in love. I'm going to miss old Heber. In fact the truck that delivered his oxygen was the largest truck that came through this town. It's funny how you can feel fine one moment and then the next you're leaning over the toilet gasping for breath. That's what a heavy meal will do to you, make you feel like Satan himself is scraping away at your insides."

Fern was drifting like a loose sailboat on a windy day.

"Can't say that Heber didn't like his food. Heber loved food and horses. That man had a heart of gold. He treated me like a real friend, despite the fact that he was so much older. I can't believe he's dead. I can't believe he wouldn't help me deliver that colt—pull, Heber, pull!" Fern yelled. "Why is it that we all only get together at funerals?"

I think that was quite obvious.

"We should have living wakes," Fern continued. "I could lie in a coffin while everyone ate and talked. Wouldn't mind at all, no sir. Staying perfectly still is something that comes as naturally as wearing pants . . . "

Sister Lynn recognized the fact that Fern was tired and lost. She carefully ended his eulogy for him.

"Thank you, Fern, now I'll pray."

She gave a nice prayer and then the party broke up. Martin rode in the hearse with the driver to the Longwinded cemetery. We all followed with our lights on.

No one cried as dirt blanketed the black coffin, and only a modest number of roses were placed on top of the grave.

There was a slight chill in the air as I drove away from the cemetery. I wanted to sigh almost contentedly, but I refused to let myself do so. Because even though I was liking certain aspects of Longwinded, I was still bound and determined to get out before I turned thirty. I would definitely die before my century mark if I had to live here alone. I liked the members, but there really wasn't anyone for me. Sister Christianson was pushing hard for me to consider her Wendy. I tried to make it clear that I never would, but that didn't seem to stop her from trying. There were a few widows around, but I made it a personal rule to never date anyone over fifty-five. I needed a miracle or the Second Coming. One would think the selection of nice single females would be much better during the Millennium.

President Wingate and his wife had not showed up for the funeral. I heard from Bob that President Wingate was calling Heber's death a direct result of our unrighteousness. When I returned my books to Sister Wingate she told me she and her husband were still Mormons, but they were just practicing the religion in its pure form.

"When the Saints come around we'll be there."

"You're too forgiving," I had said sarcastically.

Not hearing the sarcasm, she blushed in humility.

There had been one positive thing to come out of Heber's death. The religious numbers were equal again. I was thrilled that I was no longer the tiebreaker. But losing our most respected member and not having a place to meet anymore made the town alive with gossip and speculation.

The Baptist parson was having a heyday with the fact that the Mormons had no place to meet.

"Would God leave his disciples stranded?" he would petition his parish.

So even though the numbers were even, the Baptists still had an uppity attitude over our state of homelessness. None of us Mormons knew what to do. Sister Lynn sent off letters to our stake president, mission president, and the First Presidency. But we weren't expecting anyone to act very quickly, and we weren't looking forward to too great an outcome. So the Baptists gloated while we existed in limbo. We had no building, no president, and no real plan. Sister Lynn tried to keep us in good spirits, but we remained a sorry bunch to behold.

Some of the Mormons in the area held a candlelight vigil in hopes of solving some of our pressing problems. The plan was to soften God's heart by sitting around with burning wicks covered in wax. Unfortunately, Longwinded Mormons and flame made a bad match. Sister Lynn's drapes caught fire and Chad suffered third degree burns from rolling over them to put them out. Plus, little Lehi smeared wax all over the once beautiful cloth chairs in Sister Lynn's formal dining room. The incident provided the Baptists with more ammo.

Orvil stopped by my place one afternoon to give me some tips and to point out a few trails he felt were pertinent to me. While he was there Martin stopped by to show me some little figures he had carved out of soap.

Orvil was extremely impressed with the soap creations.

"How long did it take you to make this one?" he said, holding up what appeared to be a shark.

"An hour," Martin said proudly.

"You the one in the Stillwater shack?" Orvil asked Martin.

"It used to be called that," Martin said.

"I'm Orvil Strongfeather," Orvil said, sticking out his hand.

Martin dusted the soap off his palms and shook Orvil's hand.

"Martin."

"You do fine work, Martin."

Orvil held that piece of soap as if it were a pearl of great price. Then without words the two of them sat down at the counter. Martin pulled out two new bars of soap and handed one to Orvil.

It was painful to watch. Here were two grown men forming a friendship over soap. Cultures meshing due to the influence of Dove. I must, however, admit that Orvil's first attempt—a bird's nest with three small eggs in it—was rather impressive.

I sat back on the heavily stuffed sofa by the table and watched the shavings fly. I tried to make myself comfortable, but I had to face it—even with the people I was growing to like, there was no long-term life for me here. I was thinking of ways to get away when a sudden feeling of suffocation overcame me. I think I was afraid that if I waited until I turned thirty, I would be too comfortable here to leave Longwinded. I could almost see Martin, Orvil, and me years from now whittling soap and making up stories.

What had I done?

I imagined my eternal mate wandering the streets of Provo right now searching for me, screaming for Tartan, but having to settle for some guy named Mike. And all because I had hidden myself in the deep green and poignantly lonely hills of Longwinded.

Life was so inconvenient at times.

CHAPTER THIRTEEN

CHARITY HOPETH ALL THINGS

Charity put the last of her things into a small suitcase and zipped it shut. Her decision to leave felt good—distance was a wonderful solution. She hadn't seen her aunt in years, but she felt confident they would get along well for the short time that she would be with her.

Charity pulled her hair back and smiled. Longfellow would do just fine for the time being. She picked up her suitcase, turned off her bedroom light, and closed the door.

CHAPTER FOURTEEN

THE CONVENIENT

I was stressed, uneasy, late, bothered, hopeful, and doubting—Sunday had rolled around again.

Sister Lynn's home had become the unofficial meeting place of the Saints. There was no room big enough for all of us, but, weather permitting, we could hold our meetings outside. The few chairs she had were set up on her lawn, and there was a card table with a pitcher of water and a loaf of bread on it.

Holding church outdoors wasn't half bad. The young kids could run around like they had always wanted to, and sitting amidst the smell of pine strengthened the spirit. Sister North laid Daniel and Zeke down on a blanket and enjoyed the meeting without her double load; that is, until Lehi tripped over Zeke. It didn't seem to hurt Zeke at all. He just sort of rolled with it. But Lehi scraped up his knee pretty bad. So we stopped the service while his cut was cleaned.

Chad and Brother Hatch blessed and passed the sacrament, while we all tried to be as reverent as possible. Even though Longwinded Saints trumpeted the fact that they had two hundred and sixty-two members, not more than ninety or so were active. The home teaching percentage was 8%, surpassed only by the visiting teaching with 11%. There were no programs for the youth (all five of them) except for the once-a-year youth fireside.

I was trying to think of spiritual things when Sister Reese's noisy van pulled up. Sister Reese was touted by the branch as the fastest quilter in the world. She could make a full-sized quilt in minutes. I had not yet seen her when she didn't have material in hand, stitching away like mad. Her faded orange van was loaded with people's old shirts, pants, towels, and other unmentionables. She was a mobile Deseret Industries. If there were any clothes you were looking to get rid of, all you had to do was call Sister Reese. She would be there with her van in a matter of minutes, and a couple of days later you'd recognize that old blouse of yours stitched into a quilt she had given to someone else.

Sister Reese quietly slipped out of her van and sat herself upon an old log that was directly in front of me. I lowered my head to give the appearance of serious contemplation of the greatness of God, while in reality I was thinking of how many quarters it would take to do four loads of wash at the Laundromat.

Twenty-four.

Another van door slammed.

Apparently someone besides Sister Reese had been in her van. Leaves and twigs crunched and rustled as someone approached from behind. I figured I was having some sort of sacrament manifestation, because suddenly an angel sat down next to Sister Reese and whispered something to her. I closed my eyes a couple times and opened them to find this manifestation still there.

She must be trying to tell Sister Reese something, I thought. Maybe Sister Reese had angels that administered quilting secrets to her. No wonder she was so fast.

I watched Chad hand the bread tray to Sister Reese and then stand openmouthed as this quilting angel took some bread for herself.

Was she real?

I started to reach out to feel if she was flesh and blood. I stopped, thinking that if by some chance she was real, my groping would make a really bad first impression.

I sort of stretched, allowing the fingertips on my right hand to brush against her back.

Solid. Yet supple.

She was real!

She was AMAZING! Never had I seen someone so absolutely, strip the lining from my lungs, stunning. Never.

She had long blond hair and a face so beautiful that porcelain dolls would have pouted with jealousy. She was somewhat under-dressed for church—jeans and a T-shirt—but I was willing to over-look those things if she would have me. The whole congregation was staring at her now. Sister Christianson gave me the evil eye as Wendy hung her head in defeat.

I started thinking of things I could say to her. I needed a suc-cessful first approach. I was tempted to tap her on the shoulder right then, but I knew I would have to wait until after the meeting.

As I was thinking, she shifted uncomfortably on the log in front of me.

An idea. I had an empty folding seat next to me that would make the perfect place for her to rest.

I tapped her on the shoulder.

She turned and looked me straight in the eyes, her red lips turn-ing up into a smile.

I used the maturity of a twenty-nine-year-old to muster up the courage to speak. "You're welcome to this chair," I whispered, point-ing to the empty one next to me.

She nodded what I took to be her thanks.

"Thanks," Sister Reese said, jumping up from her seat on the log.

I hadn't meant for Sister Reese to take me up. There was only one empty chair next to me. I guess Sister Reese thought I would give up mine. My plans were ruined. I had envisioned this beauty sitting next to me throughout the meeting, hoping that by the end of the meeting we would be so comfortable with each other she would insist we never part. But now here was Sister Reese wanting me to give up my ace card.

I stood up and reluctantly seated myself on the log while they settled into my old spot.

This was the worst thing I could think of. I hated having people behind me. The only place they had to look was directly at my back. Was my hair messy? Did I look stupid from their angle? Did I have dandruff? Did I stink? Was my shirt untucked? If I shifted to get comfortable would I look dumb? Could she see my elbows? No one has nice looking elbow skin. This was awful.

I sat there completely rigid, never shifting or moving the rest of the meeting. A large fly tormented me, somehow knowing I would never shoo it away. I could only imagine how stupid shooing looked from behind.

The meeting seemed to last forever, and by the time I had enough courage to stand up and turn around, they were gone. They must have been sickened by my elbows and fled in fear. The only trace of them now was the tail end of Sister Reese's van off in the distance. I asked everyone as coolly as I could if they might possibly know who Sister Reese's mystery friend was, but no one seemed to know. Even Sister Lynn was in the dark about it. She couldn't remember Sister Reese mentioning any guest or visitors who were coming. Never had the members known so little about someone else's life. I was truly disappointed.

I stopped to listen to Brother Hatch and Sister North argue over just who our new branch president would be and when we would get our building, when I suddenly had a brainstorm.

Bob.

Bob would know who she was. Bob knew everything.

I excused myself from the conversation I wasn't even involved in, jumped into my truck, and sped to the police station.

Bob wasn't there.

There was a note posted on the door to notify anyone interested that Bob was helping Mary Longfellow paint her ceiling. There was a map attached to the note.

I had heard that Mary was the one remaining Longfellow in town. She was a Mormon, but didn't come out to church.

I wrote down the directions Bob had left and then drove to Sister Longfellow's house. Her home was long and rambled off in all directions. I wondered why we didn't hold church out here. Maybe Sister Longfellow would come if she only had to travel a few steps. But as soon as I stepped through the door it became clear why they couldn't hold church here. There was so much stuff in her house you could barely find passage from one room to the next. Books and trinkets and furniture were stacked from the floor to the ceiling. An older woman led me through the piles into what was probably the living room. Bob was suspended by two scaffolding towers, lazily painting the ceiling. I wondered how he got the scaffolding in here and why he didn't just stack up some of this junk and climb up on it to paint. The old lady pointed to Bob and then left.

"Tartan," Bob said.

"Hey, Bob."

"What brings you here?" he asked.

"Well, I was sort of hoping you might know something."

"Shoot," Bob said, shifting his footing and lying back on one of the scaffolding boards.

"Sister Reese was at church today with a girl about my age. No one's quite sure who she is. Any idea?" I asked. "I just can't wait until I bump into her, I need to know who she is now."

"That would be Charity," Bob said.

"No, actually I think the word's *patience*," I replied, referring to my need to know now.

"No, her name is Charity, Charity Hall, I believe. She's Sister Reese's niece."

Charity Hall. The mere mental pronunciation made me a better person.

"What's her story?" I asked.

"Guy trouble. She came down to take a break from things for a while."

"What sort of guy trouble?"

"Well," Bob said, shinnying down the scaffolding and taking a seat on top of a pile of old phone books. He set his paintbrush down and leaned into me. "You know I don't like to talk about others, but I don't like to withhold information either. Here's what I know. Charity grew up with this boy in question. Friends their entire early childhood, and when it came time to start courting, well, they tried that out as well. Good kids, kept their noses clean as they fell deeply in love with one another. Howard went on a mission to Austria, and she waited for him until he returned. When he did, they set a date to get married and everything looked perfect. Then Howard meets a girl at the library he decides he likes more than Charity. Breaks it off with Charity, becomes engaged to this other girl, and two weeks later they're married."

"Amazing," I said.

"I'll say. Sister Reese, seeing that Charity might enjoy some time away, invites her up here to stay for awhile and the rest is history."

I couldn't believe it—a girl on the rebound. My chances looked pretty good.

"Do you know anything about her personally?" I asked.

"Not much," Bob said. "She's twenty-five, likes to read, ski, and write. Broke her collarbone once when she was ten. Just your average stuff."

Twenty-five. That was perfect.

"I guess this makes the Mormons the majority again," I said.

"Actually, Betty Ann, the Baptist treasurer, just gave birth to an eleven-pound boy last night, so the numbers are still even."

"Perfect timing on Betty's part," I commented.

"I'll say."

Bob stood back up and surveyed the half-painted ceiling. He then handed me a paintbrush. "Could you help for a while?" he asked.

I reluctantly agreed to do so in hopes of Bob remembering something more about Charity as we applied brush strokes. I took off my tie and put on a pair of plastic coveralls. I then scaled the scaffolding and lay down on my back. With the wood ceiling inches away now, I could paint fairly easily. Bob made himself comfortable on the other scaffolding. For some reason we were painting a yellow ceiling blue. Both colors were personally offensive in my opinion.

"Is she paying you for this?" I asked.

"Who, Mary?"

"Yes," I answered.

"No, I was over here the other day trimming the shrubs and noticed how faded the ceiling was."

"You volunteered?"

"I guess so."

"Doesn't this interfere with your work?"

"It's like this," Bob said, paint dripping from the ceiling onto his cheek. "If a person can't help out his friends, what kind of person does he think he is?"

What? Bob's sage advice was hollow and confusing. And he had left my question dangling.

"Tartan, the people of Longwinded recognize me first as a friend, and second as a cop. You have to gain people's trust before you can plow their fields."

I was trying to make sense out of Bob's philosophizing when somewhere off in the house I heard a dull thud.

Thud.

I dismissed it. I leaned over and dunked my brush into more paint.

"Any idea how long Charity's planning to stick around?" I asked.

Thud.

Bob set his brush down and took a sip of his nearby drink through a straw. I sat up and looked in the direction of the noise. Normally, I wouldn't have been too concerned about it, but this thud carried a sort of ominous feeling with it.

"The way I hear it is that she'll be staying until—"

Thud.

"What was that?" Bob said, jumping and knocking his drink off the scaffolding and down to the floor. "Oh, no, please don't let it be."

Thud.

Shuffle.

"Start painting!" Bob screamed.

"What?" I asked, confused.

"Don't ask, just paint."

THUD.

SHUFFLE.

They were coming more frequently now, and much louder. I hit my head hard as I tried to start painting again. Bob was temple-white in the face and painting as if his life depended on it.

THUD.

SHUFFLE.

THUD.

SHUFFLE.

I turned to look, knowing that whatever the source of the sound was, it was very near. There in the doorway stood the meanest looking woman I had ever seen. Her gray hair, wild with life, twisted and stuck out everywhere. She had some sort of dress on, but it was hard to see very much of it due to the four aprons she was wearing over it. Her black eyes stared straight at us, and her lips twisted as she held tight to a gleaming silver walker. Bob swore under his breath. I kept painting, not understanding what was going on.

"Bob!" she screamed. "What in Sam's name do you think you're doing?"

"Mary, I was just trying to help—"

"If I had needed your help I would have asked—now get out!" she yelled, coming closer. The older lady who had let me in came into the room and tried to get Mary to leave us alone.

"Do you want to keep your job, Erma?" Mary asked harshly. Erma hung her head and left the room quickly. Mary set out toward us, her walker knocking piles of stuff all over. I started to climb down but Bob said I was safer where I was. She reached the scaffolding and locked one leg of her walker onto one side of Bob's scaffolding. Then as if she were possessed, she began shaking her walker violently. The two scaffolding towers were loosely connected by a couple of boards. They collapsed almost instantly.

"Ma . . . Ma . . . Ma . . . Mary!" Bob yelled as his platform gave way. The whole structure started to tip toward me. Mary unhooked her walker and then gave one final push on Bob's tower. It slammed into mine, knocking me and my scaffolding over. Bob and I went flying into piles of old clocks and board games, with the scaffolding breaking and bouncing everywhere.

Things seemed to fall on me for several minutes, and when they finally stopped I looked up to see Mary smiling. Bob picked himself up and then started scrambling for a way out. I followed close behind. I think Mary tried to chase us, but she probably couldn't get past the dam of junk we had created. We both fell on the ground outside and tried to catch our breath.

"What was *that*?" I finally said.

"That was Mary Longfellow, direct descendent of old Wally himself."

"Didn't she ask you to paint her ceiling?"

"No, Erma and I just thought it needed it. Erma promised that Mary would be in a medicated sleep all day. We didn't want to repeat what happened when I fixed her kitchen sink."

"If she doesn't want you to help, then why do you?" I asked angrily.

"Well, I'm just being neighborly."

Longwinded needed more crime. That, or one less policeman.

"My tie is still in there," I said, as if I were a mother telling the firemen about my child trapped in a burning building.

"What do you want me to do about it?" Bob asked.

"You're the cop; go get it."

"I'll buy you a new one," he pleaded.

"Forget it," I said, slipping out of my paint suit. "Someone should get that woman some help."

"Mary?" Bob asked naively.

"Yes, Mary," I yelled.

"Oh, she's harmless. She just doesn't like people butting into her business, is all."

I was about to tell Bob that he needed help as well, but I was stopped by . . .

Thud.

She had made it over the dam. I had never seen a short man run as fast as Bob did to the safety of his police car. And of course I wasn't far behind.

Bob started the car up and was about to pull away when I remembered my truck.

"Wait," I yelled, "I can't leave my truck here."

"Go get it, then," Bob said, pressing the automatic door locks.

I could see Mary standing in the doorway of her home. She stood there looking fiercely triumphant. I glanced over at my truck. It was a good twenty feet away from us, and about ten feet away from Mary.

"Think I can make it?" I asked Bob.

"She's fast," Bob said, "but I'll try and distract her."

I looked at Mary. She looked straight at me and then glanced playfully at my truck. It was as if she were challenging me to go for it. She took what looked to be a feeble step toward the truck. It was now or never. If I waited too long she would make it to the truck and probably slash the tires and shatter the windows.

Like an Olympic skier at the top of some great slope, I psyched myself up. Bob gunned the engine for effect, and I bolted for my truck. Bob was right—Mary was fast. But fortunately for me, not fast enough. Bob did a poor job of distracting her; all he did was honk his horn a couple of times as he sped away. It didn't matter in the end. I started the truck and kicked up dirt as I made my escape.

I could see though my rearview mirror that Mary was making her way back inside the house. I would have sworn she was almost strutting. What a woman.

I found out later that Mary was the only remaining Longfellow still around. She lived off the checks she received from children and grandchildren, who for some reason refused to come and see her.

CHAPTER FIFTEEN

THE CHAPEL

That afternoon I couldn't get Charity off my mind. Never had I felt so desperate to meet someone. I tried to replay over in my mind just how she looked. Perhaps I might be making her out to be more than she really was. Martin, who had come over to borrow some cheese, meat, buns, and any extra condiments I might have, stayed around and talked me into drawing a picture of Charity. I was so consumed by the thought of her that I consented.

"This is what she looks like?" he mused.

"Well, she's not quite as skinny as that," I said referring to my stick figure.

"She's only got, one, two, three, four, five, six, seven, eight, nine, nine strands of hair?"

"I couldn't draw every strand," I explained. I was certainly no Picasso.

"I'd watch it if I were you," Martin counseled. "Women are women are women."

"I know. That's why I like them," I said, adding a few more strands of hair to my picture.

This had been the longest Sunday of my life, and it was still only two in the afternoon. I was about to break out the Uno cards when the phone rang. It was Chad.

"You've got to come down to Sister Lynn's right away," he said excitedly.

"Why?" I asked.

"Brother Stolt, our high councilor, is here and he's got our new branch president with him."

"You're kidding."

"Nope, dead serious. He told Heber he would be here today, but Heber didn't deliver the message. Brother Stolt had no idea that Heber was even dead. So hurry down; everyone will be here. Going to start the meeting in about an hour."

I hung up very happy—certainly Charity would be there. I found a tie and flung water through my hair to give it that wet look. Martin didn't want to come but agreed to stay around and watch Albert. I drove quickly to Longwinded and broke the Sabbath by picking up a pack of Certs at the Stop & Shop. The ox was in the mire as far as my breath was concerned.

The news of our new president had spread, and Sister Lynn's home was busier than I had ever seen it. One side of her road was crowded with cars belonging to the Baptists, and the other side was filled with cars belonging to the Mormons. The Baptists had come to see who their new rival leader would be. They were all clustered together behind the Mormons, who were spread out on quilts and self-importantly taking up all the chairs. Someone had stacked some boards on top of some cinder blocks, creating a makeshift stage on which three people were sitting. There was an older man filling one of the three chairs—I figured that he must be the high councilor. I also figured that he had never interpreted the Word of Wisdom to have anything to do with overeating because he looked to weigh at least four hundred pounds. Next to him sat a young kid who looked like he was in his mid-twenties. I hadn't seen him around before, but I assumed he was a Longwinded resident. A beautiful woman sat next to him, whom I deduced to be his wife or girlfriend, because of how close they were sitting.

Sister Lynn and Sister Hatch were trying desperately to keep things in order. Like sheepdogs, they were nipping at people's heels, herding them into the fold. The Baptists didn't like Mormons telling them what to do, so they would wander where they shouldn't as soon as Sister Lynn turned her back. Willie, from the filling station, stepped into Sister Lynn's flower garden, and Sister North told on him. Things started to unravel from that point. The meeting needed to begin.

Brother Stolt stood and waited for everyone to quiet down. When no one did he began clapping his hands. This amused some of the younger kids, who began to clap along, but it did nothing to quiet the adults. He looked disgusted, as if he couldn't comprehend people acting this way. Sister Lynn went to the front and started yelling at everyone. A few people stopped talking, but it wasn't until she screamed something about a new building that everyone shut up.

"Brother Stolt," she said, turning all eyes and ears over to him.

He stood again, straightened his tie—which, if measured end to end, probably equaled two yards—and began to speak.

"Brothers and Sisters . . . "

"And Baptists," a Mormon heckler screamed.

Brother Stolt laughed just enough not to be stuffy, but not enough to offend the Baptists. "The stake presidency has asked me to come here today," he began.

I had heard from Sister Lynn that our stake presidency didn't come out to Longwinded very often. Apparently there had been some problems in the past. So, Longwinded rarely saw the stake president, and Brother Stolt was assigned to be our advocate with the stake.

"This is most unusual," Brother Stolt continued, "that the Church would act so quickly, but the brethren have heard the prayers of the faithful . . . "

I wondered to whom he was referring.

" . . . and the blessings are about to pour forth. First we would like to thank President Wingate for all his service and for bringing the Saints to this brink of hope. All those who can give him a vote of thanks for his selfless service please do so by raising your right hand." Everyone raised their hands high, even the Baptists, not wanting to be left out. I turned around, as is customary, to make

sure everyone was in accordance. A couple of people had the wrong
hands up, but things looked okay. Then suddenly, as if all extrane-
ous sound were gone, a lone noise called to me. It was the sound of
a needle being pushed through material. There was Sister Reese,
covered in fabric and stitching away. And there beside her was
Charity in every sense of the word. I turned back around, catching
my breath and looking forward to the moment when we would sustain the new president so I could turn around and catch another
look at her.

"Brothers and sisters, it has been made clear to your leaders that
things need some work here."

The Baptists smiled in sync.

"So after much prayer, and some friendly conversation with
Heber, God rest his soul, we have come up with a plan we feel the
Lord approves of."

Lofty words.

"The name of the person that we propose to be your new
president is Ian J. Smith."

The crowd whispered fiercely.

"Brother Smith and his lovely wife live about an hour away, just
outside of Meadow Lane. They are members of the Meadow Lane
Ward but have been called to be your new branch president and
wife. It is my deepest desire that you may all embrace them. This is
a great time for Longfellow; I can feel that things are heading in the
right direction . . . "

Brother Stolt continued to talk as I let my gaze wander over to
our new branch president.

Poor thing, I thought. I had no idea how Longwinded would
handle an outsider, especially one so young.

I caught a nice long look at Charity as we sustained President
Smith. I would try for eye contact next time. Brother Stolt was just
getting his second wind when someone from the audience yelled.

"What about the building?"

Brother Stolt paused, almost as if he were waiting for inspiration.
Apparently some came, because he started back up again.

"As many of you may know, the Church purchased two acres of

Longfellow's best land a number of years ago. And I am happy to say this land will remain barren no more."

The crowd ahhhed.

I knew the land well. It was a small plot just past the library—and almost directly across the street from the Baptist church.

People began asking questions at random.

"Who's going to build it?"

"How big's it going to be?"

"What will it look like?"

"Will it have a font?"

That question came from Sister Theo. She was convinced the reason we didn't have more Mormons was because we didn't have a font. "How can we grow without a font?" was her weekly war cry.

"People, people, is all of that important?" Brother Stolt naively asked.

"Yes!" came the unanimous reply.

Brother Stolt suddenly looked worried. "The Church has really gone out of its way to see that you will have a new place to meet. And they have decided . . . What they have done . . . "

Suddenly everything was "they."

"They have purchased a nice, new double-wide trailer that will function nicely as your building for the next few years."

The crowd went wild, weeping, moaning, and gnashing their teeth as if the end of the world had arrived.

"We don't want no trailer across the street from our beautiful chapel," Pastor Stevens shouted.

"It's not a trailer," Brother Stolt said loudly, "it's a mobile home."

"More like a Mormon Moan," Mr. Benderholden yelled.

"Don't we merit a real building?" Sister North hollered.

I saw Fern get up and go sit back with the Baptists.

The Baptists started yelling things about Christ's church having a firm foundation, not wheels.

President Smith looked worried. His wife clutched his hand—things were getting ugly. Brother Stolt gave up after a few minutes of trying to quiet people down and sat back in his seat.

It was total chaos now.

People were pushing and yelling at one another while others

were just trying to get out from the middle of it all. I was trying desperately to make my way to Charity amidst the commotion. Just when I was about to reach her, everyone suddenly stopped doing what they were doing and shut up.

I turned to see what had stopped them.

President Smith stood silently up on the stand, looking calmly at the crowd. People started sitting back down and hushing their children. I took the only open seat around—a seat which happened to be right in front of Charity.

Great, I thought.

"I know you don't know me yet," President Smith started out, "but I am here to help the Saints and the community move ahead."

President Smith spoke for about an hour about the grand principle of making something from nothing. He prophesied some things pertaining to gratitude and talked of mending and picking up where old Wally Longfellow, the town's founder, had left off. It was the strangest thing to look around and see everyone giving their undying attention to this young guy who no one knew. Even I was impressed. He had no air of superiority; in fact he seemed quite humbled by his new calling. By the time he sat back down everything was different. The Mormons, including myself, were hyped and excited for their new building, and the Baptists made no snide remarks as they slinked away, leaving the Mormons alone.

President Smith's wife gave the closing prayer. I'm sure it was good, but I was thinking about how to turn around and address Charity after the prayer was over. I would not be able to wait until next week to see her again—I had to know what she was like now! I would hate to spend the next week daydreaming about her only to find out that she couldn't speak English, or spit when she talked, or used the word *like* too often. I needed to find out if she was normal.

"Amen."

I turned slowly, planning to tell Sister Reese all about some clothes I was getting ready to discard. Sister Reese wasn't there any longer, but Charity was.

"Hey, hey, hey," I said without thinking. It sort of sounded like I was scolding her, and made a very poor first impression I'm sure.

She smiled at me.

"Nice meeting," I said calmly.

"I agree," she replied.

She spoke English.

"I'm Tartan."

"I'm Charity."

I could think of absolutely nothing else to say. I felt as if we had covered all major conversation points with just eight words. An uneasy pause grew to monumental proportions before God had mercy on me by sending President Smith over. He put a hand on my shoulder and introduced himself. I shook his hand and introduced Charity, even though she could have done a much better job telling him who she was.

"This is my wife, Bronwyn," President Smith said.

"Nice to meet you, Sister Smith," I said cordially.

President Smith laughed, "You can call us by our first names."

"Nice to meet you, Bronwyn," I corrected.

Ian was about to say something when Brother Stolt called his name.

"I guess we will talk to you two later," Ian said. He then took Bronwyn's hand and the two of them walked away from us.

"They seem like nice enough people," I commented.

"Yep," Charity said, almost bored.

I needed to dive into some real conversation. I needed to create dialogue so thrilling that she would jump at the chance to go out with me. I needed to make clear that I was different than the rest of Longwinded. I was an import—exotic and desirable. I needed . . .

"Tartan?" she said, pulling me out of my thoughts.

"Yes," I said.

"Why are you staring at me?" she asked nicely.

I hadn't noticed. My eyes had been glazed over, delving to find something to say.

"I was just thinking."

"Oh."

"Don't you want to know what I was thinking about?" I asked.

"Only if you feel compelled to tell me."

Compelled. That was the biggest word I had heard someone around here use. I wanted this girl.

I dove in.

"What do you do during the days?" I asked.

"Not much," she answered. "Help out my aunt or read."

A bored, pretty, smart girl on the rebound in a town that offered little competition. There was a bright light at the end of this tunnel.

"I work up at Flint's Peak, and I was wondering if you might like to have lunch up there with me some time?" I asked. No, I *begged*, using my most charming voice.

Silence.

Silence.

Silence.

I shifted and thought about just walking off.

"I've never met anyone named Tartan before," she said.

"Don't know many Charitys myself."

Charity smiled.

"Does that mean yes?"

"I guess so," she said, smiling. "I'll have to ask around to find out if a woman can be trusted with you alone," she joked.

"Well, pending that outcome, would Wednesday be all right?" I asked.

"That's the day they're bringing in the new church."

"Oh, wouldn't want to miss *that.* Thursday?"

"Should be fine."

"Around noon?" I asked.

"Sounds like a good time for lunch."

I drew Charity a map to my place and she left to find her aunt. I stood there completely enraptured by the presence that had just departed. Sister Christianson sneaked up behind me.

"Pretty convenient if you ask me," she whispered.

I assumed she meant Charity moving here.

"I'll say," I whispered back.

Sister Christianson stomped off toward Wendy. As I contemplated the greatness of God, Charity graced my every thought.

CHAPTER SIXTEEN

MANUFACTURED ZION

By Wednesday the Baptists were back to their old selves. In fact most of Longwinded was in an uproar over the fact that their town would soon house a double-wide. I hadn't noticed before, but Longwinded had this huge phobia regarding mobile housing. I think most folks felt that if you lived in a mobile home you weren't really committed to the area. They thought you could just pick up and leave at any moment, taking your house with you and somehow leaving the area in worse condition than when you arrived.

Years before, a Longwinded resident had tried to move a single-wide out onto a piece of property he owned. People threw such a fit that he eventually abandoned the notion and ended up groveling for forgiveness from the tolerant townsfolk. The person in question now lived in an RV. Longwinded had no qualms with RVs. Heck, they were just a glorified car, and there were plenty of cars sitting on property in Longwinded. Most homes had at least six cars parked outside; one up on blocks being worked on, one for family driving, one for hauling, and at least two that no one knew whether they worked or not.

The Mormons cleared their land and got all the hookups ready for their new building. Meanwhile the Baptists had constructed an eight-foot fence around their building so they wouldn't have to stare at the Mormon eyesore during their own well-housed services. Fern had committed to baptism with the Baptists, and they were gloating and feeling as if there had never been a better time to be one of them. Pastor Stevens was living it up; never had he had such an anti-Christ as the Mormon mobile chapel to assail.

I left my duties at about eleven Wednesday morning and headed down to welcome our chapel. The entire town was there. People lined the main road, sitting in lawn chairs and drinking warm sodas as they waited for the semis to bring in our building. The Second Coming couldn't have commanded a better turnout. Though most people were of the opinion that Longwinded was no place for a mobile home, they still wanted to be on hand to see just what a mobile chapel might look like.

Around noon Chad came racing into town to announce that the trucks were right behind him. Longwindedans started standing and talking excitedly. This was big stuff. The entire town had shut down so that everyone would have a chance to view the incoming Mormon Mobile Home. Even Sister Wingate had closed up shop and sat out in front of the library, eating purple grapes and cheesecake while trying to act disinterested. We all knew her heart was set on something going terribly wrong so she could feel vindicated in her anger towards us Mormons at the moment.

"There it is!" someone finally shouted.

I was actually getting chills; my life was pathetic.

The two semis pulled into town and honked their horns as everyone waved. Parents held their children up on their shoulders, and people of all ages waved flags and cheered. There were also bunches of people who hollered or booed. The building itself was white, with peach trim around each of the windows and doors. It had a rust red roof that in my opinion didn't match the peach trim. Of course, what did a twenty-nine-year-old, single man possibly know about the in's and out's of color coordination?

It took a few hours for the drivers to get the two sections into the right position. Fern had wheeled out his slush machine and was doing a brisk business amongst the Baptists and the few Mormons who were still speaking to him. Bob was walking around trying to act like he had everything under control and knew exactly what was going on. Sister Lynn and Ian, the new branch president, were supervising each and every thing the movers were doing and checking off lists of items that needed to be attended to. I helped level our new chapel for a bit but then gave up when I heard that Charity was around somewhere. Willie opened his station back up, and Scott started serving beer outside his bar. Bob felt confident that serving beer on the open street was in violation of some city ordinance, but in the spirit of celebration he let it slide.

I found Charity sitting by herself under a large apple tree, watching the activity as if it were a three-ring circus.

"Some show," I said.

"Amazing."

"Not much to get excited about here, is there?"

"I guess not."

"We still on for tomorrow?" I asked.

"I hope so," she replied.

She hoped!

I sat down by her. Her hair smelled of shampoo and I almost fell over due to ecstasy.

"Where's your aunt?" I asked.

"She stayed home to finish a quilt for my mother."

"That's nice of her."

"I guess."

"You guess?" I said.

"I don't want to sound ungrateful, but we must have two hundred quilts at our house. You'd think she would make us a pillow or a sampler or something. *Anything* besides a quilt. I used to be scared to open our linen closet for fear all the quilts would topple over and smother me to death."

"Couldn't you have just crawled out from under them?" I asked, unable to conjure sufficient fear of falling blankets.

Charity smiled.

"Why does she quilt so much?"

"Bored I guess; plus it stops her from overeating."

Sister Clara Reese was no size seven. In fact she would probably have a hard time finding pants that fit, even sized in the double digits. I could only imagine how heavy she would be if she didn't quilt to take away the cravings.

"She still eats a lot," Charity said, laughing.

"What?" I asked.

"I could tell you were thinking about her weight."

"I was not, I was just . . . okay, it did cross my mind. Do you two get along?"

"Most of the time. Aunt Clara gets along with everyone except Mary Longfellow."

"Does *anyone* get along with Mary Longfellow?" I asked.

"I don't know, I've never met her."

"She's a gem."

"So I've heard."

"I'll take you to meet her sometime," I offered.

"That's okay."

Charity stood and dusted herself off. I remained sitting, taking advantage of the moment to look at her. Her long blond hair was incredible; it had this relationship with the wind that most women would have killed for. The wind seemed only to blow it when it was beneficial to the mood. Charity's was the most unboring hair a person could have.

She was great—plain and simple. Simple and painfully un-plain. She was the perfect height, about five inches shorter than I. So she was tall, but she still allowed me those five inches so as to appease my single male ego. Her best asset by far were her eyes—dark brown and as deep as the most complex of souls. Every time she opened her eyes I lost all muscle function. I became a 6'2'' pile of un-responsive muscle tissue.

I stood up next to her and dusted off. She laughed at the way I extracted dust from myself.

"Hey, that's not easy to do gracefully," I said.

She laughed again, nonchalantly brushing something off my shoulder.

I could feel my straight hair turning curly as I contemplated how close she was to me.

"So what are you doing here?" I suddenly asked. I couldn't help asking; it had been weighing so heavily on my mind. As Sister

Christianson had inferred, it was awfully convenient. I had spent a large part of the previous night wondering what I had done to receive the good grace of God—only he could have sent her.

This was, after all, Longwinded.

Now if a twenty-five-year-old girl who had been divorced twice, had two kids, and was addicted to Robitussin cough medicine had suddenly swaggered into town, it would have seemed normal. But Charity? Come on, Fate, where was the catch?

"I came to see the building," she replied.

"No, not *here* here," I said, waving my hands. "Longwinded."

"What do you mean?" she asked.

"I mean what are you doing here?" I asked honestly. "You seem way too good to believe."

"Do you know me that well?" she asked coyly.

"Have you murdered anyone before?" I asked.

"Nope."

"Then what else matters? Heck I probably wouldn't even care about that. Might be kind of fun zigzagging across the country with the cops on our trail."

"Tartan, you're so unconditional."

"Aren't I though," I said. "It just seems weird that you're here."

"I think the weird thing is that you talk to me as if you know me and as if you can see a future where you and I are involved. I'm just a girl you don't even know who has come to this town to get away for a while."

"Why?" I asked, hoping to learn more.

"Don't act like you don't know. I'm smart enough to know that Bob has filled the whole town in on my pre-Longwinded life. Every other person I meet here begins their conversation with 'I'm sorry about Howard, honey.'"

For the first time our conversation turned uncomfortable.

"I'm sorry about Howard, Charity."

"Me, too, but I'm thrilled that I found out what he was before I married him. Breaking up with someone isn't the end of the world."

"No, moving to Longwinded when you're twenty-nine and single is."

"Yeah," she said, "why are you here?"

"Work."

"Was this a *promotion*?" she joked.

"I'm not sure what this was; I think I was trying to find myself."

"Well, I'm glad you're here," she said smiling.

This was good. This was *very* good.

"At the moment, so am I," I said.

"So Tartan Jones came to Longwinded to find himself. Any other reason?" she asked.

"Hasn't Bob told you?"

Charity shook her head no.

"I had to get away from Provo. I couldn't take another day of people setting me up with their daughters or giving me advice on self-improvement. Plus, I wanted to be somewhere where my childhood wasn't so intertwined with my everyday life: there's the school I went to; there's the park where I used to play; there's my first girlfriend's house; there's the alley where that big eighth grader beat me up."

"Had you been here before?"

"Nope, and I probably wouldn't have come if I had been."

"I came here once when I was nine," Charity said. "We spent Christmas with Aunt Clara. It was the worst Christmas I can remember. My mom and dad forgot to bring our gifts, so Christmas morning all we got was quilts."

"So where is home?"

"Arizona," she answered.

"Good place for quilts," I joked.

"Isn't it though?" Charity laughed.

"Where in Arizona do you live?"

"Yuma."

"It's hot there," I stated.

"It's not too bad once you get used to it."

"Same with spinach," I said, not making complete sense.

Charity smiled again.

I was openly smitten.

Sure there was Charity territory I hadn't traversed, but the landscape thus far was beautifully rocky, and the view of what lay ahead looked pretty good. I liked her. I liked the way she looked when she spoke, and I liked the way she smiled as she listened to me do the same.

Charity tilted her head and stared at me, as I stood there thinking about the view.

"Are you okay?" she asked.

"Yep," I answered honestly.

Charity stuck out her hand and grabbed mine.

"Let's go see the new building."

I consented quickly.

An invitation to hold her hand had arrived, and I would not be dumb enough to let it escape me. I took her hand, and tried to get her to walk slowly to make the moment last as long as possible as we approached the cluster of people around our new building.

Willie looked up, saw me holding hands with Charity, and leaned in to inform Fern. Fern signaled a big man with a striped shirt, who in turn whistled for Bob to come over. Bob walked slowly over to the striped man, but ran from him as soon as he had heard.

Charity and I had reached the building. We stopped and watched what was going on. Charity made no attempt to drop my hand. I was starting to worry about my palm breaking into a sweat, when I observed Bob whispering to Loni. Loni let out a small gasp and shook her head as if she disapproved. I admit she made me start to think.

Was Charity easy? I mean I hardly knew her and here she was letting me hold her hand in public. Maybe she just needed something to cling to, or perhaps she had some sort of equilibrium problem that required that she be connected to someone stable.

That was me, stable.

Certainly she wouldn't hold hands with just *anyone*. I mean this had to be a signal that she and I might just happen. Or at least an indication that I was a possibility.

Loni was quicker than Bob at getting around with the news. A few moments later Chad was by my side congratulating me, and Orvil winked at me twice.

Charity leaned into me, "Pretty neat, isn't it?"

"Yes!" I exclaimed.

"It really is a nice building."

"Oh, yeah," I said, disappointed that she had been referring to the building and not my hand.

Don't get me wrong, I didn't normally get so hyped up about holding hands with a woman. This, however, was different. For starters Charity was unlike any of the girls I had ever swapped palms with. She was magnificent and more angelic than Enoch's wife. She represented hope. It was as if God had sent down manna. Unlike the stuff Moses had supped on, this was like steaks and tossed salads being dropped down by the heavens after some angel had grilled and prepared them to a T. No gristle, no bad lettuce, but delectable enough to make the glands moisten and the throat tingle.

I was falling.

Holding her hand also gave me cause to suspect that she might just think I was all right and that just maybe she was ready to start forgetting about Howard—and move on to me. I hoped so. If I didn't have the possibility of Charity, I would have nothing.

Charity squeezed my hand.

The building's assembly was still in process, so we walked to my truck, put down the tailgate, and sat. The members were excited for the building to be done. Everyone wanted to walk inside it and check out what mobile home interiors looked like these days. Meanwhile, the townsfolk were starting to get restless, and the community was starting to show the ugly side of itself. People were running out of things to do and others to talk about.

A few non-feuders tried to get a town dance started, but they were met with opposition at all points. First the Baptists threw a fit over a dance of any sort in their town. They could see Satan himself doing the Hustle as he dragged us all down to some eternal disco. The Mormons were for the idea, but they backed out of their support when the few townspeople who had been drinking Scott's sidewalk sale dry started to get out of hand. The final problem was when Herb Walker decided to express himself by doing some sort of interpretive dance. Well, intoxication and interpretation make for strange bedfellows. Herb's dance looked just plain stupid, and Billy Pitt made that clear by shouting . . .

"Herb's dancing like a sissy. Looks like a woman."

Herb was too inebriated to really care what Billy said, but a few of the women took offense at what Billy was inferring.

Phyllis Benderholden, one of the staunchest Baptists in town, made the remark that, "No Baptist woman would ever look like that, seeing how Baptist women never tango cheek to cheek with Satan."

Sherry, from the Stop & Shop, started in on Phyllis for being such a pompous, self-righteous, ne'er-do-well and asked her to please do the town a favor by not speaking anymore. Bruce Benderholden didn't really appreciate his wife being talked to in such a way and actually slapped Sherry. Well, Orvil had been kind of sweet on Sherry for over a year now, and he flew into a rage after Bruce slapped her. Martin instantly started helping Orvil out by throwing a few punches at Bruce.

Herb, still dancing around like a loon, fell into the middle of the brawl. Billy jumped in to help Herb, and Billy's brother felt obligated by family ties to support Billy's decision. The street soon became a pile of flailing arms and kicking legs. Emotion that had been pent up for years was making itself manifest. Bob shot off his gun into the air, but no one even flinched. Folks knew good and well that Bob would never shoot one of them. He tried to manually break a few people up, but then Billy's brother socked him hard in the nose. Bob pulled back, deciding to just let the fight ride itself out.

Everyone tired after a few minutes—everyone except Bruce and Orvil. There had been some hard feelings between the two for many years now. It all stemmed from the time Orvil had appeared on *Wheel of Fortune*. Orvil got on the show but didn't win a single dollar. He kept spinning bankrupt, and when he finally got a chance to win some money he mistakenly guessed . . . "Funger sandwich . . . " instead of Finger sandwich. It was a dumb mistake, especially considering that every letter had been up on the board except for the two I's. But Orvil had never heard of a finger sandwich and thought the concept to be quite disgusting when the puzzle was quickly solved by the next contestant. Bruce made a big deal about Orvil's stupid guess.

"Funger sandwich? What the heck is a funger sandwich?"

Orvil made up some lie about the Native Americans having a ceremonial treat called the funger, but admitted the truth after Bruce began searching through books at the library. Orvil did end up with a box of Tyson potpies and a really nice hairbrush as consolation prizes, but it just wasn't the same as, say—ten thousand dollars.

Ever since then, however, Orvil and Bruce had been bitter enemies. Most people in Longwinded tolerated one another. Sure there were religious differences, and yes there was occasional name-calling. But people were still somewhat civil with each other on a daily basis. Everyone except Orvil and Bruce.

They avoided each other as much as possible and talked badly about each other every chance they got. Now they were tearing each other apart in front of the whole town and the two lucky truckers who had delivered the chapel. Sister North commented that it was nice they were at least communicating in some fashion. Finally exhausted, they both fell to the ground. No one approached them as they lay side by side, mumbling to each other.

"Did I win?" Orvil groaned.

"It depends," Bruce said. "Am I dead?"

"I don't think so."

"Well, then I'm not sure," Bruce answered.

"You have a pretty good right," Orvil moaned.

"Your left hook ain't that bad either."

"Thanks, you really think so?"

Bruce's answer was a wince.

Bob stepped in closer to the two. He tipped back his hat and leaned down on one knee.

"You boys all right?" he asked.

"Fine, Bob," they said in unison.

"I should lock the two of you up, but if you'll just shake hands and walk away I'll let this one slide."

There was no reply.

"O.K.?" Bob asked.

"Fine with me," Orvil finally said. "But could we wait a few minutes before we shake hands? Mine's kind of hurting right now."

"How's that sit with you, Bruce?" Bob asked.

"Sounds good," Bruce whispered.

Bob turned to the crowd and told them all to go back to what they were doing and to please let Orvil and Bruce rest a minute. He then retrieved a few orange street cones from the police shed and circled the two of them so that no car would accidentally run over them. Bob tended to the others with bumps and bruises and gave Billy's brother a speeding ticket for hitting him in the nose. He figured that was kinder than citing him with assault against an officer. Billy's brother didn't mind the ticket. Heck, he hadn't driven a car since he lost most of his vision falling down the stairs of Parson Stevens's home. In fact Billy's brother felt sort of good about getting the ticket. It stroked his dormant, behind-the-wheel male ego.

Martin let Loni fuss over him for a few minutes and then the two of them walked off together to talk about dogs.

Everyone ignored Orvil and Bruce, and it was about half an hour later that Charity and I saw them get up from the street, shake hands, and swagger away in different directions. The Smith boys then wore the orange street cones as hats and played some sort of ramming game with each other. A small crowd gathered and watched until Bob confiscated the cones after Jeff Smith poked Mike Smith in the right eye. Some yelled at Bob for breaking up the action, but before they could get really bored again, Ian announced that the church house was ready.

It was five in the evening now, and most of the townsfolk had gone home. Sister Wingate had opened back up for business and already shut down again. Sherry had returned to her perch at the Stop & Shop. Not only did she want to get back to work, but she also wanted to get some alcohol and cotton balls to clean up her wounds. Scott had pushed his business back indoors, and the smell of fried eggs filled the street as he started to prepare for the dinner crowd.

The two truckers pulled out of town with very little fanfare—they had done their part. Ian stood on the shaky temporary steps outside the front door of our new chapel.

Sister Lynn had tacked a purple sash across the front door. Ian took a pair of fabric sheers and ceremonially cut through the sash. Everyone walked through the place ooohhhing and ahhhhing as if this were the Smithsonian and we were looking at priceless historical displays. The Primary room with its own closet received as much reverence as if we had been viewing the Declaration of Independence.

There was a large room that would serve as the chapel/Relief Society room, a kitchen that would also function as the branch president's office, a small Primary room, a small priesthood room, a bathroom, and a tiny room that would be our library. By the time we had all finished touring the place, Lehi had broken the hinge on the chapel door, and Sister North had determined that mobile churches weren't half as spectacular as she had hoped. Aside from her, however, the overall feeling was one of thanks. We finally had a building. Charity held my hand the whole time we walked through the place. I was beginning to think she had been assigned by someone to keep track of me. I could think of no other reason for her to be so accommodating to my heart and hopes.

We had received a few boxes and chairs from Church headquarters earlier in the week, and Ian carried them in to open while we were all there. One box had some sacrament trays and a few stacks of forms. Roles, tithing slips, lesson manuals, all the exciting paperwork Church logistics required. Another box had a picture of the current prophet and his two counselors, as well as some chalk and erasers and a small recorder to play cassette tapes. There were other boxes and other articles, but it was the last box that was most appreciated.

"This one's heavy," Ian said, setting the box down on one of the open folding chairs.

Sister Lynn took out her razor blade and slit carefully along the edges of the box, while the members gathered around. To be quite honest, most of us had been disappointed by the contents of the other boxes, though I have no idea what we had all been expecting.

The last box cracked and tore as Sister Lynn pushed back the top. We all took a giant breath as she pulled out green hymnbooks. She handed everyone a copy and then tenderly broke open the one she was holding. It was just the normal green hymnbook, as recognizable and as much a staple of any chapel as the gray tithing envelopes. But here in Longwinded it was much more. Had there been another box that contained the Holy Grail or the Ark of the Covenant, these people wouldn't have cared. They had their hymnbooks. All around me pages were flipping and spines were cracking in celebration of song.

"My goodness," Charity whispered to me. "These people are odd."

I wanted to say I agreed, but I was too choked up to respond.

Ian led us all in one verse of "Count Your Many Blessings" and then "Love One Another." Willie, who had stuck around mainly just to look at Charity, was the first to suggest we all get something to eat. Most of us declined, already familiar with how uncomfortable it was to watch Willie eat. Martin took Willie up on the deal after Loni started complaining about how hungry she was.

Ian slowly ushered us all out and then locked up the chapel. The crowd had dwindled down to where it was just Ian and Bronwyn, Charity, and me. We stood there together as the sun sank ever so slowly behind one of the snowcapped mountains.

"Not bad," Ian said, in reference to what, I was not quite sure.

"Instant building," I commented.

Charity, who had stopped holding my hand a while ago, untied a long-sleeved T-shirt from around her waist and slipped it on. I felt a small tinge of jealously towards that shirt.

"I had better run," she said to all of us.

"Do you need a ride?" I offered.

"Nope, I've got the van." She pointed toward the van off in the distance and dangled her keys.

"See you all later," she said.

I was going to offer to walk her to the van, but Bronwyn beat me to it, leaving Ian and me alone.

"Well," I said, "I should be going myself."

"Could I ask you something first?" Ian asked.

"Sure," I said.

"I need a first counselor."

"I'll keep my eyes open for one," I said in response.

"Does that mean no?" Ian asked.

"No, I suppose it means I accept," I said sincerely.

"Good."

Bronwyn joined us.

"I'll call you tomorrow," Ian said as Bronwyn and he walked away.

"I have one question," I hollered.

"What?" he hollered back.

"Does the Lord approve of this?"

"Let's just say he's willing to give it a chance." The Smiths got into their Jeep and drove off.

Ian was an honest man. I knew there was no way the Lord could be totally hyped about me in a position of leadership, but I also thought him to be gracious enough to give me a chance.

I had parked my truck about a half mile down the street. I whistled softly as I strolled toward it, the stars and slight chill in the air warming my soul. I could see my truck silhouetted against the gray evening. I could also see that someone was leaning against the side of it. I had no cause to be alarmed or to suspect anything, so I continued to stroll right up to whoever it was.

It was Rich.

"Hi, Rich," I said, taking my keys from my pocket.

He didn't say anything, but remained leaning against my door.

"Could you move?" I asked.

Again he didn't say anything, so I just put my hand against his shoulder and pushed him out of the way. I had no time to play games with someone I didn't care for.

Rich stumbled. He then stood straight up, facing me and pushing his chest out as I opened my door.

"You want a piece of me?" he finally said. "You think a baby little Mormon like you can hurt Rich?"

I shook my head out of embarrassment for him and started to climb in. Rich charged towards me, shoving me back and slamming me against the truck. I turned around quickly, not giving him the chance to pin me there. He stepped back a couple of feet as if to create a safe distance between us. He was too slow. I kicked him hard in the stomach causing him to bend forward so that I could throw a punch at him.

I didn't hit him particularly hard, but he fell to the ground and curled up into a ball. I left him there to sleep it off. Eventually, however, I was going to have to do something about him. What, exactly, I didn't yet know.

CHAPTER SEVENTEEN

LAUNCH

It's no easy task deciding what to make for a first lunch with some-one, especially when that someone was Charity. All my years of being single had provided me with a decent ability to put together a pretty good meal, but at the moment I had no idea what to serve.

What meat? Did she even eat meat? What vegetables? Did she like vegetables? Should I go fancy or stay simple? Spicy or bland? So much was riding on this meal; it had to be perfect. I locked myself in the bathroom with a cookbook, determined not to come out until I had found just the right dish. I only had an hour before Charity arrived, so it had to be something that took less than sixty minutes to make.

I had narrowed it down to about eight choices when I heard some-one knocking on my front door. I figured that it was just Martin want-ing to borrow a cup of sugar or some water.

I was wrong. It was Charity!

I ran my fingers through my hair, and as I opened the door I let my eyes show just how surprised I was at her being here now.

"You're early," I said.

"You're perceptive," Charity joked.

"Perceptive is good, right?"

"Yep."

"Would you like to come in?"

"Sure," Charity said.

She came in and stood next to my couch.

"Lunch isn't ready," I informed her. "I wasn't planning on you being here for at least an hour. I figured you to be one of those fashionably late people."

"I hope you're not mad that I'm here early. I came to help," she explained. "What are we having?"

I couldn't be mad at her for coming early. Heck, I probably couldn't be mad at her for much of anything. At least I was dressed and had brushed my teeth a couple of times already today.

"I thought we could have . . . " I quickly tried to think of something I made well. "Lasagna?"

"All right," Charity said with some skepticism.

"You don't like lasagna?"

"I like it."

"But?" I prodded

"But nothing," Charity said. "That sounds good."

I was leading Charity into the kitchen when I remembered that I didn't have all the ingredients for lasagna—I was almost afraid to say anything. Things were going all right so far, but there had been a few moments of that awkward first date silence and a couple of times that neither of us knew what to do with our hands. I mean how many times can you scratch the side of your head and then put your hands on your hips without looking too nervous.

"How about having sandwiches?" I asked.

"No lasagna?" Charity smiled.

"I was just thinking about how messy I get when I eat lasagna. It's probably not the best thing for a first date."

"Is that what this is?" Charity asked.

"I think so," I answered.

"Well, it's nice that you want to stay clean for me," Charity joked.

I wanted to tell her right then and there that I would do anything for her. I could not conceive of a possible situation I would not subject myself to for her. Her blond hair, brown eyes, red lips, and flawless skin were a combination I just couldn't get enough of.

She sat down in one of the chairs at my table, making my dinette set look so much more appealing than I remembered.

"So why are you early?" I asked, pulling sandwich fixings out of the refrigerator.

"I had to get out of my aunt's house. It's so stuffy in there with all that material."

"I can imagine," I said.

"Is it okay?" Charity asked.

"As long as you still stay late."

Charity smiled.

We tore lettuce, cut meat, and spread condiments together. We agreed to see each other the next day, and when she left a couple of hours later I felt confident something would come of our relationship. I thought I had finally found the right dish.

Come on, Fate!

CHAPTER EIGHTEEN

THE SPLITTING APART

I couldn't believe it. Who could have? How did they? And most importantly, why? It was truly the darkest of days for the Saints in Longwinded. There had been a lot of dignity swallowed when we were told our new meetinghouse was going to be mobile. But we had swallowed it and embraced the temporary tabernacle that was now ours. This, however, was too much—someone had stolen half our chapel.

Bob discovered it early Tuesday morning while making his rounds. He had been checking our double-wide chapel twice a day (he figured mobile homes weren't as secure as, say, a building on a foundation), but Tuesday morning he found that instead of being broken into, our building was broken. The back half of our chapel was now missing.

A few members suggested that perhaps the back of our building may have been translated and that right now Enoch was staring out his window wondering when the eternal zoning commission had approved temporary housing. But that theory was quickly dispelled due to the deep tire tracks that clearly showed the course our building's better half had taken.

The Saints were furious, and almost all of them were convinced this was a Baptist conspiracy.

Longwinded was buzzing with speculation. Pastor Stevens emphatically denied the Baptists had anything to do with the heist. Sister Lynn did receive two crank calls from some organization called "Longwinded Instant Living Liberation" who were claiming they had done the deed. They weren't taken seriously.

Bob was having a heyday; he finally had a crime. Amazing as it might seem, no one admitted to having seen a thing. It was as if half our building had just disappeared.

Fern, out of the goodness of his heart, started taking up a collection for the missing mobile. But when he learned how expensive the thing was, he quit. He was thinking a couple of hundred dollars would patch things up.

"Forty thousand!" he raved. "For half a mobile home?"

Fern pocketed the few dollars he had collected and gave up on the cause. Ian couldn't be reached and we had no idea what to do. I tried to calm people down and to reassure my brothers and sisters this would all work out. But it just looked so hopeless. People of all faiths were sobbing over this gross injustice. There were even a few Baptists who had crossed the line and actually tried to comfort us, volunteering any help they might be able to give.

Former President Wingate was sighted six or seven times driving past the spot and smiling, and Sister Wingate was telling people that God's wrath had been manifest today.

Bob pulled me aside to help him try to get to the bottom of this mystery.

"It has to be somewhere," I told Bob.

"That's what I was thinking," he replied.

This case was going to be solved in no time.

"We could get a helicopter from the Forest Service and search the area by air," I suggested.

"That, or I was thinking we could get Pinefield to send up some of their dogs."

I could see it now. A bunch of K-9s sniffing vinyl siding and particleboard and then being let loose in hopes of finding our building.

"Don't you think a helicopter might be better?" I asked gently.

"I don't know, those dogs . . . "

Bob looked at me as I shook my head.

"Maybe you're right," Bob agreed.

I radioed Fred, who sent us a helicopter and a trained pilot. The town was an absolute zoo by the time the helicopter touched down to pick up Bob and me. This was a day most folks would never forget. People were running all over the place, competing with each other, trying to see who could spread the latest mobile mystery theory the fastest.

We got into the chopper and zipped through the air in a somewhat organized search pattern. Bob had notified cops outside our area to keep an eye on the highway and main roads. We focused mainly on the smaller roads where it would be possible to drag half a mobile home.

There was absolutely no sign of it.

The tracks the semi had left ended about a half mile from the scene of the crime, leaving us with hundreds of back road and side road possibilities. There wasn't a single trace of it anywhere.

About an hour into the search our pilot, Doug, began to get bored.

"Hold on," he said.

Doug flew the chopper as close to the ground as possible. We were almost brushing the tops of the trees. He then sped up as fast as he could, flying forward until he was forced to pull up.

"Could you see anything?" he asked.

"Only my life flashing before my eyes," I replied.

Bob commanded Doug to fly in an orderly fashion. Doug consented, turning the helicopter around and heading back to Longwinded. The flight back gave us time to speculate about just who could have taken our building. Bob felt pretty strongly that it was the Baptists, but he made it quite clear he would never openly say that for fear of making someone mad. I admired his conviction. Doug was not a believer in the single parish theory. He thought it was an inside job by the Mormons, who were then going to blame it on the Baptists and try to build up public favor. Bob and I dismissed his theory due to the fact that he was an outsider. I thought the culprit was Rich.

"Rich isn't smart enough to pull off something like this," Bob argued.

"He's mad enough," I argued back.

"It was the Mormons, I tell you," Doug said smugly.

Bob and I ignored him.

≈   ≈   ≈   ≈   ≈

By that evening there was still no trace of our building—no trace and no new clues. Someone finally got hold of Ian, and word was that he was on the way. Charity came to town around six. She, like everyone else, was wondering whether or not we were going to hold our Tuesday night activity. We all considered it canceled due to circumstances beyond our control.

Everyone except the Mormons returned to their homes sad about our loss, but not feeling personally affected. Sister Lynn was on the scene helping the members lament and vent their frustration over it all.

"We should burn their building," Brother Hatch said, referring to the Baptists.

"Don't be dumb, Conroy," Sister Lynn said, disgusted. "We don't even know if they took it."

"I know they did it," Brother Hatch insisted. "My biological compass has seldom been wrong."

I was imagining what Brother Hatch's biological compass might look like when Ian finally pulled up.

At last, I thought. I was getting tired of having to come up with answers I didn't have and solutions I couldn't foresee.

Ian would tell us what to do. Maybe he would form a posse and we would spend the night searching the mountains for our runaway building. Or maybe he would insist on Bob finding the guilty party and prosecuting them to the fullest extent of the law. The consequences for stealing someone's building had to be similar to those for kidnapping or high treason. Heads would roll now.

We all watched Ian as he climbed out of his Jeep. He patted me on the shoulder and whispered, "Help me out here." He then shook a couple of the members' hands and bounded up to the remaining half of the building. He entered through the one available door and then shut it behind him. Everyone turned to look at me.

"What?" I said defensively.

"What did he tell you?" Sister North asked.

"Nothing," I said, "except howdy."

"Well, what's he doing?" Orvil questioned.

"I have no idea," I answered.

"I say we go find out," Sister Theo yelled.

Everyone "me tooed" together.

Sister Hatch led the way up the steps and in through the door.

Whoever had taken our building had been kind enough to cap off the pipes and loose electrical wires. So happily, we still had electricity and running water in the half of the kitchen that was left.

Ian had set up chairs and was now putting a tape in the recorder to play some mood-setting music. Everyone filed in and took a seat as if they had some idea of what was going on. After a couple of minutes of sitting there quietly, Ian turned off the tape and started to talk.

"At least it's a nice evening," he joked.

Everyone scowled.

We all sang "Because I Have Been Given Much"—the chip-on-your-shoulder version—and Ian gave a nice opening prayer that was completely void of any mention of our plight, except for a token "Please help us in our time of need." By the end of the prayer most everyone was tired of waiting. We wanted answers.

"What's the deal, President?" Brother Hatch finally said. "We didn't come here for any sort of church activity."

"Isn't it Tuesday night?" Ian asked.

"Yeah," Brother Hatch answered. "But don't tell me we're just going to go about our business as if nothing has happened. If you haven't noticed, half our building is gone," he exclaimed.

"I've noticed," Ian said, wind from the open half blowing a few of his papers around.

"Well, what do you propose we do about it?"

"What *can* we do about it?" Ian asked.

I could almost hear everyone thinking things like "Spray paint the Baptist's building" or "Let's tar and feather Pastor Stevens." Everyone remained silent.

"I can probably guess what you all are thinking," Ian said. "But none of those ideas are real solutions. We can rant and rave, spilling ill will among the group, or we can go on with our lives."

"How can we progress with only half a building?" Orvil asked.

"It'll work out," I said, jumping in for the first time. "Whoever did this intended to make us angry."

"That's right," Sister Lynn said. "Upsetting us will only make them happy."

"I talked to Bob just a few minutes ago," Ian said. "He volunteered to camp out here at nights until we can get things fixed up. I also put in a call to Brother Stolt, whom I'm sure when he hears about this will respond immediately."

The wind whipped through our congregation and blew a couple of people's hair around.

"What about the wind?" Chad asked.

"No need to worry about that," Sister Lynn said. "Clara Reese has already started on a large quilt to cover this side until we can get it fixed or find our other half."

"Good," Ian declared.

A closing prayer was offered and everyone started home. Charity and I stayed around to fill Ian in on the day's activities and wait for Bob.

Bob pulled up around eight-thirty with his camper trailer. He parked it at the open end of the building and started to make himself at home.

Charity and I left Ian and Bob, while Bob was questioning Ian about the possibility of our building having just dissolved.

"Particleboard doesn't last forever," I heard Bob say as I held hands with Charity and walked her to her car.

"I think I'm beginning to feel a little bit too intertwined with the community of Longwinded," I said to Charity.

"Is that good or bad?" she asked.

"I'm not sure," I said. "I guess it all depends on what happens between you and me."

Charity smiled.

CHAPTER NINETEEN

SINGULAR

If some grand historian ever writes a history of Longwinded—although I have no idea why any grand historian ever would—the period of time we were now in would have to be titled "The Era of Odd." Things were falling into place, except they were landing in slots and notches they had never inhabited before.

A good number of Baptists were convinced the perpetrators of the mobile home heist had been from their parish. This was creating awful fights and disagreements within the Baptist congregation. Pastor Stevens had said last Sunday from the pulpit that even if it had been a Baptist who took the building, they should support him instead of sticking up for the Mormons. This made every Baptist who had an ounce of liberal in their blood furious.

Their division grew.

We Mormons were a different story. With half our building exposed to the elements, we went forward in faith. Sister Reese kept her word and made a thick, giant quilt that spanned the entire length of our building and closed up our missing side. She stitched the image of a fireplace in the middle of it and made a tricky opening at one of the ends. It did a pretty good job of keeping the place closed up and wind-free.

Whoever had taken our building had been kind enough to push all the personal objects to the side they left. So we still had all of our chairs and materials, and most importantly, we had our hymn books. I'm not sure if it was the result of years of musical drought, or just a branch of people with powerful pipes—but when we sang, we sang! Our building shook, as adults and children alike belted out hymn after hymn after hymn. Ian started to capitalize on our desire to sing by having us sing whenever a lull occurred. For example, if Sister Rawlings' testimony dragged on just a little too long or if Brother Merrill's talk on repentance turned into nothing but a story of his former life of debauchery and womanizing, Ian would cue Sister Lynn, and she would pop up and start leading us in song. Nonmembers would comment on the fact that our quilt was always quaking due to our constant singing.

With half our building gone, sacrament meeting was pretty cramped, but we managed to squeeze everyone in. The space deficit made sitting closer to Charity a necessity. I delighted in this perk that our plight provided.

Ian's big emphasis was on being more tolerant of other religions in the area. When he announced this was what we should be working on, a few of our less compassionate members got up and left. Sister Moteah hexed us with her hands as she stormed out, putting a curse on the whole lot of us. Ian took it all in stride.

"Brothers and Sisters," Ian said. "If you could bear with me for just a moment."

Sister Paul raised her hand.

"Yes?" Ian asked.

"I was wondering if I could get a CTR ring for my daughter?" Sister Paul asked.

"Well they are supposed to be for the Primary children," Ian explained.

"I realize that," Sister Paul said. "It's just that Kathy's going through some hard times now, and I know it would be easier for her to choose the right if she had a ring."

"I'll see what I can do," Ian said.

Sister Paul sat back, happy that Ian would consider her request.

"Brothers and Sisters," Ian said. "I wanted to talk to you about—"

Lehi made a loud chicken noise.

Sister Lynn stood and put her hands upon her hips. "President Smith is trying to talk," she chastised.

The room quieted down.

"Thank you, Sister Lynn," Ian said. "I wanted—"

Ian was interrupted again, this time by Brother Hatch, who was sitting in the last row, to the side, near the quilted fireplace. Apparently Brother Hatch had forgotten the wall was fabric. Tilting his chair, he leaned back into it. His feet flew up as he pushed through Sister Reese's masterpiece. For a moment he was suspended as if he were lying in a hammock, but then the duct tape that was holding the bottom of the quilt in place gave way, dropping Brother Hatch like a big wad of wet clay. His scream ceased the moment he hit the ground.

Thud!

Everyone raced to the opening he had created in the quilt. Brother Hatch lay there silently, sprawled as if the ground were his cross to bear.

"Conroy!" Sister Hatch screamed, jumping over all of us and onto the ground. Her high heels almost stabbed Brother Hatch in the head.

"Conroy!"

Brother Hatch's eyes slowly opened. He looked at all of us leaning over the edge of the mobile home and grimaced. The chair he had been sitting in now lay a few feet to the west of him. He saw it and started to laugh.

Ian was down next to Brother Hatch now, trying to help him to his feet. Everyone else jumped off the edge of our building and came down to join them.

"You okay?" Ian asked. "Did you break anything?"

"No, I think I'm all right. Just had the wind knocked out of me." Brother Hatch's face was now regaining color.

"What did he say?" little Lehi asked his mother loudly.

"He said he had the wind knocked out of him," she explained.

"Then how come he's still so fat?" Lehi asked.

Everyone went silent.

Brother Hatch had this thing about his weight.

According to Longwinded legend, two summers ago he locked himself in the library bathroom for six days. The reason being, someone told him that for his height he was seventy pounds overweight. When he heard this, he rushed down to the library to find out for himself.

Sister Wingate helped him find the book *Fat Facts*, and there in black and white, more painful than declining a second helping, was the sad truth. Brother Hatch wasn't seventy pounds overweight, he was eighty-five! Disgusted with himself, he hid up in the library bathroom, refusing to come out until he had starved off a few pounds.

Bob was called in to help, but he couldn't see any harm in Conroy dropping a few pounds, especially if he wanted to. Sister Wingate, furious that Brother Hatch would choose to cloister himself in such a public place, and tired of him being in the bathroom for six days, called in a couple of professionals to take the door off from the outside.

What they found was not a pretty sight. There was Brother Hatch, knee deep in Twinkie wrappers (he had found Sister Wingate's secret stash in the vent), delirious from hunger, and moaning something about slow-cooked roast beef while lying in a bed of unrolled toilet paper.

Brother Hatch underwent some intense therapy for a couple of months and then spent two weeks on a diet ranch. When he returned, his wife threw him a welcome home party to show her support. It was the biggest spread Longwinded had ever seen.

"After all," Sister Hatch had said, "Conroy loves a good meal."

She was oblivious to that fact that what her husband had been trying to do was break off his steamy, passionate affair with food for a far less exotic relationship with fitness. Well, Brother Hatch gained all thirteen pounds back his first night home, and out of kindness to his mental well-being no one had breathed a word about his weight since.

Brother Hatch now stood there silently. Lehi's mother gathered him up as if she could foresee harm in his future.

"President," Brother Hatch said.

"Yes?" Ian replied, a ring of members surrounding the two now.

"Could I talk to you for a moment?"

Ian ushered Brother Hatch into our kitchen/bishop's office and closed the quilt behind them.

"We need our building back," I whispered to Charity, as others began to gossip about Conroy's fall and little Lehi's comment.

"Shows great restraint on Conroy's part to take a time-out instead of beating Lehi," Sister Hatch said. I tried to imagine their home life for a moment.

We all climbed back into the building and took our seats in our half chapel. Sister Theo started up a lively debate on baptismal fonts and the growth that had followed their installments. Where she got her statistics, I have no idea.

Ian came out of his office and motioned me to come over into the Primary room with him. I left Charity and the others to join him.

"Brother Hatch has asked for a blessing," Ian said in hushed tone.

"That was a pretty hard fall," I replied.

"Actually," Ian said, a small smile playing on his lips. "Actually, he doesn't want a blessing for the fall; he wants one to lose weight."

I smiled also. "You're kidding."

"Nope."

"Is that legal?" I said. "I mean isn't that blasphemy or something?"

"I don't think so."

"Are you going to do it?" I asked.

"Why not?"

I could think of a few reasons why not, but I kept them to myself.

"Listen, Tartan, Brother Hatch thinks this might work. So you and I need to go in there and give him that blessing without laughing."

I snickered.

"Brother Hatch asked that we don't tell anyone what this blessing is for. He said he wants to make sure that if he ends up not losing any weight nobody's testimony of priesthood blessings will be affected."

"How noble," I commented.

"Yeah, isn't it?" Ian said.

"Certainly you couldn't blame Brother Hatch's mouth for the failure. The priesthood seems like a much more sensible force to blame—will-power versus priesthood power."

"Well, I think we should do it," Ian said.

I agreed, and we walked back to the office. I could hear the blessing already: "Bless that Brother Hatch will stop after seven doughnuts and that his fat intake will always stay somewhere in the double digits. Please bless his wife that she might only include two pounds of cheese in her famous no-fuss lasagna."

We entered the office and Ian closed the quilt behind us. Brother Hatch sat there, fidgeting and darting his eyes back and forth between Ian and me.

"Does he know?" he asked Ian nervously.

"He does."

Brother Hatch dropped his gaze to the floor.

"He won't tell a soul," Ian comforted him.

We put our hands on his head.

"Aren't you going to use oil?" Brother Hatch asked.

"I think it would be best if we didn't," Ian counseled. "Besides I don't have any on me."

"I had a whole bottle at home that I've been meaning to bring to the branch to consecrate," Brother Hatch said reflectively. "I used it all up on the fried chicken, though."

"Waste not, want not," Ian said.

I could think of no better segue into a weight loss blessing than a conversation about fried chicken.

Brother Hatch shook our hands off of his head. "Maybe I should eat something before."

Ian gave him one of his branch president glares.

"Yeah, right," Brother Hatch said, settling back into his chair.

It was a great blessing.

Ian gathered us altogether after the blessing to make the announcement he had intended to make before Conroy's fall.

"I just wanted to announce that the entertainment committee and I have decided to do something a little out of the ordinary for our Fall into Winter celebration. We've decided to throw a community party."

"Whom would we invite?" Sister North asked suspiciously.

"Well, for starters the community," Ian answered.

"Just what do you mean by that?" Sister Hatch asked, giving Ian a hard stare.

Sister Lynn, our ward activity chairman, stood.

"President Smith had the inspired idea to throw a party where all faiths could have a good time together."

She needed to make the obvious a bit more obvious.

"You mean the Baptists?" Lehi's father asked.

Bronwyn squirmed in her seat, as Ian adjusted his tie and his attitude toward the open-mindedness of Longwinded residents. Charity sat perched on the edge of her folding chair, as if waiting for the first side to draw blood.

I stood.

"Brothers and Sisters, this is an inspired idea," I said. "Just think how much more charitable this will make us look than the Baptists."

I had their attention.

"We'll openly invite them to spend time with us—you know none of them will show—and in the end we appear to be the more Christlike religion." I hated to be doing this, but I could see no other way to talk some of our members into it. If in some small way they felt this was a chance to look better than the Baptists, I knew they would jump at it. "Love your enemies," I pleaded.

The room was quiet as everyone thought about this plot to outshine our rival religion.

"Where will it be held?" someone finally asked.

"Sister Smith and I," Ian said, "have decided to have the celebration at our home outside of Meadow Lane. We just built a new barn, and before we put any animals in it we want to throw a party."

"That's almost an hour away," Orvil protested. "How are we all going to get there?"

"Orvil," I questioned, "how many cars do you have?"

"Seven, but only five run," he answered honestly.

"Those who can't drive can surely find a ride with someone else,"

Ian said. "We could even post a ride board at the library. I'm sure there are some Baptists that may need rides as well."

"But none of the Baptists are actually going to show, right?" Brother Hatch asked.

Ian shook his head in disgust.

"Surely none will show, but we have to look like we are doing everything possible for them to have a chance to come," I said. "Just think, if one actually does show up we'll be so nice they'll run away scared."

"I like it," Orvil commented.

Sister Lynn, Ian, Bronwyn, and I all sighed a great sigh of relief. Orvil carried a lot of weight around our branch. It had been Orvil who had talked everyone into burning the hymn books at the Pinewood Derby. The Saints of Longwinded seemed to think that because he was Native American he had some sort of spiritual connection with the elements and God that they didn't possess.

Everyone began talking about the party and how Christian they all were to be hosting it. I could tell it depressed Ian to see the depth of his branch surface in such a manner.

When the meeting finally broke up, everyone was hyped. Sister Lynn and the Primary kids made some big posters with maps and then left to hang them up at the post office. Orvil had plans to paint up one of his cars, so as to create some sort of a moving advertisement. But then he became concerned about anti-Mormons slashing his tires or scratching up his paint. The suspected harm was too great.

"Maybe I'll just put a poster on my lawn," he compromised.

"Good idea," Ian said.

Sister Hatch had volunteered her services as food chairwoman. I could see Brother Hatch sweating over her desire to serve. All other areas of concern were quickly filled by members who were for once excited about the Fall into Winter social.

Charity and I spent some time alone at her house that night while her aunt went around collecting clothes from other people. It seemed like the right time in our relationship to kiss Charity, but instead we just talked about the barbecue.

Neither one of us could wait to see how the Baptists would respond.

CHAPTER TWENTY

REACTION

They couldn't believe it. Bob called Ian twice to confirm what the yellow sign in the post office said quite clearly.

ALL FAITHS BARBECUE
(YES, ALL FAITHS)

TIME: Saturday, August 20th From 1:00 pm Till 8:00 pm
PLACE: See Map at Bottom of Poster
PURPOSE: To Bring All People of Longwinded
Closer Together

Everyone Is Invited and Encouraged to Bring a Dish of Their Own (Meat Will Be Provided). There Will Be Games and Activities, As Well As a Talent Show

Call Gwen Hatch for More Details 888-2634

PUT ON BY THE MORMONS OF LONGWINDED
SORRY, NO ALCOHOL ALLOWED

Once again the town was abuzz.

"Good glory," Bob swore. "This could be the end of us."

But there didn't seem to be a lot of negative talk; it just seemed that people were absolutely flabbergasted that the Mormons might even consider such a thing. I was beginning to think it was a splendid idea. The people of Longwinded did get along. All week long Baptists and Mormons did business, swapped stories, and associated with each other. But it seemed as soon as Sunday arrived, all of that was scrapped so as to continue the tradition of religious feuding.

Now the Mormons had laid their cards out on the table and were bidding their opponents to fold or call. A lot of Baptists had already said that just maybe they would go—after all, the invitation included free meat. This frightened a few Mormons, but they were easily convinced the Baptists wouldn't actually show.

Sister Wingate sent Ian and me each a card expressing her strong disappointment in our decision to encourage such a thing as an interfaith barbecue. "President Wingate would have never sanctioned such an act. The Church of Christ cannot be home to hooligans or Baptists," she had written. Her Christian attitude was duly noted and then forgotten like the cards we both threw away.

After the initial shock of it all, amazing things began to happen. First Willie took down the sign outside of his station that said "Baptist discount." Perhaps he was tired of not getting the full sale from his compadres, or perhaps he didn't want to seem quite so anti-Mormon. Fern changed his mind and called off his baptism into the Baptist church for the time being. Scott started to serve Caffeine Free Coke at his counter and offered hot chocolate as well as coffee to his patrons in the morning. They weren't huge changes, but they seemed to suggest that just maybe the Baptists weren't as horribly anti-Mormon as we had thought. It was also a pretty good indication that our barbecue invitation was being viewed kindly (the promise of free beef seemed to soften hearts immensely).

≈   ≈   ≈   ≈   ≈

I was just returning from Beaver Lake when I passed Orvil. He was riding his horse he had affectionately named Dogfood. Orvil waved me down. I pulled over and waited for him to reach me.

"Brother Hatch wants to call an emergency meeting," Orvil said, short of breath.

"What for?" I asked.

"He's concerned that Loni, and maybe even Scott, might show

up at the barbecue. Apparently they've been telling folks they are going for sure. Word is that Loni's already working on a bean dish to top all the others."

A little culinary competition.

"Sister Hatch's bean pit pie is pretty hard to top," I said.

"Yeah, but Loni soaks her beans."

This was one of the stupidest conversations I had ever had.

"Have you talked to Ian?" I asked.

"Can't get hold of him. Bronwyn said he won't be home until late tonight."

I needed to make a decision.

"Would it really be so bad if Baptists showed up?" I asked, hoping Orvil would answer maturely.

"You're joking, right?" Orvil asked in return.

I sighed and let my shoulders sag. "Tell Brother Hatch, and whoever else might be concerned about the Baptists showing up, to meet me at the church Sunday morning at seven."

Orvil nodded his okay while I rolled my window back up.

"Wait," Orvil said. "Do you know if Martin is at your place?"

"I have no idea," I answered.

Orvil kicked Dogfood in the ribs and galloped off in the direction of Flint's.

I drove to Scott's and went inside for a drink. A couple of members had voiced their concerns about me (the first counselor) going into Scott's bar.

"It just doesn't look right," they would say.

But I could see nothing wrong with it, so I usually stopped by Scott's at the end of the workday and had a Sprite while Scott talked about a specific tattoo he was saving up for. Today Willie was there as well, nursing a warm beer and throwing an occasional dart.

"Hey, Tartan," Scott said as I walked in the door. Willie nodded a polite howdy as well.

"What's up, guys?" I asked.

"We were just talking about the barbecue," Scott said.

"Are they going to have darts there?" Willie asked.

"Wouldn't be surprised if they did," I answered.

"I think I'm going," Willie admitted.

"Me, too," Scott said, almost embarrassed.

Scott handed me my Sprite. "You're not going to try to change us into Mormons, are you?" he asked.

"Nope."

"I hope not," Willie said. "My Baptist heritage would be horribly insulted."

Willie was using words from Pastor Stevens again.

"It's mighty neighborly of you Mormons to invite us, however," he added.

"It should be fun," I said, mentally trying to decide what I was going to say to Brother Hatch and his band of disgruntled dissidents—the enemy was going to show.

Willie went back to throwing darts, and Scott slipped out the rear door to feed his chickens. I could already see the egg-on-egg casserole delight he would bring to the barbecue.

This barbecue was a good thing, and I could feel myself becoming more comfortable with Longwinded as everyone became excited about it. Oddly, I wasn't so scared about becoming too comfortable anymore, not with the possibility of Charity.

I was concerned, however. It seemed as if she and I were turning into good friends, but I couldn't clearly see the point where sparks would start to fly. She was beautiful—my word she was beautiful. My mind exhaled whenever she was around. I could also tell she didn't disapprove of me: she called me, she loved to do things, and she had remarked more than once about how nice it was that I was around. All this was great, but I had no desire to just be her friend until the day she might decide to leave Longwinded—and me—behind.

I knew she still had bad feelings about Howard, but she refused to talk to me about them.

Maybe tonight, I thought, as I sipped my watered-down Sprite (Scott cut every corner he could). Tonight I was taking Charity to the big city. A movie, not a video, and dinner, not lukewarm hot dogs from off the metal rollers at Stop & Shop. I sensed that if sparks were ever going to fly, they would have to start up tonight.

"Another," I said, hailing Scott to refill my red tumbler.

"So, you're going out with Charity tonight."

People knowing my business was so commonplace now that I

hardly flinched at Scott's awareness of my love life. I figured Bob had dragged it out of Sister Reese or Charity and had then traded the information to Scott for the latest on his kid in reform school.

"Hoping to impress her with the big city?" he asked.

"Something like that."

"Will you be eating dinner there?" Scott asked, setting me up.

"Yeah."

"I could fix you up something here—before you go."

"Well, I . . . "

"I ain't no big city eatery, but I have fair prices."

I could see it now: Charity and me sitting romantically at the bar while drunk men threw darts and Scott served us cold eggs and warm soda.

"Thanks," I said, "but I think we'll try out what the big city has to offer this time."

"All right," Scott said, sounding hurt.

"Nothing personal."

"Sure," he said, picking up his towel and wiping off the bar.

I tasted my refilled drink and then snuck out while Willie and Scott were discussing tires.

≈   ≈   ≈   ≈   ≈

Flint's was cloudy that afternoon, but a few early stars had enough luster to push through the bulky clouds. I washed up and put on my nicer shoes and pants.

I looked at myself in the mirror. I didn't feel like I looked twenty-nine; I thought I looked more like twenty-six. My hair was getting long enough that I needed to start thinking about getting it cut soon. I had been trying to decide if I should grow a beard but couldn't quite make up my mind. As things stood right now I had a pretty good start toward a beard and I decided to leave it for the evening.

I was going to wear a plaid shirt, but the stubble combined with the plaid was just a little too rugged for the mood I was hoping to create. I settled for a black T-shirt in hopes I would come off as mysterious.

I fixed some dinner for Albert and then sat on the porch waiting for six o'clock to roll around. A couple of minutes later Martin and

Rex popped up over the edge of the knoll and strolled toward Albert and me. Martin's blond hair was combed back into the tiniest ponytail I had ever seen, and he held a Monopoly box in his hand.

"Sorry, Martin, not tonight," I said apologetically.

"Actually I was sort of hoping . . ." He paused.

"Yeah?" I asked.

"Well, I ran into Orvil today, and he invited me to do something with Sherry and him tonight."

"A threesome, huh?"

"Well, actually Orvil said something about Loni coming along."

"Sounds fun," I commented.

"I don't know," Martin said hesitantly. "Loni is a woman."

"That she is," I said.

"You know, Tartan, Orvil and I were hoping that . . . Well, since you're going out with Charity tonight, we were hoping that we could use your place to play some Monopoly. Orvil had his place exterminated yesterday, and the smell is still pretty overwhelming. And of course my place is out of the question."

"That's fine," I said. "You won't go through my drawers will you?" I asked jokingly.

"Nah, you Mormons probably have boring drawers anyway."

That was the truth. My most private drawer housed nothing but clean underwear and old *Ensign*s. I did have that photo album with a picture of my fifty-year-old mom in her bathing suit playing shuffleboard with her friends. But that was far from a boiling blemish or exciting secret.

I got up to go.

"Take care of Albert for me?" I asked.

"Of course," Martin answered.

I went inside and got my wallet, keys, and one more application of cologne. Martin was too busy setting up the Monopoly board to notice my departure.

CHAPTER TWENTY-ONE

FLAME

I pulled up to Charity's place five minutes early. I stewed a moment, wondering if I should wait a few minutes before knocking on her door. I didn't have to stew long. Charity was walking my way. I got out to open the truck's door for her.

She smiled and I could see inside her head. Every thought she was processing at the moment was inspired. My heart pumped faster.

"Hi, Tartan," she said, squeezing my hand and getting into the truck.

I watched her smooth her skirt and bite her lip as she sat down. I then walked slowly around the front of the truck back to the driver's seat. I didn't want to walk too fast and risk the possibility of tripping in front of her. I got in and we were off.

"This should be fun," Charity said.

"Uh, huh," I said a little too enthusiastically.

She laughed.

"What?" I asked.

"Nothing," she said. "I'm just glad you're excited about tonight."

"Heck, yeah, I am."

"You have such a nice way with words." She smiled.

We made one stop at Scott's before we left town. I had felt badly telling Scott about our excursion to the big city and our plans to fortify ourselves at some place other than his. So I picked up a couple of burritos, two bags of chips, and told him Charity and I would eat them as we traveled. I had no real plans of eating the stuff tonight, but I figured it would heat up nicely tomorrow morning in my toaster oven.

There was no secret about what Charity and I were going to do tonight—I had briefed Charity on the basic format. A great dinner, followed by a good movie, and then a nice ride home. It wasn't a remarkably spectacular itinerary, but I didn't know the big city well enough to do much more. I figured I would check the place out tonight and then come on really strong and creative on our next date.

"Tell me about Provo," Charity said as we drove. "What's it like to live with all those Mormons?"

"Great," I said.

"Do you think you could expound on that thought?" Charity asked.

"It's *really* great," I said hesitantly.

"If it really is a great place then why would someone such as yourself," she said signaling to me, "trade *that* for Longwinded?"

"Isn't it pretty clear?" I asked.

"Actually, no," she replied.

"Okay, if you must know, I'll tell you."

"Good, and don't give me that same story about people setting you up."

"Well, believe it or not, that did have something to do with my decision. But if you promise not to tell, I'll let you know another reason."

"Promise," she said with mock sincerity.

"Until I came to Longwinded I had never been out of the state of Utah."

"You're kidding."

"Nope," I said.

"But Bob told me you served a mission."

"Did he tell you where?" I asked.

"No. Brother Hatch guessed it was someplace in Europe."

"Ogden's a far cry from Europe."

"Ogden, Utah?" Charity laughed.

"Go ahead, everyone else has already laughed about it. Born in Sandy, raised in Alpine, went on a mission to Ogden, and lived in Provo. I did spend an afternoon just over the Idaho border harvesting potatoes for poor people so some kid could get his Eagle. But we were trucked there and trucked out."

Charity was really laughing now. "So you thought you would break free of the Utah border, and you chose Longwinded?"

"Hey, I took the first transfer I could."

"What luck," she said.

"You're just mad because I'm here. I'm taking away valuable time you could be spending with Willie or Chad."

"A Utah psychic."

"I knew you had something for Willie," I joked.

Charity pushed her hair up over her shoulders and let it fall down her back. It reminded me of someone fanning a lengthy book. *How novel,* I thought.

"You know what, Tartan?" Charity asked.

"No, what?" I answered.

"I'm glad you're around."

Charity then slipped into some sort of silent contemplation mode. I watched her scratch her nose and then try to look at me without me knowing—which was impossible since I had great peripheral vision. I could almost see behind me out of the corner of my eye. It was the one ace I had when dating. I could see if my date was bored or if she was doing something that would indicate her mood. I broke up with a girl named Cindy once because she was secretly trying to clean her ear while we were driving on a date. She had her finger a good two inches into her ear, twisting and cleaning like mad, while I stared straight ahead pretending not to notice. Then she had tried to hold my hand.

Charity looked away.

"Glad you're around" is what she had said. I just wish she would have slipped in something like, "I'm really glad you are here. You're the greatest guy I've ever met. I mean, I barely know you, and already I'm thinking about what temple we should get married in."

"Tartan?" Charity asked, interrupting my thoughts.

"Yes."

"What are you thinking about?"

"You."

"No, seriously," she laughed.

"I'm being serious. I know we're just getting to know each other, but I can't stop thinking that God might be happy with me because he sent you."

"God sent me?" she asked.

"Well . . . "

"I hate to break it to you, Tartan, but I came to Longwinded for one reason."

"Intellectual stimulation?"

"Nope, it was so I would be hundreds of miles away when Howard got married. Not that I still wanted him or that it would just break my heart to think of him with her. I just didn't want to be there. I didn't want to have people treating me as if they knew that deep down inside I was crying and weeping because I had lost my man."

"So God didn't send you?"

"Nope. In fact he would probably have preferred that I just bucked up and remained there."

"Well, didn't you at least pray about your decision to come?"

She shook her head no.

"What about a burning feeling in your chest, telling you that you had done the right thing when you first entered Longwinded?"

She shook her head no again. "In fact I felt sort of sick."

This was just great. Apparently our fledgling relationship was founded on nothing that heaven had sent or arranged. One aging single and a beautiful woman trying to get away—that was our foundation. I would compensate by working hard to turn this into something more that just convenient.

The exit for Meadow Lane came into view. A few lights could be seen to the east, and one could be seen to the west.

"Quite a community Ian and Bronwyn live in," I commented.

"Bronwyn sure likes it," Charity said.

I could see why. Even though it was dark out I could tell that the landscape was almost as beautiful as Longwinded. Plus Ian and Bronwyn had the added benefit of being so much closer to the big city. You could already see the outer lights of the city far off in the distance.

"I can't wait to get there," I said eagerly. For some reason I was really excited. I had missed paved roads and houses with sidewalks. I also missed going to the movies. Videos weren't so bad, but the video house in Longwinded didn't get new releases until they were no longer anything close to new.

Charity smiled and almost instantaneously the truck went dead. It sounded as if the engine just stopped running. I pulled to the shoulder and turned the key off. I tried to restart it, but nothing happened.

"Don't tell me you ran out of gas." Charity grinned.

"There's plenty of gas; I don't know what's wrong."

I jumped out and popped up the hood. Things looked all right. Nothing was smoking or loose. "I can't believe this," I mumbled. I stepped back into the truck and turned on the hazards.

I tried to start it again.

"It won't start," I meekly informed Charity.

"Sure," she teased.

"I'm not joking; the thing won't start."

I picked up the radio and called Fred. His voice indicated he was annoyed.

"Stranded?" he asked.

"Yes, I wouldn't have called unless it was an emergency."

"Is anything on fire or is someone in personal danger?"

"No, Fred, but we'd rather not spend the night here."

"Well, what do you want me to do about it?" Fred was in a bad mood. I made a mental note to never call him after dark again.

"Have him call Ian," Charity suggested.

"Listen, Fred," I said, trying to sound commanding. "Will you do me a favor and make a call for me?"

Fred consented. I gave him Ian's number and explained to him where we were. We then waited patiently to hear back.

"This stinks," I said to Charity.

"Could be worse," she stated.

The radio crackled to life. "Tartan, you there?"

I picked up the receiver and spoke. "Go ahead, Fred."

"No one answered, but I left a message on the machine for you," Fred informed me. "Told 'em you were stranded just past the exit."

"Thanks, Fred."

"Don't mention it." The radio went dead.

"Nice guy," Charity observed.

"Isn't he though? Normally he's not this bad." I reached back behind the seats and pulled out the burritos and chips.

"Dinner?" Charity asked.

"Afraid so."

"What if Ian and Bronwyn never get the message?" she asked, not seeming to be overly concerned.

"I'm sure Fred is on his way here right this moment," I said. "I could tell he was just sick with worry."

Charity laughed to make me feel good and then opened up one of the burritos. I thought for a brief moment about saying a prayer for help—and for the food—but I didn't know how it would go over with Charity. I'm sure she liked to pray, but was it too soon in the relationship to suggest something as spiritual as asking for help? Would I look weak? I was hoping to detect a spark of romance tonight, not remind her of her father.

Charity adjusted her seat back a bit and started nibbling on one of the burritos. She handed me the other one. I was somewhat reluctant to dig in. Sure, she looked all right eating hers. She was beautiful. However, I would not be a pretty picture eating a burrito. I couldn't take small feminine nibbles; I would be required to take big male bites. I had planned to be eating a steak tonight, or something I could cut up and debonairly swipe into A-1 Sauce.

"Aren't you going to eat yours?" she asked.

I picked up my burrito, pushed about one-third of it into my mouth, and bit down.

Either Scott hadn't heated up the beans, or they had mysteriously frozen as we had driven. Charity laughed, as she had detected the frozen beans through a series of probing nibbles. I had no idea

what to do. I could chew and swallow, but some of the beans were
so frozen they were like ice. I could roll down the window and spit
this lump of re-fried ice out into the street, but I had a strong feeling
that would look bad. I gazed pleadingly at Charity.

"Do you want some chips?" she asked, handing me a bag of
Dorritos. I pushed the mass of beans to my left cheek with my
tongue and tried to fake swallowing. Charity started eating her
chips.

I waited until she looked to the right for just a moment and then
spat the gob of melting beans into my chip bag. There was some
noise that accompanied my action, but I felt I was successful at hiding my poor social graces from her. She continued looking away.

"You don't want your chips?" Charity asked after finishing hers.

"I want them," I said defensively.

"Oh," she said, shifting to face me.

I looked into my bag. There was my burrito bite resting on the
top chips.

"Can I have just one?" she asked nicely.

"No."

She held out her hand—what wonderful palms she had. I could
trace her love line all the way up her arm, across her perfect neck,
and up to her pouting lips.

"You already had yours," I said weakly.

"Just one?"

"No."

Heck, if that wad of beans hadn't been in the bag I would have
gladly turned them over to her. She could have anything she wanted
from me, especially at this moment. Here in this stalled vehicle, with
cars and semis whizzing by us, she never looked better. I thought
about offering her my wallet or my watch, anything to get her mind
off of the chips.

She looked to the right for a moment.

I pushed open my door, leaned out, and scraped the beans out
of the bag. The frozen beans plopped down onto the asphalt. A few
chips had to be sacrificed, but I had no other choice. I leaned back
in and shut the door, hoping she hadn't understood what I had
done.

"Chip?" I asked holding the bag out to her.

Charity had lost interest. She fiddled with the knobs on the radio and made sure her window was rolled up tightly. The highway was traffic free for a few moments, providing us with a nice silence.

"This isn't what I had planned," I finally said.

Charity smiled.

I tried to start the truck again. Nothing.

"I'm sure help will be here at any moment," I said, feeling that I needed to explain.

Charity just stared off into the distance.

"I guess we could walk, but I'm sure the closest house is miles away."

Charity remained silent. For a brief instant I was concerned that the sheer nothingness of the date so far might have struck her dumb.

"This actually is sort of nice," she said, dispelling my concerns.

A huge semi sped past us, leaving the truck rocking in its wake.

I looked at Charity. I let the realization of what a great situation I had sink through my thick skull and saturate my brain.

Alone.

Together.

"This *is* sort of nice, isn't it?" I said. "Unplanned, but nice."

"So where were we going to eat?" Charity asked.

"I thought we would decide when we got there."

"Well, what movie were we going to see?" she asked.

"I thought we would decide that as well."

"You don't like making decisions do you?" Charity asked, smiling.

"I don't mind making decisions. It's the results of those decisions that frighten . . . Wait a second," I said jokingly, "don't tell me that you're one of those girls who likes guys who can make a decision."

"Howard was the king of decisions," Charity said. "He loved to make decisions for everyone."

"Well, I'm the prince of indecision. I break out in a sweat choosing between all the different brands of toilet paper at large grocery stores."

Charity laughed and continued to stare out into the night.

A touch of awkward silence crept into the truck and attempted to smother the comfortable atmosphere we had been building.

"I know that we have things to talk about," I said, trying to break up the silence.

"I'm sure we do," Charity agreed.

"Important things."

"Like what?" she asked.

"How about Howard?" I said.

Charity winced.

"How about your mom?" Charity suggested.

"You're alone with a twenty-nine-year-old single man and you want to talk about his mother?" I asked.

"You've got a captive single girl in a parked car and you want to talk about her ex-fiancé?" Charity replied.

"Are you comparing my mom to Howard?"

"This really has turned out to be an important conversation," Charity laughed.

"All right," I said. "We'll talk about something besides Howard or my mother. We'll talk about how much more you would have liked me had our date gone as planned."

"Would I have been impressed?" Charity asked.

"I was hoping you would be."

"How impressed?"

"Impressed enough to write something like 'I have found the one' in your journal tonight when you got home."

"The one, huh?"

"Yep, that's me."

"I don't keep a journal," Charity said.

"In that case I guess it doesn't matter what happens tonight." I was going to babble on, hopelessly searching for something worthwhile to talk about, when I realized that Charity was now staring at me. It wasn't just a normal stare. There was something behind her eyes that made every bit of me go haywire. My knees started to hurt, and my fingernails felt loose upon my fingers. It was as if she had changed our relationship from casual to serious with just a glance.

I tried to inject some levity.

"Journals are nice."

"Tartan," she said.

"It's a commandment to keep one," I said, remembering that journals aren't really a subject of levity.

Charity's dark brown eyes shone through the gray night, awakening dusty parts of my soul and rusty regions of my spirit. I felt like the tin man in the *Wizard of Oz* as Dorothy applied the oil. Charity was loosening up hinges and bolts that my life so far had not allowed me to use. Her gaze was an awakening, and her smile was a filling that left my soul stuffed.

"Tartan?" Charity asked.

"Yes," I said softly.

"I'm not sure I've ever felt as comfortable with someone as I do with you."

"Shoes are comfortable."

Charity ignored my joke. "I hate to start sounding like you, but there is something about us that I like."

She was opening up.

"Like?" I questioned.

"I probably would have said *loved* if I hadn't seen you spit that burrito out earlier."

She had seen?

"It was frozen," I tried to explain.

"I'm sure it was," Charity said. "I was thinking after you spit it out about how I didn't want to go out with you when I first met you."

"You didn't?" I said, sounding crushed.

"I thought that the last thing I needed in my life was some guy. I came to Longwinded to be alone."

"Should I leave?" I asked. "I could just open my door and step out into traffic. I'd be out of your life forever."

"That is the exact opposite of what I do want."

"What is it you want, Charity?"

"When I agreed to have lunch with you that first day I think I wanted nothing but to forget about my real life for a moment. I wanted to forget about Howard and to forget about home. But now I can feel my perspectives shifting. My thoughts keep involving more and more of you. This is real life, Tartan."

A huge moving van dragging a car zoomed past our stranded truck. Charity and I swayed back and forth as the truck did the same. I stayed quiet, thinking about what Charity had just said. She was by far the most impressive person I had ever been out with. Beauty aside, she was one spectacular view. I could feel the figurative floor dropping out from beneath me. I was falling. And like a good book whose new spine I had just cracked, my existence pleaded with me to read on.

"It's getting kind of cold," Charity said, rubbing her arms.

I was just about to put my arm around her, tell her how much I liked her, and open up. I was just about to kiss her when a pair of headlights pulled up behind us.

A couple moments later Ian rapped on the truck window. I quickly stepped out of the truck, carefully avoiding my spat out beans.

Ian and I looked under the hood of my truck and then decided to tow it to his place. When we got there Charity ran in to say hello to Bronwyn as Ian and I pushed my truck up next to his garage.

"My truck has never done this before," I complained. "It has over one hundred and fifty thousand miles on it and I've never, until tonight, had a single problem with it." If I had been a cowboy, right now would have been the time when I would take my hat off and slap it against my thigh while saying something like "Gol darnit" or "Don't this beat all?" Instead I rubbed my hand against the stubble on my face and kept silent.

I looked around the outside of Ian's home. It was a very impressive spread. He had a nice-sized house and well-kept lawns and gardens. The house sat just right, giving you an inspiring view of the mountains and valley round about.

"How did you get this place?" I asked with no little amount of jealousy.

"Inherited it," Ian answered.

"No kidding?"

"Nope."

"Some people are so lucky," I lamented. "The only thing I stand to inherit is my mom's upright piano. Which, by the way, is missing two keys and leans to the left."

"Pianos aren't cheap," Ian said.

"This one is," I added, dusting my hands off and following Ian into his house.

Bronwyn made something for Charity and me to drink. She offered to make us a couple of sandwiches, but we declined the invitation. We both felt we had imposed enough already. Ian volunteered to drive us home.

Charity and I said good-bye to Bronwyn and then went out and got into the Jeep. Ian told us he would join us as soon as he made a quick phone call. Charity and I sat alone in the backseat of the Jeep, waiting patiently. Despite all that had gone on it was still a beautiful night. Stars blinked though the blackness to some undefined rhythm.

"I didn't mean for this night to turn . . . " I started to explain to Charity.

Charity stopped me midsentence.

"Shhh," she whispered, putting her finger up to her red lips.

"Well, I . . . "

Charity leaned into me. She put her right hand behind my head and pulled me to her. She then put those perfect lips on mine and kissed me. Every single fiber of my body was convulsing as my heart flopped around inside my chest like a pair of wet tennis shoes in the dryer. The backseat of the Jeep started to cave in and then expanded to everything I had ever hoped and dreamed of. I knew Ian would be upon us in a moment, but I didn't care. I threw my arms around her and kissed her back.

It was heaven!

Charity ran her hand through the back of my hair as we kissed.

My fingers were starting to tingle.

She whispered my name.

My ankles began to pulsate.

Never had I been kissed like this. Never! It only lasted a moment, but it felt just shy of forever.

Ian bounded out to the Jeep and into the driver's seat. It wasn't until we were awkwardly trying to cover up that we had been kissing that he even noticed anything.

"Sorry," he said.

"We were just . . . " I tried to explain.

"I should have taken longer to make that call."

"Amen to that," I agreed.

Charity and I kept comfortably quiet as we drove home, throwing knowing glances at one another whenever possible. When Ian finally dropped us off—Charity first—there was very little to be said.

Sparks had flown.

Finally!

For a single Mormon approaching thirty it was about time.

Ian did say something kind of branch-president-like when I finally got out. I think he felt it was his responsibility to do so. But I had caught his smile in the rearview mirror when he first realized Charity and I had been kissing. He couldn't hide the fact that he was happy for me.

It took me two hours to fall asleep that night. It's difficult for the soul to settle down after being awakened in such a way. Very difficult.

CHAPTER TWENTY-TWO

THE SANCTITY
OF SUNDAY

The emergency meeting was held Sunday morning at seven A.M. Ian decided not to come. He had experienced just about enough intolerance for one lifetime and didn't care to hear Brother Hatch whine about having to share chip dip and stage time with those of a different faith.

"They're coming," Orvil prophesied. "Heard Willie telling Sister Wingate about a new shirt he was going to wear."

"I knew this would happen," Brother Hatch said, wringing his hands as he paced back and forth. "I knew it."

"We invited them," I argued.

"Yeah, but you told us they wouldn't come," Sister North complained. "If I'd known they would show, I would never have given my support."

"Nor I," Brother Hatch said.

"Same here," Orvil added.

There were only a handful of people at the emergency meeting besides Charity and me. Brother and Sister Hatch, Sister North, Orvil, Sister Theo, and Sister Lynn, who had come with the express intent of helping me keep things under control.

"We need to remember what Christ would do," I lectured.

"What's that?" Sister Theo answered.

"Get along," Charity answered for me.

"What we need to do, is remember that it was a no-good Baptist who stole half of our building. They have defaced the Lord's mobile home," Brother Hatch shouted.

"No one knows if it was the Baptists, or even *a* Baptist," I reasoned.

"I can feel it," Sister Theo said. "Had a dream a few nights back about a crow."

There was a long pause as I waited for her to continue.

"And . . . " I finally said.

"And what?" she asked. "That's it."

"What does a crow have to do with all of this?" I questioned.

"Nothing, it's just that I can't stand them—they pick at my tomatoes."

Sister Lynn did what she did best and brought the discussion back to where it was supposed to be.

"I know it's extreme, having a meal with the Baptists, but I think it's about time we started to get along. Things are different now. People seem kinder than they were just weeks ago. We have to forget about our missing building and foster these feelings of goodwill."

"What goodwill?" Orvil scoffed.

"Orvil, who are you worried about showing up?" Sister Lynn asked.

"Well, Willie was talking about his shirt, and . . . "

"Orvil, where did you spend last night?" she asked.

"Playing pool."

"With whom?"

"Scott, Martin, and Willie. But this is different; this is *church*."

"Like wind it is. This is a barbecue for everyone. The Baptists here don't bite. We all know that. It's time we started to mend the rift."

Brother Hatch started to huff and puff.

"Calm down, Conroy," Sister Lynn commanded.

"Well this whole thing is crazy. They don't believe in Joseph Smith," he said, as if it would finalize things.

A couple of people whispered between themselves about what a good argument Brother Hatch had brought up. I looked at Charity and made the international sign for crazy by twirling my finger around my ear.

"You talk to them, Tartan," Sister Lynn said, throwing her hands up into the air.

I stood and pushed my fingers through my long hair. I could use a little inspiration I thought, trying to shift the dirty work onto the shoulders of God.

"This Saturday there is going to be a barbecue at the home of our branch president," I said. "I will be there, and I hope Ian's barn is packed with Baptists. Anyone who is un-Christian enough to let this keep them from attending will only hurt themselves by missing out on a really good time, not to mention being extremely cowardly. I for one am not afraid of a single Baptist. In fact, I like 'em. Sister Lynn is right when she says we need to mend this stupid religious rift. Even if it were a Baptist who took our building, which I personally don't think it was, then it's up to us to forgive them. Let's move on, for goodness sake. Aren't we all just a little tired of this ridiculous fighting? I know I am, and I haven't been here a fraction of the time most of you have. We should be the bigger people."

Brother Hatch looked up, thinking the last line was directed toward him personally. I quickly added something else.

"If we do this, our burdens will be made light, I promise you."

It was bold, it was straightforward, but it was what I felt prompted to say. I walked out, slamming the quilt behind me.

"Aren't we going to have a closing prayer?" I heard Sister North ask, confused that the meeting had been closed without any benediction.

The meeting was adjourned.

Church went well that Sunday. Those who had attended the early morning gripe session were quiet throughout most of the service. It appeared that they were contemplating how they should feel, or just how they should to react to the real possibility of having Baptists at our barbecue.

Our sacrament speaker was Sister Reese. She spoke on the gospel and how it is the fabric of our existence. She passed out little cloth swatches afterward, with the saying "Swatch what you do" stitched upon each one. However, she turned a cute talk into a real downer when she ended her sermon by saying she had never had a husband and felt doomed to always be single.

"Are you going to come over tonight?" Charity asked as we held hands after the meetings.

"I have a couple of visits to make with Ian and then I'll be over."

"I'll be waiting," she said, walking away from me and getting into her aunt's van.

I counted the times I had been out with Charity on my hands. I then used those same fingers to wave good-bye to Charity as she drove off.

Ian had a couple of interviews and a setting apart to do, so we didn't leave the chapel until much later than I had hoped. We were walking toward Ian's Jeep, on our way to do our visits, when we heard . . .

"Pssst."

"What was that?" I asked.

"What was what?" Ian asked, pulling his car keys from his pocket.

"Pssst."

"That," I said, certain he had heard this time.

The noise was coming from a large cedar bush just over the Church's property line.

"Pssst!" it went again.

"Who is it?" Ian asked the noise.

"Do you think I'd be whispering if I wanted everyone to know who it is?" the voice answered back.

"Sister Wingate, is that you?" I laughed.

"For lands sake, Tartan, keep your voice down."

Ian and I approached the bush.

There was Sister Wingate, crouched beside this overgrown shrub, her head covered with a shawl as if she were playing the part of

Mary in the Christmas pageant. I think she was trying to be inconspicuous.

"I heard about the meeting this morning," she said. "I'm glad to know you are finally doing something about all of this. Sorry I had to miss it, but President Wingate hates a cold breakfast. Anyhow I wanted to find out what was going on to nip this thing in the bud."

"What thing?" Ian asked.

"Why, the barbecue of course. You're not actually planning to go through with it, are you?"

"We are," I said.

Sister Wingate's eyes expanded to the size of compact discs and then contracted until they were no bigger than small pinpoints.

"Mary Longfellow is going to have both of your hides. You realize that, don't you?"

"Is she coming?" I asked nervously.

"Not on your life. Mary might be a bit inactive, but she still has her convictions."

A car drove through the forest behind Sister Wingate. Her eyes darted back and forth, scared that she might be seen.

"How's President Wingate?" Ian asked kindly.

"Never been better," she said smugly.

"Have you two talked about coming back to church soon?"

Ian's question caught Sister Wingate by surprise. She had come out here to scorn, not to be interrogated.

"And what business is that of yours?" she asked indignantly.

"I'm just concerned," Ian explained.

Sister Wingate pulled her shawl tightly against her head. "Concerned? I have a hard time believing that anyone who could willfully invite the kind of trouble this barbecue is going to bring is concerned about anything besides leading each of us into the mists of darkness. I've got the rod, Brother Smith," she said, raising one fist to the air. "I've got the rod, and your great and spacious building can't block my view of the tree."

I shook my head in disgust.

Sister Wingate threw the end of her shawl over her shoulder, and like some sort of overweight, out-of-fashion Batman, stalked off into the forest.

Ian and I looked at one another and smiled, then walked back to Ian's Jeep and drove off to do our visits.

We parked the Jeep down at the end of the lane and walked the half mile to Brother Bender's cabin. Brother Bender lived out on the edge of nowhere. I had never met him, but I had heard from others that he housed a rather unique personality. The area in which he lived was beautiful—thick trees and wild brush covered everything in one shade of green or another.

When we got to his cabin it was boarded up and there was a chain across the front door.

"No wonder he's never been to church," Ian said. "He probably hasn't lived here for months."

"Did you talk to Bob about him?" I asked.

"No. I should have, though. Bob would have known he was gone."

We turned to leave, but stopped when we heard a loud crashing noise come from inside the cabin.

"Something's in there," I said, stating the all too obvious.

"Brother Bender?" Ian shouted.

The reply we got was two shotgun blasts right over our heads. We dropped immediately to the ground.

Ian shifted around on his belly and frantically tried to crawl away. He was kicking up leaves, which were filling my mouth as I tried to talk.

"Brother Bender!" I yelled.

Ian stopped squirming and braced himself for another shot.

"I don't want to have to shoot no one today," Brother Bender hollered. "So you two best get on your way."

"Come on, Tartan," Ian whispered fiercely.

I didn't want to go. This was the most exciting Sunday I could remember.

"We're from the Church," I yelled.

"Tartan!" Ian demanded.

"Which church?" Brother Bender asked.

I could see he was staring at us through a knothole. His shotgun was sticking out of another hole a few inches down. The barrel was angled up, pointing towards the sky.

"We're Mormons," I answered.

"Men of God?" he questioned oddly.

I looked at Ian and shrugged.

"Yes," I yelled.

The chain across the front door started to rattle, then dropped loudly against the wood porch. The door opened just a crack and a large arm popped out, waving us in.

"Should we go in?" Ian asked, looking to me for answers.

"He seems friendly enough," I joked.

We got off of our stomachs and dusted dry leaves and twigs from our bodies. The waving arm waved for us to move faster. We walked up to the door and then cautiously entered. If it hadn't been for the two burning candles, it would have been pitch black in the room, due to the boarded-up windows. The best I could make out was that Brother Bender was a big man, big and scruffy. He looked like an unshowered, extremely frazzled Grizzly Adams.

He held his shotgun up to us and nodded for us to sit down. He sat himself down in a large, matted, greasy looking fur chair that stunk of mildew. I was grateful for the wooden bench he had offered us—dust and splinters I could handle.

"I'm Mormon, also," he stated, watching for our reaction.

Ian had composed himself and was looking every bit the branch president.

"We know, Brother Bender."

"Clark," he said. "Call me Brother Clark. I heard that's what old Brigham Young used to do. He used to call everybody by their first name. 'Brother Bill, Brother Clark, Sister Sarah,' much more personal, don't you think?"

Brother Clark set his shotgun down. Ian and I nodded in agreement.

"Brother Brigham was a good old boy," Brother Clark said. "He knew how it was. Of course, he had all them wives; bet he always had clean socks."

Ian and I laughed uncomfortably and then introduced ourselves.

"God sent you here—I know he did," Clark said.

Ian and I just nodded.

"He's mighty mad at me, I know that. I ain't so ignorant as to not know that."

At least his ignorance was limited, I thought.

"Why do you say that?" Ian asked.

Brother Clark leaned in toward us and with complete seriousness tried to explain.

"He threw rocks at me."

"Rocks?" I asked.

"Rocks," he answered. "I was out trying to get me a little critter to eat, hunting where I know I shouldn't be hunting, and God started throwing rocks at me." Brother Clark folded his arms and leaned back in his chair, looking almost proud that God had picked him to pelt.

I was intrigued. "How do you know it was God?"

"I ain't saying it was him directly. It could have been some angel or one of his helpers. It was the dead of night, and I was completely alone when it happened. I had just knocked off a nice sized buck and was dragging it home when all of a sudden rocks the size of mice started hitting me. They were coming at me from all directions—scariest thing I've ever been through."

"I can imagine," I said, suppressing a smile.

"That's why my windows are boarded up. Rocks can't go through wood," he said matter-of-factly.

Brilliant observation, I thought.

"Were you standing near a cliff?" I asked, wondering if perhaps some pebbles hadn't accidentally broken loose and fallen on him.

"Nope," he insisted. "The rocks came directly from heaven."

Ian decided to use this situation to our advantage. "Brother Clark," Ian said, "that is the reason we are here. We need you to start coming to church, and we need you to start living in such a way that you can be worthy of repentance."

Brother Clark was listening real closely, and Ian was running with this.

"Besides illegal hunting, what other negative things have you been doing?"

"I been sipping the spirits pretty heavy, but I haven't had a smoke since the rocks."

"Anything else?" Ian asked.

"Awful fond of women," he said.

Ian looked at me and cringed.

"Brother Clark, I want you to come to church next week," Ian said. "I also want you to stop drinking."

"What about the rocks?" he asked.

"There will be no more rocks," Ian answered. "So you need to take these boards off of your windows and let some light in here."

Clark nodded. "What about my women thoughts?"

I tried not to imagine what those thoughts might be.

"We'll talk about that later. For now just try to control them."

"I knew you would come here," Clark said. "I knew something was going to happen. I just knew it. God don't throw rocks at just anyone."

Ian read him Doctrine and Covenants 3:8 and changed "fiery darts" to "rocks."

> *Yet you should have been faithful; and he would have extended his arm and supported you against all the rocks of the adversary; and he would have been with you in every time of trouble.*

"Wow!" Clark said in amazement. "The scriptures say that?"

"In a sense, yes," Ian answered.

We helped Clark take down his boards and pour out his liquor. We then blessed his house and left him with my scriptures. He promised he would come to church next Sunday and the barbecue on Saturday if we could find him a ride.

"My truck just can't make it all the way to Meadow Lane," he complained.

"We'll find you a ride," Ian assured him.

Clark walked us to the Jeep, talking a million miles an hour and constantly looking over his shoulder or above his head for falling rocks.

"Should have brought an umbrella," he said when we finally got to the Jeep.

"There will be no more rocks," Ian said.

He turned and started a slow jog home.

"What a visit," Ian commented, as we were driving to our next stop.

"You're not kidding."

"Do you believe that story about the rocks?"

"He probably just had a little too much to drink that night," I reasoned.

"A little too much?" Ian asked.

"The Lord works in mysterious ways," I commented.

"Amen to that."

∾   ∾   ∾   ∾   ∾

Ian didn't tell me we were going to visit Mary Longfellow until we pulled up to her place.

"No way," I said, locking my door as Ian climbed out.

"Come on you big chicken."

"At least I'm an alive chicken."

Ian stood in front of the Jeep waiting for me to grow up. I shrugged my shoulders in defeat and reluctantly climbed out. Ian straightened his tie and put on a serious face. I wrung my hands and tried to suppress my anxiety. Mary was not the kind of person you just visited, not unless she was tied down. She was the kind of person you ignored, a neighborly enigma, a person shrouded in rumors and greatly embellished stories about her never coming out in the day, or lingering too long at the raw meat nook at the Stop & Shop.

Ian knocked sharply on the door.

"Maybe she's not home," I said, hope tainting my dialogue.

"Wishful thinking," Ian whispered, as the door before us was pulled open.

Erma looked particularly frazzled. Her clothes were wrinkled and sloppy, and her hair was flat on one side of her head and sticking up on the other. We had obviously awakened her from a Sunday afternoon nap.

"Hello, I'm President Smith from the Mormon church," Ian said politely. "We were hoping we could visit with Mary for a few minutes."

"You were?" Erma asked, surprised.

"We were," Ian said.

Erma glanced at me nervously. I opened my arms as if to gesture "don't look at me, this certainly isn't my idea."

Erma pushed open the screen door and let us in. The house looked the way I remembered it, rambling and cluttered. Erma led us to a relatively clean room with giant windows on all sides, which permitted a large amount of sunlight to enter. The sunlight did a great job of exposing the layer of dust that lay thickly on every flat surface in the room.

"You might want to sit," Erma said. "It'll take Mary a spell to get here."

I sat down in a plush purple velvet chair. Dust rose up in protest to my sitting where it had settled. I pulled some cushions in front of me for protection should Mary come at me with her metal antlers. I looked around the room for something I could grab to fight her off if it came to that. I spied a large walking stick leaning against the far wall. If she didn't cut me down with her walker, I could easily grab it and buy enough time to get out. I'd have to leave Ian behind, but I figured since he got me into this, it was only fair that he fend for himself.

"It's going to be all right," Ian said, picking up on my nervousness.

"Just wait," I warned, sounding like some doomsday prophet.

Mary's coffee table was covered with copies of *National Enquirer* and *Glamour* magazines. Ian picked up a copy of the latter and thumbed through it. I felt as if I were in the waiting room at a dental office (the fear level was the same). Erma ran past the doorway, obviously scurrying about doing some task for Mary.

"Quite a house," Ian commented.

"Yeah, a king-size collection of clutter."

"She could throw one heck of a garage sale."

"Yeah," I said, "I can just see some poor soul trying to haggle her down twenty cents for some piece of junk and her beating him to a pulp for even suggesting it was worth one dime less than she had marked it." I pulled at the corner of one of the cushions I was holding and then softly punched it.

"No one could be that bad."

"Mary is," I said.

"Couldn't be," Ian insisted.

I thought about making a bet with him but I didn't know if he, as a branch president, would be willing to wager.

Ian put down the *Glamour* magazine he was reading and picked up a *National Enquirer*.

"OOH, listen to this," Ian said excitedly. "It says here that there is this lady who beats people to death with her walker and then hides their bodies underneath piles of junk."

"Funny," I said.

"Thanks," he laughed.

"You won't be laughing when you meet—"

THUD.

"Oh, no," I whispered fiercely, jumping up into my chair, acting as if I were a frightened woman who had just spotted a mouse.

"What?" Ian asked, looking behind him.

THUD.

"She's coming," I tried to say calmly.

"Good," Ian said.

THUD.

Mary was close. I could sense her presence, near and unnerving; like a huge pimple forming under the skin, she was about to erupt. Like pus, she would soon be upon us, and no antiseptic on earth could fight the fear she brought with her. Brother Bender's loaded shotgun was far less worrisome.

THUD. SHUFFLE.

THUD. SHUFFLE.

Even Ian looked a little unsettled now. He had picked up his scriptures and was clenching them tightly. We both closed our eyes. Ian was probably praying that we might be able to help Mary, while I was trying with all my might to will her away.

THUD.

She had arrived.

I opened my eyes slowly. Ian was standing up and moving toward her. The poor fool had no idea what he was doing. I looked at Mary.

The walker was the same, but everything else was different. Her silver hair was beautifully combed and styled with some sort of antique hairpin. She wore a clean red blouse and a dark skirt that looked as though it had been professionally pressed just moments before. She had makeup on and appeared to be at least ten years younger than when I had last seen her. I wondered for a moment if by chance she might have struck some bargain with the devil to regain some of her youth. Of course, just a couple of minutes back, I had thought she and the devil were one and the same.

Ian helped her into a wicker chair and then introduced himself.

"And this is my counselor, Brother Tartan Jones," he said, pointing toward me. Mary smiled a bright, sincere smile. She looked like the kindly grandma we all wished to have. I myself almost felt like crawling into her arms.

Maybe I had been wrong about her. Perhaps she had just been overly medicated when I last saw her—medicine can do strange things to a person. This woman here clearly couldn't harm a soul. I nodded a friendly hello, confident she most likely didn't even remember me. Ian winked at me as if to say, "See, I told you this would go fine." I nodded back as if to say, "You know, I think it just might."

"Yes, President," Mary said kindly. "Brother Jones and I have met before, haven't we, Brother Jones?"

Any comfort I had felt seconds before was gone. Those few words had an edge to them that made every fiber of my body take cover, and there was a glint in her eye that told me that I was in trouble. I softly whimpered as Ian started up a conversation with her.

"Sister Longfellow, we just wanted to stop by and let you know we are willing to help you in any way possible. I realize you have a hard time making it out to church, but I want to see if it might be all right for my wife and me to stop here each Sunday on our way to church and pick you up."

"Oh, that would be great, President," she said, clapping her hands together in joy. "Wouldn't that be great?" she asked me.

"Great," I said nervously.

Ian looked away for a moment and Mary shot me a cold glance. She was playing with us.

"This is marvelous," Ian said enthusiastically. "I am so happy you will let us pick you up."

"Me, too, President," Mary said, dabbing her now-moist eyes.

She was quite the actress.

Ian pulled out his day planner and penned in his new responsibility. Mary looked at me and mouthed some word. I couldn't quite make out what her wrinkled lips were saying.

She did it again, this time breathing life into it.

"Run."

Ian didn't see her say it, but I certainly did. I could feel blood draining from my face. Ian started to chat with her again. I tried desperately to get his attention and warn him of the impending danger. But he was so elated by how this visit was supposedly going that he never looked at me. I waved my hands and coughed for at least five minutes before he gave any attention to me.

"Is something wrong, Tartan?"

"Yes, Brother Jones, is there anything the matter?" Mary said, oh, so sweetly.

"Well . . . I . . . no, I'm all right, it's just that . . . "

"Yes?" Ian questioned.

"Please, Brother Jones, let us know what's wrong," Mary said, sounding sooo concerned.

"No, nothing," I stuttered. "I'm okay."

Ian told Mary a few more things and then started to wrap up the visit.

"Well, Mary, it has been such a pleasure meeting you, and I look forward to getting to know you better."

"Same here, President," she chirped.

"Sister Longfellow," Ian said. "Would it be all right if we had a word of prayer before we leave?"

"I would love that," she said.

Ian sat there proud as an unrighteous Nephite, thrilled by what appeared to be his most successful visit ever. Unfortunately for him, while he was gloating, things started to unravel.

"You know, President, before you give the prayer could I ask you just one question?"

This was it, I thought. I could tell by the tone of her voice that her question wasn't going to be something friendly, like, "Since you will be giving me rides to church, could I help pay for gas?" No, I knew her question would be much more sinister.

"Shoot," Ian said.

Shoot me first, I thought.

Her voice was soft and low at first, but by the end of her question it had reached such a fevered pitch that you could almost feel the skin melting off your body. "I just wanted to know, President, if it was your idea or the idea of Lucifer himself to throw a barbecue and invite the Baptists?" Mary had raised herself so that she was now standing up behind her walker. Her hair was falling out of its clip as she shook her head and flung her spindly fingers at us. Ian's mouth was hanging open and his eyes looked painfully surprised. The veil had been lifted, and Mary's true colors were beginning to bleed all over the room. I wanted to tell him "I told you so," but I was too busy fearing for my life. "I can feel the hot breath of Satan himself," Mary continued, "breathing down the neck of Longfellow. Wally Longfellow will have your soul for this, and he'll have it on a golden spike!" she spat.

Mary was screaming so loudly that Erma came to investigate. When she saw Mary's state, she simply turned and walked away. I stood up and started making my way to the door.

She swung her walker up, blocking my progress. "And you, bad Brother Jones," she vented, "do you sustain this barbecue?"

I shook my head no. Ian looked at me as though I had hurt him. I changed my no to a yes.

"You will burn, Jones, oh, yes, like swine on the griddle of Scratch you will fry. For the sheep that follows is nothing but next day's lunch to Lucifer." I had no idea what she was talking about, and I didn't want to stay around for an explanation. I tried to make my way out again but she stomped her walker in a spastic rage.

"It's just a barbecue!" I yelled.

"With Satan as the chef!" she screamed back.

"Sister Longfellow," Ian pleaded.

She held her walker up in front of her as if she were a trumpeting elephant. I dove for the walking stick. Too slow. Her walker came down on my legs. Finally realizing just how vicious she was, Ian took off his kid gloves.

"Mary, stop that this instant," he ordered.

She lifted the walker off of my legs and turned her rage toward Ian. I got up and scrambled through the door. Mary turned to try and stop me, but she was too late—I had escaped. Mary swore, cursing herself for letting me slip away. I ran into the next room and found a large throw pillow. I picked it up to make sure that it was heavy enough for my purpose, pleaded with fate to guide my hand, and then ran back to rescue Ian.

Normally, I wouldn't set out to hurt an old woman. In fact, I was the kind of guy who helped them cross the street or carried their groceries. But Mary was different. Mary was not your cookie-baking, bingo-playing, average senior citizen. She was more like the love child of all that was unholy.

Mary now had Ian trapped in a corner. She was thrusting her walker at him and stomping her orthopedic shoes. Ian was holding his day planner over his face while trying helplessly to push himself even deeper into the corner. I took aim and then let loose with my weapon of minor destruction. The pillow hit Mary on her left side, dust exploding from it at impact. She sprawled into the big fluffy chair I had been sitting in earlier, scrambling and wiggling like an overturned cockroach.

"Run, Ian!" I screamed. He didn't need to be told twice. He bounded out of the room.

"Help me," Mary whimpered.

I wasn't going to fall for it. Ian, on the other hand, was.

He stopped in his tracks and turned to look at Mary. She was lying still in the chair now, her walker by her side, smoldering.

He looked at me. "Come on, Tartan, we can't just leave her."

"Why not?" I asked, wiping sweat from my brow.

Ian ignored me and started to walk back into the room. He was stopped by a voice coming from behind a large pile of shoes. It was Erma.

"Don't go in there."

"But she needs help," Ian argued.

I must admit she looked pitiful; slumped over in that chair, her body appearing almost lifeless.

"She's faking," Erma said quietly.

"I heard that, Erma. You're fired!" Mary said, suddenly coming to life.

"Go," Erma urged.

Ian and I ran all the way to the car, and it wasn't until we were a few miles down the road that we dared to feel safe.

Ian was the first to laugh.

I joined in almost instantly.

"Did you see her when that pillow hit her?" Ian laughed. "I've never seen anything funnier than her falling into that chair."

"I don't know," I said. "You should have seen your face when she was backing you into that corner."

"I was scared to death. Why didn't you warn me about her?"

"Funny," I said. "Are you going to try and pick her up next week?"

"Are you kidding?" Ian asked, stepping on the gas and pushing us farther and faster away from Mary's home. "We're going to have to do something about her, though."

❧   ❧   ❧   ❧   ❧

Our next and final stop was the home of a Robert and Sarah Crimsal. Neither Ian nor I had met them before, so we were unsure just what to expect. We were encouraged when we pulled up to a beautiful home with well cared for lawns and perfectly manicured gardens.

The garage door was open, exposing two very expensive cars. It was disturbing to see how clean their garage was. Tools were neatly hung on the wall, and cherry wood shelves housed cleaners and household supplies. Never had roach killer been more aesthetically displayed.

This is how every garage should look, I thought.

There was a drop cloth draped over a third car. It was the whitest drop cloth I had ever seen. It seemed to radiate and glow. What kind of people had the ability to keep a drop cloth so clean? The robe

Moroni wore when he appeared to Joseph Smith couldn't have been whiter.

I laughed, thinking of the story people told about Sister Milton in our branch. A few months back she had gone into the big city to buy some material to make clothes for herself and her family. Disgusted by the high price of fabric and finding that Wal-Mart sold six drop cloths for ten dollars, she bought twenty of them. Now her family all wore drop cloths sewn into pants or shirts. She had even used a magic marker to draw pockets and seams.

The whole story was rather funny except for the time she and her kids got stuck out in the rain—drop cloths become quite heavy when saturated with water. The weight of the clothes actually forced her smaller kids to the earth, pinned down by their economical wardrobe. I heard it had been some sight to see her trying to peel her youngest off the ground while trying to prevent gravity and her rain-soaked jumpsuit from sentencing her to a similar fate.

I smiled trying to picture it.

"What are you smiling about?"

"Sister Milton," I answered.

"I was just thinking the same thing," Ian said.

I rang the ornate doorbell and we stepped back a few feet. A nice looking older woman opened the door, smiling. I assumed it was Sarah Crimsal.

We were invited in and ushered to a room that was so clean and perfectly decorated, I was afraid to enter. I sat, somewhat reluctantly, upon a stark white couch. I put my arm up on the arm of the couch and then took it down. I crossed my legs but then uncrossed them when I saw how dirty my shoes were. Footwear like mine shouldn't have been allowed in a sanctuary such as this.

Ian didn't seem to care that we were sitting on a white couch. He shifted in his seat and brushed off the leg of his pants. Sister Crimsal left the room to retrieve her husband.

"This place is spotless," I whispered.

"Far cry from Brother Bender's place."

"I think I felt more comfortable there," I said, somewhat ashamed to admit it. I was certainly no socialite. I fit in better with people who vacuumed seasonally, not daily. Not that I was a slob.

No, I kept my surroundings nice and clean. I just wasn't obsessive about it, or so confident with my domestic skills as to actually own a white couch.

Sister Crimsal returned with her husband.

Ian told them exactly who we were as they settled into large armchairs across the room from us. Although Brother and Sister Crimsal were in separate chairs, they reached to one another and held hands as we conversed. Without knowing much about them I could tell they were in love. They looked to be the perfect older couple. I could practically see their history. Met when they were children and nurtured a growing relationship all throughout their adolescence. He went off to war while she waited for her soldier to return. Upon his return, they married and had five kids who were all taught the value of work and now had successful jobs at different places around the country. He retired from medicine a few years back, and now they were enjoying their time together, as well as a growing number of new grandchildren who visited them all through the year. They were perfect.

What a testimony to good living, I thought.

"Could we offer either of you a cup of tea?" Brother Crimsal asked.

"Well . . . ," Ian started to say.

"Oh, that's right. Mormons don't drink tea. I should know that," he said. "After all, I am a Mormon."

We both laughed uncomfortably.

"A soda perhaps?" he asked, getting up to retrieve us some sort of drink.

"That would be fine," Ian said.

As Brother Crimsal was walking away, Ian asked Sister Crimsal how long she had been a member.

"A member of what?" she asked.

"Of the Mormon church," Ian said.

"Oh," she said. "I don't much care for any religion."

Ian looked perplexed. He looked over at me and shrugged his shoulders.

"I just assumed you were a member," Ian said, embarrassed he had even asked her.

"I think Robert's fifth wife was a Mormon," she said.

My picture perfect image of them was beginning to fray.

Robert came back into the room and handed us all our drinks. The conversation halted as we sipped our sodas. I set my glass down on a coaster provided me by Mrs. Crimsal. Brother Crimsal was the first to start speaking again.

"So what brings you boys out our way?" he asked.

"We just wanted to get a chance to meet the two of you," Ian said. "Brother Crimsal, how long have you been a member?"

"All my life," he replied.

"Have you ever been out to the branch here?"

"Branch?" Sarah asked.

"It's a small ward," Robert said, hoping to explain.

"And a ward is?"

"It's what the Mormons call a congregation."

"Oh."

There was more silence as we each in turn took another drink.

"So, Brother Crimsal, have you been out to the branch?" Ian asked again.

"No, I stopped practicing Mormonism years ago. Don't get me wrong. I still think the Mormons are okay. I know there are plenty of folks out there who still need that kind of guidance. But just between you and me," he leaned in as if to tell us a secret. "Between you and me, isn't religion just something to keep the masses in line?"

Robert and Sarah smiled at each other.

I think he was in some way calling us simpleminded sheep. Ian handled the question well.

"The gospel of Jesus Christ is much more than religion."

"I'm sure it is," he said.

I felt prompted to change the subject. This one was starting to feel uncomfortable.

"So, how long have you two been married?"

"Six months," Sarah blushed.

"Newlyweds," Robert boasted. "Sarah here was the receptionist at a small company I forced into bankruptcy. The moment I saw her, I knew I was in love."

Six wives, too good for religion, and he squashed companies for gain. My first impression of this man had been very wrong.

"Isn't he great?" Sarah giggled, dropping the sophistication she had played so well.

"Well," Ian said, "would it be all right if some home teachers came to visit you?"

"Home teachers?" Sarah asked.

"Yes," Robert said. "They're people who come teach you at your house."

"Teach you what?" she asked.

"Religious fodder," he explained.

"It's more than that," Ian jumped in. "They would also be able to help you out if you ever needed anything. Like if you needed someone to help carry boxes when you're moving."

"But we're not moving," Sarah said, confused.

"Well, if you were," Ian reasoned. "We would also like you to have some visiting teachers if that is all right?"

"Whom do they visit?" she asked.

"You," I answered.

"Why?" she questioned.

"To bring you muffins and spreads," Robert joked. "Or maybe they'll teach you how to make a quilt or something."

"I do like to sew," she said, warming up to the idea.

"Actually it's much more than that," Ian explained. "They are representatives of the Relief Society and will be around to help and to friendship you."

"Is there a cost?" she asked.

"For what?" Ian questioned.

"To join this Relief Society."

"Nope," I jumped in.

"Doesn't sound too exclusive," she said.

"It's for everyone," Ian reasoned. "Everyone needs help."

"With what? Moving?" Sarah asked.

Ian put his head in his hands.

I thought about giving the example of the big stake women's conference that was coming up to show her some of the more spiritual things that the Relief Society did. But I knew we would be here for hours trying to explain "stakes" if I did.

"Brother Crimsal," Ian pleaded, "would it be all right if we assigned you and your wife home teachers?"

Robert rubbed his chin as he thought it over.

"I suppose so," he finally said. "But I'll have no talk of religion while they are here unless I bring it up."

"Fair enough," Ian consented, standing up to leave.

I stood up and checked to see if I were leaving the couch as clean as I had found it.

My heart stopped.

There on the cushion where I had been sitting was a spot about the size of a silver dollar. I sat back down as quickly as I could.

Ian looked at me oddly. "Are you ready to go?" he asked.

"I . . . " I had no idea what to say.

"We really should be going," Ian said.

There was no way I was going to stand back up.

"What about a prayer?" I asked, trying to buy time.

"That would be nice," Ian said, realizing he should have suggested it before. "Brother Crimsal, since it is your home would you like to call on someone to give a prayer?"

"I'd like to give it," I blurted out.

"Well, Tartan, that's up to Robert here."

"Please, Robert," I begged.

I had ulterior motives. If I could give a long enough prayer I might have a chance to clean off the spot while everyone had their eyes closed.

"If you would like to that much, go ahead," Robert said.

"Thank you," I said. "We all need to make sure we close our eyes out of respect for the one we are talking to."

Ian looked at me as if I were crazy.

All three closed their eyes and I began my plan. I started the prayer like any other prayer, but while I spoke I felt around for what I had spilled.

I knew it—my consecrated oil vial had popped open. I had filled it up this morning in anticipation of these visits, and now it had done me in. My dark pants didn't show the stain, but the oil had leaked down the side of my pants and onto the couch. I continued praying as I tried to figure out what to do. I needed a solution fast. I was running out of things to pray for.

"And bless us that we might all be able to find the joy we wish we had, that we might know assuredly this earth is a place for us to live and to dwell one with another, brothers and sisters in harmony . . ."

No one was peeking yet, but I felt certain they were all growing weary of my prayer. I slowly stood up still praying and examined the stain. It wasn't huge, but there on that pure white couch cushion it looked to be the size of one of my mom's old vinyl records.

I was having a hard time keeping my voice directed toward the Crimsals. I needed to be able to turn around and clean the cushion.

" . . . help us to understand the true blessings of tithing. And let us know what thou preferest we pay on, gross or net. Guide us as the seasons change . . . "

Facing them I put my hands behind my back and tried to flip the cushion over. It was no use. The cushion didn't fit unless it had the stained side up. I quietly pulled the cushion in front of me and then sat down on the couch where the cushion had been. Amazingly everyone still had their eyes closed. With the cushion in my lap I used the end of my tie to try and lift the stain out.

" . . . we're thankful for today, that it's not tomorrow, and that there is still the possibility of the next day." I was scraping the bottom of the prayer barrel. "And let us be wise enough to make an extra effort in all we do, that no task will be left undone in the presence of others. And that time will treat us kindly, taking us from one point to the next smoothly and with peace of mind."

It was no use, I wasn't doing anything but making the stain worse. I scrubbed harder.

"And, and, and bless the weather that it will be nice this week, and that, and that if it's not we won't complain . . . "

Sarah was the first to peek.

She nudged her husband who in turn looked over at me in confusion. There I was, a grown man sitting where my cushion should have been, about six inches lower than Ian, scrubbing one of their couch cushions with my tie while praying for things so vague that even God must have lost interest.

The Crimsals started to whisper between themselves. Ian hearing their whispering cracked his eyelids and turned to look at me.

"Amen," I quickly said.

"What are you doing?" Ian asked.

It was no use, I had to fess up. I hung my head in shame.

"I got some oil on your couch," I said, defeated.

Sarah jumped up and ran to the kitchen. Robert rubbed his temples, vividly recalling why he had chosen to disassociate himself with the Saints years ago.

Sarah came back with a bowl full of yellow liquid and a white washcloth. I handed her the cushion with little or no ceremony and she quickly applied the concoction with the cloth.

"Where did the oil come from?" she asked.

"It leaked out of my vial," I said apologetically.

"Your vial?" she asked.

"Well . . . " I looked to Ian for help. Help came from Robert, rather than Ian.

"It's for blessings, Sarah," he explained. "The members of the Church carry oil around with them so they can anoint the sick and bless them."

"Oh," she said, as if she comprehended.

"And the stain?" I asked, afraid to hear the answer.

"Coming out," she declared.

I wiped my dry brow and smiled. "I'm so sorry."

I guess my prayer was sufficient because we didn't offer another. I shook Brother Crimsal's hand and then Sarah's.

"Oil, huh?" she asked.

"Oil," I answered.

"For blessing the sick?"

"Yep."

"Amazing," she said, turning from me to shake Ian's hand.

Amazing was right. We were finally out of their house and finished with our visits. All in all I would say it went rather . . . well, I'd rather not speculate. At least we were through for the day. Neither Ian nor I said much as he drove me back to my truck at the chapel.

❧   ❧   ❧   ❧   ❧

Ian pulled up next to my truck and turned off the engine.

"Some visits," he commented.

"Sorry about the prayer," I said.

"Hey, it was a great prayer."

I pushed open my door and started to climb out.

"Wait," Ian said.

I sat back down.

"What is it?" I asked, wanting to get out and on with what was left of my day.

"Do you think this barbecue is a dumb idea?"

"No, not at all."

"Have you ever seen people like these here in Longwinded?" Ian asked in a perplexed tone.

"Yeah, these people here are just like those in my ward back in Utah. Granted, my ward in Utah had normal people as well. I think the ratio was one eccentric to every twenty normals. Here it seems to be just the opposite."

"I guess that's true," Ian said. "I've just never seen so much contention over a barbecue."

"The thing is," I explained, "that it isn't just the barbecue—it's this building thing. These people have wanted a real building for so long and when they finally get it, half of it is stolen. You know that deep down every Mormon really does think it was a Baptist who did it."

"I don't," Ian protested.

"Not at all?" I asked.

"Maybe a small part of me thinks that."

"See?" I taunted.

"Well, I just can't imagine who else could possibly want half of our building."

"I can't imagine where that half might be," I said. "It's like searching for Noah's ark. Maybe the Lord did take it up. I mean we have to live in something beyond the veil."

"You may be onto something," Ian said sarcastically.

"Well, I was supposed to meet Charity an hour ago," I said, looking at my watch and trying to get out of the Jeep.

"She seems like a nice person."

"Nice?" I questioned. "Sister Lynn is nice. Charity is much more than nice—she is exaltation in a tangible form."

"Like her, do you?"

"What's not to like?"

"Too bad about Howard," Ian said sadly.

"You know about Howard?"

"Of course."

"Bob?" I asked.

"Actually Charity came to me to talk about him."

"Why you?" I questioned.

"I am her branch president."

"Oh, she came to see you officially."

"Yep," Ian said, almost gloating over the information his priesthood position made him privy to.

"Anything you can tell me?" I asked curiously.

"Not a thing."

Oh this was great. A teaser. It was like holding a piece of stinky meat out in front of a salivating grizzly and then telling the bear he couldn't actually have any. I was a counselor in the branch presidency. Wouldn't it behoove the branch for me to know everything that was going on? How could I really support the members if Ian was keeping secrets from me? Didn't I deserve to hear all the facts so I could adequately comfort and help those in need? Wasn't Charity's business my business just by virtue of my calling? Where was the justice in this world?

"Anything I should know as your counselor?" I asked hopefully.

"Probably," he said. "I'd tell you if you weren't somewhat involved with her."

"Involved?" I scoffed.

"Oh, sorry, I think I meant to say smitten."

"So, if I wasn't slightly infatuated with Charity you would tell me what she has told you?"

"I would."

"Would you believe me if I said I can't stand her?"

"Not at all."

"What if I told you I cared for her like I care for my sister?"

"You don't have a sister."

"I know. That's why I want Charity to be my sister."

"So, that was your sister you were kissing in the back of my Jeep?"

"Stepsister?"

"I'm not telling you what Charity said."

"What if I asked you true or false questions?"

"Tartan."

"You just have to nod your head yes or no. Okay?"

Ian shook his head no.

I asked anyway.

"Does she still like Howard?"

"I'm not saying."

"Just nod," I said forcefully.

Again Ian nodded no.

"Is that a no she doesn't like Howard, or a no you won't nod?"

"The latter."

"Would your answer to the first part have been the same?"

"Tartan."

"I just want to help her," I pleaded.

"I can tell."

"All right, I give up," I said, defeated.

"Good."

"Just tell me one thing, in your opinion, and not in the opinion of Charity's branch president, do you think I might have a real shot with her?"

"What do you mean by shot?" Ian joked.

"Come on, Ian, don't play stupid games with me. I am twenty-nine years old and living in a place so odd the town bird is a flying squirrel. As cute as that is, a squirrel is still not a bird. Do you understand?"

"Too deep for me."

"You fit in here, Ian," I said with some disgust. "It's a shame you don't actually live in Longwinded. You would make the perfect mayor. I could see it now. You calling the entire town together outside of Scott's place and making the proclamation that from this day forth, the red speckled garden snake will be the town flower."

Sensing my state of mind wasn't exactly one of harmony, Ian tried to make me feel better. "Hey, Tartan, you don't need me to confirm she likes you, do you? It's evident to all of us bumpkins here in town that the girl is plumb sweet on you." Ian said the last bit in his best western drawl.

I stayed quiet hoping he would say more.

"The best thing that could have happened to Charity was for her to find out what Howard was really like before she was committed to him. She might be sad about the situation, but I know she is thrilled to be rid of him now."

"Thrilled?" I asked, raising my left eyebrow.

"Happy at least. Anyhow, it is now up to you to convince her that coming to Longwinded is the best thing she could have done." Ian started the Jeep.

"Do you think I'll have a hard time convincing her, Ian?"

"Nope, not unless you do something incredibly stupid."

"Thanks," I said, stepping out of the Jeep and closing the door.

Ian waved and drove off.

"What a day," I thought, looking forward to spending some time with Charity now that my visits were over. I tugged on my tie, trying to remove it as I walked to my truck.

"Pssst."

I hung my head, afraid to look for the source of that now familiar "Pssst." I used my peripheral vision to see if it was indeed Sister Wingate. There she was, back by the bush, calling me over like some ghost of situations present.

"Pssst!"

I pulled my keys out, acting as though I hadn't heard or seen her.

"Tartan Jones!" she demanded.

It was no use. I had to acknowledge her now. I turned and walked sheepishly over to her.

"I thought you went home," I said.

"Do I look like I'm home?" she asked.

I shook my head.

"I knew you would have to return for your truck. It's not safe to leave it here overnight. I mean if the Baptists can steal a chapel, they can certainly steal a truck."

"Sister Wingate," I complained, fed up with her blaming the Baptists for everything.

"Listen, Tartan, I wanted to talk to you alone. I feel you have a better head on your shoulders than Mr. Smith. You've been here longer, Tartan. You know these folks, and you know this barbecue is a precursor to rural strife like we have never known."

"I've only been here a little longer than Ian," I protested.

"God made the earth in only seven days," she debated.

"Well, not literally," I debated back.

That was it. I had said exactly the wrong thing. The last thing I wanted to do was discuss gospel philosophy with Sister Wingate, but I had thrown down a gauntlet the size of Utah County.

"Mr. Jones," she hissed, "unless you choose to take back that last remark I will have to personally inform Church headquarters that you, one of their ambassadors, are willfully preaching blasphemy. Willfully! Preaching! BLASPHEMY!" Her mouth trembled and her eyes flashed as she chastised me.

"Sister Wingate," I said, coming to my own defense. "There is quite a bit in the Bible that we shouldn't take literally."

"Oh!" she screamed, "heads are going to roll." Her face, red with rage, looked so contorted I had to snicker. I felt like a small child laughing during an important prayer. But I couldn't help it.

"What, pray tell, are you laughing about?" she demanded.

"Nothing, I just—"

"You were laughing at me," she declared.

I couldn't deny it. I nodded my head yes.

"Why you little . . . " Her rage from moments before was nothing compared to what now boiled over. She reached into the cedar bush and broke off a long branch. I didn't realize what she was doing until she started to beat me with it.

"Ouch!" I yelled. "Sister Wingate!"

"Don't Sister Wingate me," she screamed, swatting and poking me with such force that it was really beginning to hurt.

I started running toward my truck with her following close behind whipping that long branch against me. I know I was making matters worse by continuing to laugh, but despite the small amount of pain, the entire day had just been too comical for me to contain my laughter now.

I opened the door and jumped into the safety of my truck. With the door closed behind me, I burst out laughing again. This was so absurd!

Sister Wingate was outraged at her inability to swat me.

"Step out of the truck and face me like a real Mormon," she baited me.

"No way," I yelled, starting up the engine.

"You chicken!" she screamed. "You certainly are no Porter Rockwell."

I had no idea what she was talking about. I had no desire to be Old Port. In fact, at the moment I had no desire to be young Tartan in this situation. I threw the truck into reverse and looked over my shoulder to back out.

THUDWAMP!!

I turned back around to see Sister Wingate sprawled on top of my hood, her large face pressed up against the windshield. I did the only thing I could think of.

I stepped on the gas.

She beat her right fist against the window as she held on for dear life with her left. She was screaming like mad, but I was having a hard time making out any of her words. At one point it sort of sounded like she said, "Tartan spelled backwards is Satan." But that didn't make any sense (of course I think she had been on the committee that elected the flying squirrel to be the town bird, so maybe in her mind, it did make sense).

I drove into a large grassy field and brought the speed of the truck down to where we were just barely moving. Feeling confident she could keep her balance at this speed without having to hold on, Sister Wingate began using both fists to beat on the window.

This, of course, was what I was hoping for.

At just the right moment I turned sharply, causing her to roll off the hood and onto the grass. She was a sturdy woman, so I felt confident the fall wouldn't do more than bruise her ego and maybe give her a few scratches for all the ones she had inflicted on me. I must say also that her rolling across my hood in such a way, her scarf blowing everywhere and her large hands grasping wildly for a hold, was one of the choicest sights I had ever witnessed. I know it was incredibly wicked of me to enjoy such a moment, but I just couldn't help it. I made a mental note to ask for forgiveness later.

After she had tumbled off, I slowed to see if she was all right. In my rearview mirror I could see her get to her feet and begin running after me. I pressed on the gas and sped away.

Once on the pavement, I finally felt confident she couldn't catch me. I flew past Bob, who was parked on the side of the road watching for speeders. I flashed him an, "I'm not in the mood for a ticket" glance, so he didn't pursue me. I knew that a couple days from now he would approach me with a ticket for jaywalking or some other lesser offense. He would patiently wait for me to calm down before my reprimand. Good old Bob.

✎   ✎   ✎   ✎   ✎

Charity and I spent the evening laughing about my visits. It took me a full hour to convince her I wasn't embellishing the facts. It was tough getting her to believe the absurdities I was describing were the truth, the whole truth, and nothing but the truth.

Oddly enough, by the time I left Charity's place we both seemed to like Longwinded just a little more than we had.

CHAPTER TWENTY-THREE

BUMPY

The day had finally arrived. After all the squabbling, after all the frustration and run-rampant speculation, it looked as though the barbecue was going to occur. A handful of Baptists had committed to attend, and just over a handful of Mormons had committed not to participate.

I picked up Brother Clark Bender and brought him over to Charity's house. Martin, Loni, Clark, Sherry, and Orvil were all lined up to ride with Charity, Sister Reese, and me. It would have been a decent plan had Sister Reese's van worked.

We men all stood over the engine pretending to know what was wrong.

"Great," I said.

The only other vehicle we had was mine. Orvil and Sherry had ridden over on horseback, and I had crammed Clark, Loni, and Martin into my truck and brought them here.

"If we miss this barbecue," Loni said, holding her large casserole dish full of beans, "I'll just die."

Martin put his arm around Loni to comfort her.

"We'll find a way to get there," I said.

"Sherry and I could go get our cars," Orvil offered.

"You'd better," I said, seeing no other option. Surely we would be late, but at least we would get there.

"Or you could use the truck," Sister Reese said, suddenly right there beside us.

"What truck?"

"The truck," Charity said, smiling.

I looked around for any sign of a truck.

"It's back behind the old main house," Sister Reese said, nodding her head toward an older home farther back on the property.

"Does it run?" I asked.

"It does," she replied.

"What are we waiting for?" Sherry asked, heading toward the old house.

We all followed closely behind her.

I had pictured in my mind that "The Truck" was a large Suburban or Bronco. In reality, it was an old 28-foot U-haul truck. Sister Reese unlocked the back door and pushed it up. There was about a two-foot-high layer of clothes covering the entire floor.

"My word," I said.

"The clothes are all clean and rodent free. This truck is practically airtight," Clara Reese said, banging against the side of it.

"Should I go get the cars?" Orvil whispered to me.

I was sure it was illegal, but I was also certain we were going to be late if we didn't leave as soon as possible.

"No," I whispered back.

"What do you propose we do, then?" he asked.

"Hop in," I said.

I suppose if I had really thought about it I wouldn't have let everyone crawl into the back of that truck, but I didn't really think about it. For some reason this particular combination of people and their prepared food dishes didn't seem like a bad mix. Everyone climbed in, and I pulled the back door down and shut the latch.

"It's dark in here," Orvil yelled.

"You'll manage," I yelled back.

"What are we suppose to do the whole ride?" Martin asked.

"Pray," I said, only slightly concerned for their well-being, as Charity and I jumped into the cab and revved up the engine. It roared to life, sounding like my Uncle Herman coughing after he had eaten a dairy rich dinner.

"Think this is all right?" Charity asked.

"I hope so."

I could tell by the time I had the truck on the main road that it was most likely one of the first vehicles ever invented.

It was at least that old.

It had a stick shift that extended so high my arm was practically chin level whenever I shifted. It had only four gears and jerked like crazy whenever I tried to move from one to the other. Of course being so old, it could only dream about having power steering or brakes. It took everything I had to bring that thing to a stop or turn a bend or corner.

The blinkers didn't work.

Our seat was nothing but bare springs.

You couldn't roll the windows down.

The dashboard was cracked and falling apart.

The gas pedal stuck.

The gas gauge didn't work.

There was no radio, and the cab was permeated with an overwhelming stench of what smelled like bad fruit.

The drive was slow and rough. Try as I might, I couldn't get the stupid thing to go over thirty-five miles an hour. We would have arrived earlier had Orvil and Sherry gone back to get their cars. True, on the downhill stretches, I couldn't keep the truck from going around eighty. But after finally managing to slow the thing down, it would take what seemed like hours to get it back up to thirty-five miles an hour again.

I hit a large boulder that caused the truck to almost bounce off the road.

Charity casually bit her lip.

"I can't help it," I reasoned. "This road is so bumpy."

"I just hope everyone in the back is all right," she said.

"I'm sure they're fine. They have all those clothes for padding."

"I guess that's true."

"Yep," I said, hitting another large rut. "Where did your aunt get this thing, anyhow?"

"She bought it at an auction."

"Why?"

"She was going to buy a storage shed to hold all of her projects, but on the way to the big lumber store she came across this thing at an auction. I think it cost her two hundred dollars." Charity braced for a bump that was visible in the road ahead.

"Does she drive it often?"

"Nope, just uses it for storage."

"Well her storage facility could very well be the death of us all." I turned hard to make a wide turn. It was close but we made it.

I was wiping sweat from my brow when Charity suddenly started in on a conversation about Howard.

"I think I'm officially over Howard."

"What a great accomplishment," I said. "Does it come with a certificate or something?"

"Nope, just peace of mind."

"Oh, there's an expensive prize."

"No, really, I'm over him."

What could I say? I was elated, ecstatic, overjoyed, and intoxicated. I had been wanting forever to get this out in the open, to talk about Howard. But Charity had always shied away from the subject. Now, here she was bringing it up herself, and she was basically saying, "Tartan, I'm ready for you." I was hyped, happy, and downright smug, but there was no way I was going to let her know that.

"Do you mean you weren't over him a couple of days ago?"

"I mean even minutes ago I still felt a small tinge of sadness over him dumping me. But right now, at this exact moment, I am over it."

"So when we kissed you were thinking about him?"

"Okay, there were a couple of moments there where I forgot all about him. But it wasn't until just this second that I became completely over him."

I leaned back in my seat and let the thrust and hum of the engine dominate the conversation for a moment. Even though I hated still being single, it had some advantages. When I was sixteen, it took everything I had just to look a girl straight in the eye without running away scared. When I was eighteen, I was so consumed with the desire to have a girlfriend I would say almost anything, making a complete fool out of myself whenever I spoke. At twenty-one, I was so set on being cool that I would hardly speak at all on a date unless I had something really neat to say. Twenty-four brought that awkward "I have no idea who I am" stage. And after my mission, every date was sort of like a pity party, spent either in fits of depression or in being concerned that the next word I spoke would scare this girl off and ruin my chance of ever reaching the celestial kingdom.

Now that I was twenty-nine, however, it just didn't matter. I could say what I wanted, when I wanted, without having to worry about what people thought. I was old enough to be confident about who I was. Acne was a thing of the past; adolescent awkwardness, ancient history. I had come out of my youth with ample self-confidence and very few negative-self-esteem-induced pockmarks. It was great to be with a girl and just say what was on my mind.

"Is the girl Howard married pretty?" I said, breaking the spell of the engine.

"I guess," Charity said, giving me a weird look. "Why do you ask? Are you thinking of leaving me in Longwinded to go see her?" she joked.

"No way. I just can't comprehend what would possess a man to leave you for someone else."

"Did I tell you she worked at a library?"

"Oh, that changes everything," I said. "Did he have overdue books and as part of his obligation for repayment had to marry the librarian?"

"You just don't know Howard," Charity said.

"Are you sticking up for him?"

"No, but he always had to be doing something shocking. If his parents expected him to attend school, he would drop out and join up with Greenpeace. If someone told him his hair looked nice, he would shave it all off. That's Howard. I remember when he asked me to marry him. We had always been friends and had been going out on and off almost our whole lives. I liked him. In fact, I liked him a lot. I wanted to marry him mainly because it would be so easy and comfortable. It would have been how it always was. I knew I didn't really love him, but I was certain that with time, I would.

"Well, we were at a friend's house one night watching a video and just hanging out, when one of his buddies made the comment that Howard would never get married. He said Howard just wasn't that kind of guy.

"The next night Howard asked me to marry him." Charity looked at me to make it clear she wasn't sad about any of this anymore.

"Look, no tears," she said.

"I'm impressed," I said softly.

"Anyhow, after we sent the announcements out, booked the reception hall, and ordered the flowers, Howard met Annie. The horrible thing is that it was as if there was some written rule—one of the few rules Howard actually followed—that said you could no longer be friends once you'd been engaged and then broken it off. I've maybe said five sentences to Howard since we called it off. How can it be so easy for him to just end such a long friendship?"

There were tears now.

I thought about saying something like: "You're too good for him, anyway" or "You wouldn't want someone like that as a husband. Think how he might have treated your kids." But those things lacked everything I needed to express.

"You're over him, remember?" I said kindly.

"Oh, yeah," she said, smiling, "and I'm into something much better."

I pushed hard on the brakes as a corner approached more quickly than I anticipated. It took everything I had to maneuver the huge steering wheel to turn the tires. We made it again.

The dirt road turned to pavement, but the transition caused us to bump higher than before. We could hear thuds coming from the rear as everyone fell back into place. A couple of seconds later, everyone was banging on the dividing wall. I assumed they were upset with my bad driving, so we ignored them, figuring that now that we were on the pavement things would be all right.

They stopped banging after a few minutes.

We got to Ian and Bronwyn's place right on time. People were just arriving as we pulled up. Charity and I got out and opened the back of the truck.

It was awful.

Not only was Sister Reese covered with beans, but she was in the arms of Brother Bender, who was one visibly shaken man. I'm sure he interpreted the entire truck ride to be another sign from God for him to clean up his fantasizing. Orvil's hair had what looked to be marshmallow all over it, and Martin's pants were soaked with Sherry's famous limeade. Loni looked clean but frazzled. All of them looked to be out for blood—my blood!

I helped each one out of the truck, apologizing.

"It was a bumpy road."

They all headed quickly into Ian's home to try and clean up and salvage their one-time culinary works of art.

I took Charity's hand and together we joined what was later labeled the social event of the century. Had I known what was to occur, I might have turned and hightailed it for home.

FIRE ON THE MOUNTAIN

It was the perfect day for a barbecue. The sky was blue, a gentle breeze was blowing, and the temperature was hovering somewhere in the low eighties. Most of our gang had washed up nicely after our hectic drive. The real tragedy was the fact that Loni's beans had been reduced from twenty to seven servings.

Ian, who had greeted us at the barn door, informed us that Loni was the first Baptist to arrive; then he ran off to finish a few final barbecue details. Some of the Mormons regarded us unkindly for bringing Loni, but who cared when there was meat cooking and the air was filled with the fragrance of clean straw. Straw had somewhat of a calming effect on me. I'm not sure why, but I like to think it had a connection to the Christ child's first bed. It was a nice spiritual explanation. The truth, however, was probably that I just felt at home in a barn.

We Mormons were well represented. Not only were most of our regulars there, but a nice number of inactives had shown up as well. I think they mainly came to see if the Baptists would show. I spent some time greeting unfamiliar faces and picking at the platters of food we would soon be served.

While Charity helped Bronwyn, I had a nice long talk with a

brother by the name of Earl Hodgins. He was a contemporary of Mary Longfellow and held as much contempt for her as most folks in our area.

"I'm not the only person Mary has chased away from church," Earl said.

I could sense he was beginning a story, so I took a big drink of my pre-meal punch and let him continue.

"I had a cousin from Delaware who came down to stay with me one summer. This was back in the summer of . . . well, it was some time ago. Anyhow, my cousin, Bert, had lost one of his hands in some sort of farm equipment accident. He got along fine but always felt he had to overcompensate for having only one hand. You know what I mean?" Earl said, elbowing me.

I looked at both my hands, wondering if maybe I had lost one on the way here. Both of them were there. Maybe Earl thought I was lacking in some other area.

He continued his riveting story. "Bert hadn't been a member for too long. I'd say a year minimum."

"Maximum," I corrected.

"No, no, it had just been a short time. Bert was like a little child in the gospel. Well, back then we didn't have any sort of classes or programs for new members. I certainly wasn't going to take Bert to Sunday School with me. No sir, we were going to be discussing the Holy Ghost and tithing, stuff way over a new member's head. Like the scriptures say, don't throw no diamonds at pigs."

"Pearls before swine," I said.

Earl looked around as if I were calling someone. "Huh?" he asked.

"Oh, nothing. Continue."

"So we sent Bert to Primary. Would have been a fine idea had Mary Longfellow not been giving a lesson on 'I'm thankful for my hands.'" Earl shook his hands in the air. "Most insensitive woman I have ever known. She knew very well that Bert was missing his hand. Bert never went back to church. Can you blame him? I tell you, in the eyes of God, Bert is as innocent as a little child. Mary, however, is a different story."

"I'm glad I won't be the judge," I said.

"She drove me away from the Church as well," Earl said. "Did I tell you about that?"

"You mentioned something."

"Well, let me tell you the whole story." I looked around for an excuse to leave but found none.

"I was teaching a lesson on Joseph Smith in church one Sunday. Even though I was teaching all about Joseph Smith I liked to pick a sort of focus topic and zero in on that."

I wished he would do that now.

"So I was teaching about honesty by using stories of Joseph's life. I had just told the story of where Joseph Smith chopped down the cherry tree, when Mary started in on how my story was wrong. What did she know? Women shouldn't have their hands in recounting doctrine anyhow."

I held my tongue.

"She said that it was George Washington who chopped down the cherry tree."

I let go of my tongue. "It was."

"I know that," Earl said defensively. "But Joseph Smith chopped one down as well. It was part of the 'Cherry Tree Prophecy.'" Earl spit all over as he said "Cherry Tree Prophecy."

I was unaware of the Cherry Tree Prophecy but very aware of how much I wanted out of this conversation. I spied Ian setting up chairs and tables.

"Earl, I hate to interrupt, but Ian needs some help."

"He looks like he's doing fine to me," Earl commented.

"There are lots of chairs," I argued.

Earl probably would have protested further, but he saw Orvil, someone he obviously knew, and decided to go talk to him.

"Orvil," Earl called out.

I saw Orvil mentally reprimand himself for allowing Earl to spot him. Obviously, Orvil knew Earl well.

I finished my drink and helped set up some chairs and tables. Ian had told me he had built the barn himself with the help of some friends and family.

I was impressed.

It was nice and big with stalls on each side and a large center area where the chairs and tables were now being set up. Just outside the east door was a built-in barbecue. Bronwyn and Charity were busy turning ribs and hot dogs.

With everything set up, the clock showed it was now a couple of minutes past our announced starting time. I figured the rest of the Baptists to be no-shows. But no sooner had I counted them out, when I saw Scott stick his head around the corner of the far barn door. Seconds later Willie had his head in the door as well. I walked over to the two of them. They both pulled back out when they saw me coming. I stepped outside.

"Are you two coming in?" I asked.

"Looks like a lot of Mormons in there," Willie observed.

"A few," I said. "Nobody you don't already know."

"Meat smells good," Scott said, trying to make conversation.

"Come on in, you guys," I said, prodding them to make up their minds.

"Well, I didn't buy this new shirt for nothing," Willie said, puffing out his chest and preparing to enter the barn.

"I'll follow you," Scott said, licking his palms and attempting to slick back his hair.

They slipped in unnoticed, but as soon as Willie went for the punch, they were spotted. Everyone quieted down until Ian strode up to Scott and Willie and shook their now sweaty hands.

Talk resumed and the few members who had been assigned to greet people tried to make Scott and Willie feel comfortable. They were beginning to feel at ease when the large Benderholden van pulled up.

Everyone was speechless.

The Benderholdens?!

Never in anyone's wildest imagination were they expected to show. But here they were, and their van was filled with other Baptists.

It was a miracle.

I watched Ian try with all his might to suppress a smile as I freely displayed mine. Mrs. Benderholden walked straight to the refreshments. She was reaching for a cookie when she realized all eyes were on her.

"What is everyone staring at?" she asked. "We were invited, weren't we?"

Every Mormon instantly said yes, trying to dispel the awkwardness their staring had initiated. I watched as Ian patted Mr. Benderholden on the back; Bronwyn hugged Mrs. Benderholden; Orvil started throwing darts with Scott; and Willie carried on a conversation with Charity, Sherry, and Sister Lynn. But the truly amazing sight was that of Brother Hatch cutting a thick piece of homemade bread, covering it with a heavy coat of real butter and fresh strawberry jam, and then handing it to one of the Baptists who had come with the Benderholdens. It was like watching the Arabs and Israelis shake hands over a peace treaty. Then, when I thought I had witnessed all the miracles I could handle for one day, Brother Hatch left the bread table without having a piece himself.

Moses would have been flabbergasted.

A few more Baptists arrived and made themselves comfortable amongst our Jell-O and ribs. Ian asked Mr. Benderholden to offer the opening prayer. The crowd went wild with whispers as Bruce came front and center.

Bruce's prayer was pretty nondescript, all except for . . .

" . . . and may the Baptists shine tonight. Let our glow give luster to the light of Mormonism. Amen."

The Mormons let his comment slide.

Much food was consumed that afternoon, and any differences the Mormons and Baptists may have had were buried under mounds of beef and potatoes. People ate together in harmony. Salt and pepper were freely passed, from one religion to the other.

With full stomachs, we all mellowed to the point of comfort and familiarity. We talked freely as three young women from our branch cleared the tables of paper plates and plastic silverware. A large slice of peach cobbler, smothered with real vanilla ice cream, was passed to everyone with remaining room in their stomachs.

Once dessert was devoured, we started setting up for the talent show. Tables were pushed aside and a crude stage assembled. Ian had borrowed a microphone from the school where he worked. I plugged it in and we were ready to go.

The first act was little Lehi. He got up and read a poem about dogs and then spent a few minutes making noises with his hands.

Mrs. Benderholden did what you might call a dramatic reading of a poem. You might also have called it melodramatic or overdramatic or a number of other things that would probably be less kind. It must have been divine intervention that kept me from bursting out laughing. Never had I seen anyone sway and warble as she did during her few short moments on stage.

Phoebe North tried to do a skit with her two sons and husband. She sat Zeke on her knee and her husband had Daniel on his. It was a long skit intended to be funny. It was amusing to watch them try to convince us their kids were actually speaking, but the skit itself was nothing to laugh at.

A Mrs. Wallow got up and gave a demonstration on good hygiene. She showed how to clean the ears, wash the hands and face thoroughly, and clip the finger- and toenails. She ended her demonstration with a personal story about her brother Clifford who had to wear shoes two sizes larger than he needed because he never clipped his toenails. I thought for a moment she was going to cry, which surely would have prompted some tips on how to properly wipe away tears.

Sister Theo sang "Somewhere over the Rainbow" in some key over the normal person's pain threshold. It was a good thing that we had used paper—instead of glass—cups. The floor would have been littered with shards of glass rather than sawdust after her performance. She tripped while bowing and had to be taken into Ian's home for some doctoring on her knee.

Bruce Benderholden surprised us all by clogging. He made Herb Walker's interpretive dancing on the day of the mobile home move-in look almost normal. His arms and legs were flying at such a jumpy pace I feared they would be ejected from their sockets. It was obvious, however, that one of the main reasons the Benderholdens had shown up was because deep in their hearts they believed they were talented.

Sister Lynn played the spoons and played them well. The only other time I had seen silverware fly so fast was watching my Uncle Herman eat cake at one of our family reunions.

Willie's talent was the ability to stand on his head for almost ten minutes. We all wondered why he had been hiding his light under a bushel for so long.

Fern, however, was the show stopper. He astounded us all by sucking a wet spaghetti noodle into his mouth and expelling it through his nose. The crowd loved it. Then Fern told the extremely engrossing story of how he came to develop such a talent.

"I was in the army, stationed in Munich, Germany. I had encountered some problems over my name so I was put on the kitchen staff," Fern explained. "Don't get me wrong. We were kept busy. But not busy enough to prevent us from experimenting with wet noodles."

Of course, I thought. I mean the army might be slightly uncivilized, but who could deny a person time for wet noodles?

"And even though I make it look easy, don't be fooled," Fern continued. "We almost lost our senior chef when he tried this with a lasagna noodle." Fern quickly pulled the pasta out of his nose and shook it at us.

Everybody eeewwed.

Wendy Christianson took the stage and tap danced to the theme from *Chariots of Fire*. She was wearing a neat homemade costume that was made entirely of rubber. It looked like a tie-dyed wet suit.

Ian was about to end the talent show when Bob pulled up outside. He apologized for being late and asked if he could still perform. Ian, of course, consented. I was glad Bob had come. He was such a staple in Longwinded, no event felt complete or had that Longwinded stamp of approval without him.

Bob needed a couple of minutes to set up, so we all used that time to pick at the leftovers and chat. Charity sat down in front of me and asked me to braid her hair.

"You do know how to braid hair?" she asked.

"Of course," I lied. I had no idea how to braid hair. I had never had the opportunity to spend my sacrament meetings braiding the hair of my older or younger sisters. Like knowing how to fill out a four-generation pedigree chart, braiding was a must know for any real Latter-day Saint—yet I had no clue. I decided to give it a go, hoping Charity's perfect hair might make it easy for me.

I took two clumps of hair and started twisting them together. At first I thought I was doing it the right way, but about halfway down, her hair started to look horrific. I undid that and tried tying it in a knot a bunch of times. That definitely wasn't right. It was a lot harder to undo my knot try.

"What's the matter?" Charity asked.

"I'm just trying to get it really straight."

Since I had experienced more success with the two clump system, I tried that again. But this time I wrapped the hair around the opposite clump each time they crossed. The result can best be described as awkward.

Charity, thinking I was at the bottom of the braid, handed me a rubber band to tie it off. I took it from her and sadly finished what I had begun.

"Is it straight?" she asked.

I eyed it carefully.

"It's pretty straight," I replied.

"Pretty straight is good enough for a barbecue."

Charity stood up and turned to model it for me.

"Nice," I said weakly.

When she turned back around I could see her eyes were slightly bulging, due to the fact that I had tied her hair too tightly.

I looked quickly around the barn for any mirrors I might need to cover to prevent her from discovering my hair monstrosity. None. Apparently horses and cows had very little vanity.

Charity was about to walk off and show Bronwyn when Bob announced he was ready. She sat down next to me on a bale of hay.

"This ought to be great," she whispered.

"I can only imagine."

We all knew Bob had some talents. He could spread news faster than Ma Bell and CNN combined. He could cut shrubs into the shape of animals. He could write a ticket and whistle "Moon River" simultaneously. He could sleep with his eyes wide open, and he was one of the area's fastest eaters. But none of us knew about the talent he had for us today.

Ian introduced him.

He read from a card Bob had given him. "Presenting the Amazing Bob."

Catchy entertainment name, I thought.

Suddenly, with a small puff of blue smoke, there was Bob. He wore a black top hat tipped ever so slightly to the left and a black cape lined with red satin. His big hands were covered with white gloves, the left one holding a cane. The rest of his outfit wasn't quite as slick. He obviously had gained weight since he last wore the pants. They were at least six sizes too small, and his white shirt was missing two buttons, causing open gaps in the shirt and exposing his fleshy belly.

But we all clapped like crazy as he strode to position in front of his table.

Normally, I don't like magic. Something about that and clowns makes me physically sick. The tricks are always schmaltzy, and the impressive ones are usually explained away by some annoying person sitting next to you. How many times must a person sit through the ring trick or the handkerchief trick in their lifetime before mercy strikes them dead? Too many in my opinion.

Bob's show was different—but not in a good way. Most of his tricks had at one time made a home for themselves in the bottom of a cereal box. Bob went on and on with the lamest, most elementary magic tricks I had ever seen. Then after each one he would stop and explain how each one was done.

"I want to share the joy," he would say after each explanation.

Bob performed the "cut off finger" trick as his last bit and did the "I've got your nose" magical extravaganza as his encore.

All and all it was one spectacular talent show.

The activities began after the show. Horseshoes were tossed, footballs thrown, races held, and Ian gave some of the younger kids rides on his family's new pony. Sister Lynn had hoped to have a hayride, but they couldn't find a wagon to use. Luckily for everyone, we had Sister Reese's U-haul. We bounced around Ian's eight acres with everyone piled in the back on top of all the clothes. Baptists and Mormons jostled about in joy. Everyone was having a great time.

Until the fire.

I thought at first I was just fondly remembering the smoky meat I had eaten earlier, but as soon as I heard Sister Theo screaming, I knew something was wrong. She was the only person who had stayed back at the barn—she felt impaired due to her scraped knee—and was now running like a mad woman towards us. We were at the far end of Ian's property, but we could see the smoke now, rising over the trees. Ian jumped out as I tried to turn the huge truck around. At first it was just a little whiff of smoke, but soon it was a giant billow of dark black smoke with huge orange flames underneath it.

The barn was on fire!

I could hear everyone banging against the truck walls as I raced to the scene. I screeched to a halt and jumped out to help Ian, who was frantically trying to turn on his hose.

It was too late.

The barn was history—all that hay and wood had provided the perfect fire food, and the fire grew in strength, its orange arms reaching for anything it could possibly devour. We worked on clearing away anything it might latch onto. Only low winds made it possible to keep the hot menace contained.

Everyone was doing whatever they could to help out, but with only one hose and no real hope of saving the barn, there wasn't much to do.

Charity commented on what a good job I was doing fighting the fire. I then slipped back behind the blaze and rubbed some soot onto my face for effect.

She winked when she next saw me.

I guess the soot suited me.

Sister Theo explained to all of us how the fire had started. Apparently she was helping herself to some of Mrs. Benderholden's mint casserole when she suddenly smelled gasoline. She walked outside just as Rich was throwing a match to the gasoline. She yelled at him, but it was too late. The flame had caught. Rich ran off scared and she ran to tell us.

I had been right about the potential damage I thought Rich could cause. After notifying the fire department and seeing to it that no one was hurt, Bob took off in search of Rich.

The fire was dying by the time the fire department arrived. They turned their hoses on for effect, but at this point the flames would have ceased without them.

After it was over we all just stood around dumbfounded! What had seemed to be the perfect activity had ended in disaster. The Baptists gave their condolences and quietly shuffled off to their cars and headed home. Most of the Mormons did the same.

Ian and Bronwyn were incredibly upbeat about the whole thing. I had the feeling they were mainly upset that such a good time had been ruined.

Everyone who Charity and I had driven to the barbecue found other rides home, so eventually it was just Ian, Bronwyn, Charity, a few firemen, and me.

"Quite a party," I observed.

"No kidding," Ian said, still holding the hose on some smoking embers.

"I can't believe this happened," Bronwyn said sadly.

"I can," Ian commented. "It's just my luck." Ian laughed a small, slightly cynical laugh.

"Don't pay attention to him," Bronwyn said. "He just has this problem with things burning down on this property. The first home he had up here burned down as well."

"At least you're consistent," Charity said.

Ian laughed. He turned off the hose and put his arm around Bronwyn. "So, Tartan, are you going to help me build a new barn?"

"Sure," I said, using the moment to slip my arm around Charity. "The Baptists are going to have a great time with all this, you know."

"I hope they're kind about it all," Ian said.

"I'm sure they will be," Charity said sarcastically. I put my arm on her shoulders, and she put her arm around my waist. It was a nice arrangement. After a few moments of silence, stars by the thousands suddenly appeared in the night sky.

"Nice evening," Ian commented.

"I wonder where Rich is right now," I said, gazing up at the Big Dipper.

"Wherever he is, I hope he's cold and having a hard time building a fire," Ian said.

Charity and I left Ian and Bronwyn alone with the firemen and headed home. Driving the U-Haul home proved harder than driving it to the barbecue. The darkness of the early night made each turn harder and each pothole and rut a surprise.

I had planned in my mind to drop the truck off at Charity's place and take her back to my place to watch a movie or something. Instead, our plans were altered the moment we entered town. People were walking around in the streets, and Bob's patrol lights were flashing as his car sat outside the Stop & Shop. I pushed my foot hard against the brake and managed to bring the truck to a halt just past the library. I could see Sister Wingate inside the library talking to a cop who must have been called in from somewhere else. The two big windows on the front of the library were shattered and glass lay everywhere.

"What's going on?" Charity asked.

"I have no idea," I said, taking Charity by the hand and walking over to the Stop & Shop.

Scott came running up to us.

"What happened?" I asked.

"Rich went crazy," Scott said. "Broke into the Stop & Shop and stole a bunch of food. Then he threw rocks through just about every window on the street. He broke three of mine," Scott said angrily.

"Did they catch him?" Charity asked.

"Nope," Scott said. "Bob called in some of his buddies from Pinefield to help look for Rich."

"And they're sure it was Rich?" I asked.

"Yep," Scott answered. "He wrote his name with Cheese Whiz across Sherry's floors, and Sister Wingate was in the library when Rich threw two big rocks through her windows. She said she would have tried to stop him but was afraid for her life."

Someone called Scott's name and he ran off in that direction. Charity and I walked over and talked with Bob.

"What a horrible crime," Charity said.

Bob looked her up and down and then guffawed as if to say

"amateur." "This is no crime," Bob said soberly. "This is a crime *spree*."

"Can we help?" Charity asked.

"I'm afraid, missy, that this is a time for professionals," Bob said.

Bob looked every bit the professional, standing there in his too-tight magic outfit, wearing a milk mustache he had obviously just acquired.

I took Charity and her aunt's U-Haul home. I then radioed Fred and filled him in on all Rich had done. Fred agreed to come into town to meet me and see if we could assist Bob in some way.

Despite all of us there to help Bob, nothing turned up. Rich had given Longwinded the slip. Bob was disappointed he didn't get his man. Me? I hoped Rich would never show up again. Things would be much better around here without him.

CHAPTER TWENTY-FIVE

QUESTION ON THE GREEN

Two weeks later Rich had still not been found. In fact, there was no trace of him. Everyone suspected he was hiding out somewhere in the surrounding forest; Rich had never really been anyplace else. But despite his suspected nearness, still no show. He was, however, third after UFOs and Elvis on the list of frequent sightings by those who seemed a few bricks shy of a Longwinded load.

Bob had conducted what I thought to be a very thorough search of the area, but it bore no real fruit. He had shaken down Rich's friends, but the few he had didn't like him enough to harbor him in his now fugitive state.

Most people had put their religious feelings on hold since the barbecue. It seemed as if everyone was avoiding church talk. Even Pastor Stevens had cooled down. He had made no harsh comments in public toward the Mormons for a few days. Of course I heard through the grapevine (Bob) that in private it was a very different story.

So, life in Longwinded was just sort of there, with people avoiding each other's toes and waiting for something to happen so we could start acting uncharitable again. A few times I caught the tail end of locals conversing about the barbecue and how much fun it had been. However, because of the fire and Rich's crime spree, folks just didn't bring the barbecue up unless it was in a private, guarded conversation. It was very difficult for a town as apt to talk about each other as Longwinded to keep their mouths shut regarding such a hot topic. Rich's deeds had the makings of enough possible loose talk and rumors to slake our nosy souls for years. Still, for some undefined reason, people were holding their once-wagging tongues.

There was one real loss to come out of all this; Chad left Longwinded for good. He was a single Mormon male just over thirty—with no possibility of marital bliss anywhere on the Longwinded horizon.

So he called it quits.

The fire was just what he needed to light a fire under himself. He headed back to the great state of Utah where his parents still lived. It was too bad; I liked Chad. And even though I had never gotten to know him really well, he had always been a normal person here amongst the odd.

The Mormons were now down by one.

It could have been a moment of triumph for the Baptists if it weren't for the fact one of their members had gone crazy and was now possibly hiding in the surrounding mountains or valleys. So, the Baptists trumpeted their slight triumph with muted trumpets and minor whispers.

Despite all that was going on in Longwinded, Charity and I were cementing our relationship by spending every spare moment together. Talk of marriage had even surfaced. We both understood how incredible our relationship was and had a pretty good idea in which direction it was heading. We were growing more and more committed to each other with every passing day, hour, minute, and second.

In fact, I felt committed enough to our relationship to finally take her miniature golfing in the big city. I had always felt miniature golfing required a great amount of trust. I mean, what if I said a perfectly normal male thing, and she interpreted it wrong (a perfectly normal female thing)? It would just be too handy for my date to then have a metal club at her disposal. And even if my date didn't have the heart to hit me over the head, there was always the potential of golf ball welts.

I don't know why I obsessed over this; I just did. I suppose it could have had something to do with the time I went miniature golfing with my aunt and uncle. My Uncle Herman said something about my aunt's arms looking cute when she swung, or when they swung. My aunt then proceeded to chase him around the course until she cornered him and showed him just where she could put her putt.

But I had no fear when it came to Charity. She was over Howard, and her emotional state seemed to be just where it should be. No fear. In fact I looked forward to showing off my golfing skills to a girl who seemed to really like me.

I was just about to send my purple ball through the legs of a giraffe and up the ramp into the mouth of a chomping hippo, when Charity asked:

"When are you going to get married?"

We had been talking about school and the amount each of us had digested. I had no idea why she brought up this subject. The only reason I could think of was to throw off my game.

It worked.

My purple ball ricocheted off the belly of an alligator and missed the ramp altogether.

"Shoot."

Not that I really minded the topic of choice. I was much happier getting things out in the open than having to continually guess about them.

"Well?" she asked, setting her ball down for her shot.

"I don't know. Is there some reason why I should be concerned about it right now?" I asked.

"I was talking to Bob this afternoon . . . " she took a swing and sent her ball rolling through the legs and up the ramp.

This was great! Not only was she beating me, but she had talked to Bob. I knew exactly what they had talked about. I shook my head, disgusted with myself for discussing with Bob anything I wanted kept private.

It was about three days before at Flint's that Bob and I had sat down to tuna salad sandwiches and a couple hours of talking. I was in a good mood because Fred wasn't going to stop by as planned and Charity had just invited me over to her place to spend the evening. So, I suppose I was a little bit giddy, and I guess the giddiness combined with a full stomach caused me to say a little more than I normally would have. Anyhow, somewhere in the conversation, I had told Bob straight out that I wanted to marry Charity. I then spent the rest of the conversation begging him not to tell her or anyone else.

Bob had no mercy. I could tell by the smile on Charity's face he had told all.

"What did he say?" I asked, while taking my second shot up the ramp.

Charity put her arm through mine and walked me to the next hole.

"He said you wanted to marry me," she said, as if it were no big deal.

"He's getting old," I tried to offer as an explanation.

I hit my ball through a loop and then straight into the hole.

"Impressive," Charity commented.

"I'm sure his mind isn't what it used to be," I said, referring to Bob.

Charity knocked her ball through the loop. It missed the hole by at least four inches.

A stroke of luck.

"So it's not true?" she asked.

"That's beside the point," I said.

"Beside *what* point?" she asked.

"I don't know, some point somewhere that represents what I'm comfortable talking about right now."

"So this subject matter makes you uncomfortable?" she asked, sensing weakness. She then made her short putt and picked her ball out of the cup.

I set my ball down at the next hole and teed off of what looked to be a little elf.

Hole in one.

I needed to start missing my shots so Charity could catch up.

"You didn't answer my question," Charity said, postponing our game to wait for an answer.

I sat down on the little bench provided at this particular hole. A large plastic pig sat in the background, spraying water out of his mouth—providing not only a romantic setting, but causing a difficult shot on hole seven.

"It's just that my expectations, my view of where you and I are right now, might be so different from yours," I explained. "Laughably different."

"Are you saying you haven't thought about us getting married?"

"I'm saying that part of me is so logical it feels there is no way I could even be considering something like that when I've only known you for six weeks."

"That must be the boring part of you," Charity joked.

"If so, then the exciting part of me thinks about it all the time, praises God for sending you to Longwinded, rejoices in the fact that you are the most stunning creation I have ever beheld, and makes my right arm tingle at the mere mention of you."

"Tingle, huh?" Charity asked, skepticism tainting her tone.

"A powerful tingle."

"So which side of you is more persuasive?" she questioned.

"They both make a pretty good case for themselves."

This sitting around discussing our future allowed a bunch of high school students to catch up to our hole. We let them play on through.

"How old are you, Tartan?" Charity finally asked.

"You know," I stated.

"How old am I?" she asked.

"I know."

"So what is our problem?"

"With what?" I asked.

"We're both single; I love you; I think you love me; and like you said earlier, neither one of us has ever murdered anyone."

"You love me?" I asked, surprised she had said it so nonchalantly.

"I do."

"How can you?" I questioned. "Six weeks. How do you know that

I don't have some sort of weird problem that makes me go psychotic for one week every seventh week of my life?"

"We'll work through it together," she teased.

"You're so compatible," I quipped.

"For someone so sure of himself you sure are chicken."

"You really do love me?"

"I think I do," she said softly. "There is something about you that makes me feel things will be all right. You have something about you that could cause a girl to settle for a place like Longwinded just because you're there. I'm not saying I need you in order to be complete or that I would follow you anywhere. I'm just trying to describe a feeling I've had about you from the start." Charity stopped a moment to see how I was reacting.

I smiled. It seemed appropriate.

"Remember," she continued, "when they were putting in the new chapel and you came over and talked to me?"

"Of course."

"Remember how we held hands as we toured what was then the double-wide?"

I nodded yes.

"I could tell exactly what you were really like that afternoon. I saw the way you looked at others as they looked at us. I saw the small smiles when you thought I wasn't looking. And, of course, I noticed the thumbs up sign you gave Chad as he signaled his congratulations to you. But more than anything I could see inside your head as you wondered if my holding your hand meant something, or if I could possibly like you as much as you were beginning to like me. I could see everything. It was amazing."

I felt so naked. I put my hands up to cover my brain.

"The only reason I'm saying this is because it's so different from how it usually is for me. Never have I known what Howard or any other boyfriend was thinking."

"Maybe I'm just incredibly simpleminded," I interrupted.

"That's just the thing you're not. You are perfectly complicated," she said.

Perfectly complicated?

"Perfectly complicated and apparently chicken," she added.

She was right. For someone who came on so strong at the start, and professed to want to be married so badly, I sure was hedging.

"So, what are you thinking?" she asked.

"I'm just not sure I can fathom your feeling this way after only six weeks. What if underneath my clothes my whole body is covered with tattoos?"

"Well, as long as they aren't obscene."

"What if they were?"

"They can be removed these days," she said, laughing.

"Well, what if we did get married and after a little while I left you?"

Charity stopped smiling.

"Now we're getting somewhere," she said. "You're not your father, Tartan."

"I know, but I bet when he married my mother he didn't plan on leaving her one day. He was probably totally in love with her."

"Maybe," Charity said, prompting me to go on.

I waited while another set of golfers played through. The small wooden bench was making my backside sore, but I didn't let that stop our conversation.

"I can't begin to tell you how much I like you," I said. "Sometimes I almost pass out when I think about you and me—and us. But there is this giant chalkboard in my head where I keep writing 'this is too convenient to be true, this is too convenient to be true' over and over again. Then there is the part of me waiting for you to tell me that this is all just a joke. I know the moment I tell you I love you, a bunch of strangers with hidden cameras and big signs that say Sucker are going to jump up and yell something about this being one big blooper."

Charity rolled her eyes.

"What?" I said defensively.

"I think the only thing keeping you from getting down on your knees right now and proposing to me, in fact the only thing that's truly kept you from not getting married sooner, is your father. None of this tattoo, psycho, tired of being set up with girls garbage. It is all your father. Here I am, Tartan, and I'm over all the Howards in my life and into you. How long do I have to wait for you to get over someone you haven't even seen in twenty-nine years?"

She was pushy.

My backside was really hurting now. I stood up and stretched my arms into the air. The cool night made the air thin and my thoughts jumpy. Charity stood and led me by the arm to the next hole.

I put my ball down and prepared to swing.

"So when you told Bob you wanted to marry me you were just talking big with the boys?" Charity asked.

I stopped my swing midway.

"No," I said turning to face her. "When I told Bob I wanted to marry you, I was dead serious."

"You wouldn't think it by the way you are acting tonight," Charity said.

This was turning out to be one serious game of golf. I could see if I were not very careful with what I said next I could possibly damage the relationship Charity and I had been working on. The question wasn't if I loved her or not; it was whether or not I was ready to commit to something I feared. Not that I couldn't commit. No, in fact my every action was committed to Charity. I just had such self-doubts.

Once when I was eight I left my mother. We had been out back working on our lawn and planting some new flowers. We were cleaning up for the day, putting our tools and supplies into the small shed we had in the back. Well, just for fun, I shut the door on my mother, trapping her inside. It was just supposed to be a joke, but she instantly started to scream at me.

"Tartan, you open that latch right now! Tartan, I'll spank your hide if you don't open the door right this minute! Tartan, I can't get out by myself!"

Mom's voice still bounced uncomfortably around in my head. I was so scared I was going to be in trouble that I just took off running, leaving my poor mother locked up in a Tuff Shed prison. She had needed me and I had deserted her. I hid out by the dry creek at the end of our street until I could muster up enough courage to go back.

When I finally went home, Mom was in the kitchen crying. I

found out later that our neighbor had heard her banging and screaming and had let her out. My mom yelled at me that night. Even at the young age of eight I could tell Mom was stressed out about much more than what I had done, and unfortunately she used me to vent. It was the first and only time she ever compared me to my father.

I vowed right then and there to never ever do anything again that would invite that comparison. Still, in the back of my mind I was always scared, feeling that I really did have the potential to leave someone I loved.

Just like my father.

I swung hard. My ball bounced off one of the moving windmill blades and rolled right back to me.

"Lack of concentration," Charity commented.

Charity swung, sending her ball through the windmill and down onto the next Astroturfed green. We then walked silently to where our balls had ended up.

I could tell Charity was trying to give me some time to think things over. She was so patient. I took my next shot; my ball did just as I wanted.

"What if I did ask you to marry me and things didn't—"

"Tartan," Charity interrupted, "I don't want to hear one more 'what if' or 'I'm worried because' from you. If you don't want what I want, I can live with it."

"If I asked, would you say yes?" I asked, hoping to find out what my options were.

"I'm not answering that," Charity said.

"But you do love me?"

"I've said enough on that subject already."

"Would you be happy with me?"

"There is only one question I will answer at the moment," Charity said defiantly.

"Do you want to move on to the next hole?" I asked, hoping that was the question.

She stood firm in her silence.

I knew exactly what question she wanted me to ask; it was the big one. The one that could only be followed by one of two answers:

"Yes, I will."

Or . . .

"No, I won't."

I wished we were living in the days when I would have had to fight some would-be suitor for her hand. That to me seemed like a better way to handle these things. I could battle some poor chump to the death with golf clubs, and in the end it would be clear I was the man for Charity. And if by some chance I died in the duel, it would be just as clear I wasn't the one for her. Fate could make the decision for me.

I stood there waiting for fate to do something.

A small child chasing after one of his wayward balls ran over my toes.

Was that a sign?

Charity shook her head as I whined about my run-over toes.

Was *that* a sign?

Our golf game had been put completely on hold. Charity stood there with her arms folded, waiting for me to do something.

"Do you want to just skip the rest of the game and go straight to dinner?" I asked.

"That's not the question."

"Let's just go," I said, reaching for Charity's hand.

She shook her head, her perfect hair flinging just right.

"You want to keep playing?" I asked.

"That's not the question."

"Charity," I moaned.

"Is that a question?" she asked.

She was the most persistent person I knew. How could I ask her to marry me on the grounds of Putt-Putts Wacky Golf Course?

"I know you wouldn't," Charity said.

I stared at her blankly.

"I know you wouldn't leave me, and I know you wouldn't ever stop trying to make me happy," Charity said seriously.

"How did you know what I was thinking?" I asked.

"That's a question."

"Ahhh," I screamed out of frustration.

Charity smiled, apparently happy over my nervous state of mind.

Regardless of how she knew what I was thinking, she had a pretty good point. I would never leave her; I just couldn't be that way.

Come on, Tartan, just ask her, my mind begged.

There was the possibility of a negative reply, but if that were the case, I could just move in with Fern and be a bachelor the rest of my life. At the moment, anything seemed better than not knowing.

"You really want me to ask that kind of question on a miniature golf course?"

She remained silent. This too was not the question.

"Charity?" I said, my heart suddenly racing.

I took her warm hand in mine and coaxed her into looking into my eyes.

"Yes, Tartan," she answered, sensing I was finally about to ask the right thing.

Someone hit a ball into the bonus bin at the end of the course and set off the winner's alarm. The air was suddenly filled with a high pitched whistle and the recorded voice of someone screaming over and over, "You're a winner! You're a winner!"

I could imagine no finer moment than now to ask.

"Charity, will you marry me?" I pulled back a bit and waited for a reply.

She smiled.

Her top lip curled up, then went back down.

A long strand of blond hair blew across her face. She moved it back into place with her right hand.

She smiled again, her red lips driving me crazy and her brown eyes peeling back the edges of my soul.

I thought that possibly she hadn't heard me over the winner's alarm so I asked again, "Charity, will you marry me?"

"I heard you the first time, Tartan," she said with a laugh.

She then pushed herself up on her toes and pulled me closer. It was only a whisper, inaudible to any outside ear, but I heard it loud and clear as she moved her lips toward mine.

"Yes."

She then kissed me until I was afraid my heart might burst into a million sloppy pieces. I pulled back from her and looked deep into her dark brown eyes. The alarm at the bonus bin stopped, giving us a moment of silence, but only a moment. Someone else made the impossible shot into the bonus bin as well, and once again "You're a winner" screamed out.

"Can we leave now?" I yelled.

She nodded yes.

As we left the course we could hear the guy who had just become a winner talking to his friends. "Did you see that shot? I tell you this must be my lucky night." He then picked up his drink and finished it off in one giant gulp. "Yep," he said, his wet lips spraying soda all over, "this is the kind of night most people dream about."

He had no idea how right he really was.

CHAPTER TWENTY-SIX

SOMETHING TO TALK ABOUT

Longwinded loved it that Charity and I were engaged. Finally, they had something to talk about besides Rich.

Charity's aunt had already made us three quilts, a dust ruffle, and two of the frilliest pillowcases I had ever seen. She probably would have sewed twice that much, but lately she had been giving a good amount of her time to Clark Bender.

Good old Brother Clark was so sweet on Sister Reese he was becoming a new man. He shaved, bathed, and, according to Sherry, had purchased at least four new articles of clothing for himself in the last two weeks. Everyone in town was certain Clark's women-thoughts at the moment were mainly about Sister Reese. The ill-fated U-Haul trip had thrown two people together who would most likely have never met otherwise, and it provided Longwinded with another hot discussion topic.

My mother had a fit when I called to tell her I was engaged.

"Who is she?"

"I told you about her, Mom. Her name is Charity and—"

"Tartan, marriage isn't something you just jump into," Mom lectured loudly.

"I'm not jumping, Mom."

"Sounds like you are to me."

"Mom, I have never been more sure about anything. Doesn't that mean something to you?"

"Yeah," she said indignantly. "It reminds me of the time you wrangled me into buying you that guinea pig from your friend."

"Mom, I was eight," I complained.

"Maybe so, but you said you knew you could take care of it, and then you let it cook itself to death in the hot car while you and your friend swapped baseball cards."

"I remember what happened, Mom. I forgot he was still in the car."

"One can rationalize anything if they need to," my mom said.

"Mom."

"Well, what if after a few weeks of marriage you become more interested in something else?"

"Mom, I'm not going to forget and leave Charity in the car. Besides, she's a big girl and can unlock the car door for herself."

"You're missing the point, Tartan."

"Mom, I'm not making a point. I just called because I wanted to tell you I was getting married, and here you are trying to talk me out of it."

"I was married once, too, you know."

"I'm well aware of that, Mom. The man you married is my father," I said with just a touch of sarcasm.

"Does this girl know you come from a divorced home?"

"You mean crazy home?"

"Tartan, don't be funny with your mother."

"Mom," I said somewhat bothered, "she knows."

"And she is all right with it?"

"She's fine with it."

"Well, maybe she doesn't quite understand what it means to be engaged."

"Mom, she's been engaged before."

This was the wrong thing to say.

"What?"

"Well, she . . . "

"Oh, Tartan, I don't like the sound of this."

"Everything sounds fine, Mom," I said, unable to think of anything else to say.

"You know I just want what's best for you," Mom said, starting to sound a little bit choked up.

"Oh, Mom," I moaned.

"Is this even for sure? What if she decides to back out of this engagement as well? What if this is all just a game to her?"

"She won't," I said. "Besides, she wasn't the one who broke off her first engagement."

"So she's on the rebound?" my mom asked with alarm.

"No."

"I'm wondering if you have really thought this through."

"I have."

"I wonder."

"Mom, I'm twenty-nine years old. I'm not asking for your permission, nor am I calling to get your input. I just wanted to make you aware that come November 20th, I am getting married in the Mesa Temple."

"Mesa?"

"Yes, Mesa."

"But we have so many lovely temples here in Utah. The Mesa Temple is so square looking. It doesn't even have an angel Moroni on it."

"Charity's from Arizona," I informed her.

"What about that San Diego temple? It's so stunning. It's like getting an earthly glimpse of the celestial kingdom."

"Have you been there?" I asked, somewhat fed up with the whole conversation.

"No, but I've seen pictures."

"November 20th, Mom," I said, trying to end the conversation.

"It's not too late to think this through, Tartan."

"Mom, I'm twenty-nine; I'm running out of time."

"So, this is an act of desperation?" she asked.

"Bye, Mom."

She was still talking as I hung up. I wanted to throw the phone or scream over her being so stubborn and noncongratulatory. But I pretended instead that deep down she was really happy for me.

I took no comfort in the fact that Charity's parents had been equally unexcited over our proposed union. But they had agreed to get the marriage ball rolling and were now busy with the early details of marriage preparation. Charity and I planned to go to Yuma in a couple of weeks so I could meet her parents in person.

Life seemed incredibly hectic at the moment. I was glad we were going to wait a couple of months before we actually got married. It would give us enough time to get things done right.

≺   ≺   ≺   ≺   ≺

I was lying on my couch listening to the rain beat melodically upon the roof, thinking about how crazy the sleepy little town of Longwinded had made my life, and trying to envision myself in tails, when someone started banging at my front door. I wondered for a moment who could be knocking on my door so late at night.

Whoever it was started banging harder.

"All right, all right, I'm coming," I yelled as I reached for the door.

"Tartan, it's me, Bob," Bob screamed back through the door.

I opened the door and Bob came bounding in. He was soaked and dripping like a wet dog after a long bath.

"My word, Bob, what are you doing?"

He leaned against one of my kitchen chairs and tried to catch his breath. "It's Rich," he finally said.

"What about Rich?" I asked, interested.

"I found him," Bob said.

"Where is he?"

"I lost him again."

Bob sat down on the couch and tried to compose himself.

"I was camped out at your chapel, as usual," Bob started. "I was just about to doze off when Fern tore into the parking lot and started banging on my camper. He was screaming something about Rich and Mary Longfellow. Couldn't make out a word he was saying. Some people just don't handle confusion well."

Bob would know, I thought.

"Get this," Bob went on. "Apparently Fern and Erma have been seeing one another for some time now."

I gasped. Not necessarily over the fact that they were seeing one another, but over the fact they had been able to keep it a secret.

"That's how I reacted," Bob said, referring to my gasp. "Anyhow, Erma had been giving Mary a little stronger dose of her medicine at dinnertime so she would be sound asleep when Fern came over."

"Fern and Erma?" I said, finally realizing just how unrealistic that seemed.

"Fern and Erma," Bob said, flabbergasted.

"How old is Erma?" I asked.

"She'll turn seventy-one next November."

"And Fern?"

"Eighty-six in February."

"He's robbing the cradle."

"That he is," Bob said, as if he couldn't comprehend that kind of behavior. "Anyhow, Fern went up to see Erma tonight and instead of finding her with open arms, she was bound, gagged, and tied to one of Mary's good chairs."

"You're kidding."

"I wish I were," Bob said. "Guess where Fern found Mary?"

I shrugged my shoulders.

"Dead! Dead's where he found her!" Bob's big eyes were on fire.

"You're kidding," I said again.

"Nope. I'm so serious I could be the Pope's bishop."

"Did Erma overmedicate Mary?"

"That was my first thought," Bob said. "No, actually, I hadn't thought about that."

Colombo he wasn't.

"So what happened?" I demanded.

"It was Rich. I guess he had been breaking into Mary's place and stealing food and other small things of value. Erma thought she had just been misplacing things, but noooo, it was Rich. He had been slipping in while Fern and Erma were cuddling and Mary was medicated. I guess Rich was getting desperate because tonight he went for the antique watch Mary was wearing. It's one of those nifty kinds that has the sun rise when it's daytime and the moon rise when it's night. I had one sort of like that, but somehow with daylight savings things got out of whack. Never could quite get that thing back in sync. Watches and I aren't the best combination. Once when—"

"Bob," I said sternly.

"Oh, yeah, Rich. Well, he was trying to slip the watch off Mary's wrist when Erma decided to check up on Mary. When Erma turned on the light and found Rich wrestling with Mary's arm, she screamed so loudly, it woke Mary up. I guess the shock of Erma screaming and waking up to find Rich pulling on her was too great. Mary's heart gave out."

"My goodness," I said softly, reminding myself of my mother.

"Tragic, tragic loss," Bob said.

I don't know if I would go so far as to say it was tragic, I thought, thinking back to my encounters with Mary.

"Rich ran after Erma and caught her. She would have escaped except for the huge pile of TV trays that seemed to jump out at her."

"Incredible," I said. "Is Erma all right then?"

"She is."

"Where's Rich?" I asked.

"He got away," Bob explained. "I looked for him for a little while, but there was just no sign."

"Why did you come here?" I asked.

"After Rich tied Erma up, he spent some time thinking out loud and pacing in front of her. Erma said he was pretty shook up about Mary dying. He was going on and on about how everyone was going to say he had murdered her and how none of this would have happened if Joseph Smith had never been born."

"Good argument," I said sarcastically.

"Yeah," Bob said, "that's what I was thinking. Anyhow, Rich also said that it seemed to him that all this," Bob swirled his hands around in the air for effect, "his life falling apart, all seemed to coincide with you coming to Longwinded."

"Me?"

"Yep," Bob answered. "Erma said Rich was spitting mad when he left, and that the last thing he said was something about you."

"And what was that?" I asked.

"I'm not sure, but you can bet it wasn't something nice."

"Or in the form of a complete sentence."

Bob ignored me and went on. "That's why I'm here, to protect you."

I laughed a small laugh.

"Listen, Bob," I said. "I know there are a million things for you to do, what with Mary dying and all. So don't feel you need to stick around here to help me. I'm a big boy; I can take care of myself."

"Still," Bob said, "I think it would be best if I just hung around for a little while. I could even sleep on your couch here."

The last thing I wanted tonight was to have a sleepover with Bob. I was about as frightened of Rich as I was of my shadow, and I could see no reason why Bob would need to stay and protect me.

"Bob, what about Fern and Erma?" I asked. "Someone needs to watch after *them*. I'd hate for Willie to be the one to tell everybody about their secret romance. Willie has such a hard time getting his facts straight."

"That's true," Bob said reflectively. "News like that should be delivered by the law."

"I'll be all right here," I said.

"You sure?" Bob asked.

"Positive."

"I called in Ralph Cooney from Pinefield to help me with Rich. I probably should be at the station when he arrives."

"Sounds protocol to me."

"Scott's watching Mary's body until the coroner gets there," Bob said. "I should probably call Mary's family to let them know."

"It's pretty late," I commented.

"That's true," Bob said. "I'd hate to wake them up just to tell them something that could wait until tomorrow."

The only family Mary had lived far away from Longwinded. I felt certain they would prefer not being disturbed by news they had been expecting for years anyway.

Bob got up from the couch, a large wet spot marking the place he had occupied. "If you need or hear anything, let me know."

"I will," I said, opening the door for him.

Bob stepped out into the wet night. Rain was falling hard and heavy as he got into his car and drove off. I was about to shut and lock the door when Albert wandered over to me wanting to be let out. I pushed the door open and let him out.

I called Charity and told her about Fern, Erma, Mary, and Rich.

"Fern and Erma?" she asked.

"That's what I said. I can't believe it."

"You think you know someone," Charity said. "Poor Mary."

"I'll bet she's never been happier," I said, suddenly feeling sorry for all the angels above who were now having to deal with her.

I-love-yous were exchanged, and then Charity and I hung up.

I made myself a big cup of hot chocolate in honor of the freezing rain, sat down in front of my small TV, and vegetated. Thanks to the mountains, my TV only picked up two channels. I switched back and forth for a few minutes trying to decide between a rerun of "I Love Lucy" or a program on male pattern balding. I had plenty of hair at the moment, which finally persuaded me to choose Lucy.

I would have completely forgotten about Albert if it weren't for a dogfood commercial that came on during my show. I got up and went to the door. I opened it and yelled for Albert a couple of times.

It was still raining hard, making the air smell so good you could taste it.

"Albert!" I yelled.

The loud rain almost caused me to miss hearing Albert's cry off in the distance. I could tell from the direction of his cry exactly where he was. There were some rabbit holes a little way off, at the base of one of the biggest pines around. Albert would dig and scrape until he could get his head into one of the holes, but then he would be trapped by the roots when he tried to pull back out. It was a weekly ritual for Albert. Beagles were not heavy on brains.

"Stupid dog," I mumbled as I slipped my boots on.

I grabbed a flashlight and headed out after my dog. I was completely drenched before I was ten steps away from the cabin. I thought about going back in for a raincoat but knew it would just be a few seconds before I had Albert and was heading back.

I could hear Albert clearly now.

"I'm coming, I'm coming," I said loudly.

I wiped rain from my eyes as I approached the big pine. I couldn't see Albert anywhere.

"Where are you?" I yelled, expecting him to answer me.

He whined again. I walked in the direction of his whine.

"Albert?" I called, sensing for the first time that things didn't feel right.

"Albert, are you there?"

Albert yelped as if in pain. I started running toward him. The rain was letting up a bit, but with my clothes completely soaked, I was moving slower than usual. A horribly painful bark rang out, followed by a loud thud, but my puny little flashlight did little to light the way. I sent my tiny beam scanning frantically for any sign of Albert.

I envisioned Albert maimed by a bear or with a broken leg from falling down a cliff or into a hole.

My beam finally picked up Albert laying atop a huge rock. There was no movement when I finally reached him. I gently poked around him trying to sense any sort of life. I could feel he was still breathing, but it was shallow, last-breath type of breathing. I could see no blood or lacerations anywhere on his body. He was just a very wet, very close to death dog. I was somewhat hesitant to move him for fear I would make matters worse.

I stood and looked up to the rain. I had heard of people giving blessings to their animals, but it was something I didn't think I would feel comfortable doing. I said a small prayer but before I could finish it, something hit me across my shoulders, sending pain to every corner of my body.

I fell over Albert and rolled to a stop at the bottom of a small slope. I tried desperately to get back on my feet and find out what had hit me. But before I could, a foot pushed my head against the ground.

Wet grass pushed up against my face as I tried to catch my breath. I reached above my head and grabbed the leg that was pushing my head down. With one quick grasp, I pulled the leg off my head and pushed someone over. I had caught whoever it was off guard, and whoever it was fell to the ground, rolling farther down the slope.

I pulled myself up.

I strained my eyes to see who had assailed me. Lightning struck on cue, lighting up the night and giving me a pretty good glimpse of Rich. He was about twenty feet away, and I could see from the expression on his face he was confused about whether he should run or fight.

I helped make up his mind by charging toward him. Rich took off running. With clouds blocking the moon and stars, the night was very dark. But I could make out Rich's form and was chasing after him with all the energy I had. There was no way I was going to let him get away, not after he had burned Ian's barn, wasted Sherry's Cheese Whiz, broken Scott's windows, made fun of Joseph Smith, and beaten my dog. There are certain things people just don't do.

Running downhill made finding footing difficult. I blinked and Rich was gone. I only had two seconds to consider his whereabouts before I ran off the edge of a ten-foot drop. I crashed hard against the wet ground and rolled with the fall. Rich, who had discovered the drop in about the same fashion, was on his feet now. He kicked me in the stomach as I tried to get to my feet.

"Stay put, you Mormon dog," he screamed as he kicked.

His kick sent me back to the ground. He then took off running again instead of sticking around to kick me some more. I got up and deliberately disobeyed by running after him. Rain made the mountain terra mushy and hard to maneuver on. I stumbled a number of times as I tried to catch up.

Lightning struck and Rich looked behind to see if I was coming. He saw me and began running faster. Just when I felt I could go no farther, Rich stumbled, giving me just enough time to catch up to him. I tackled his legs, pulling him down to the ground. He wiggled like a wet fish in soapy hands trying to get free. I finally got a grip on him, but he kicked me in the chest, sending me back a few feet. I frantically tried to catch my breath. Rich got to his feet and grabbed a large broken tree limb from the ground. I sat there unsure of what to do.

"You've ruined my life," he growled, holding the limb above his head as if he were about to strike me. Where was Bob when I needed him?

"Things were nice around here before you came and messed them up."

I sat there gulping in huge amounts of air trying to catch my breath.

"What would you say if I told you I was going to finish you off?"

"Don't be stupid, Rich," I managed to say.

"Stupid? Stupid? I'll show you stupid," Rich screeched, as he brought the limb down. I tried to roll out of the way, but Rich still managed to hit my left shoulder. I could hear my collarbone crack.

I wanted to scream, but my lungs wouldn't let me. Rich lifted the limb again. He was a bit closer to me now. I pulled back my right leg, then kicked as hard as I could. His legs flew out from under him, flinging him forward onto me. Our heads knocked as he fell against me on the ground. I pushed him off with my right arm and scrambled to my feet.

I had no idea where I was going—I just ran. My broken collarbone made running so painful it got to the point where I thought I was going to pass out.

I stopped and looked around for Rich—I couldn't see him. The rain began letting up until it was nothing but a fine mist. I hoped I had lost Rich, but my hopes were dashed when out of the corner of my eye, I could see him sneaking up on me. I played dumb, using my peripheral vision to the fullest. Rich had the same large branch with him, and I had no doubt that once he got close enough, he would take one final swipe at the back of my head.

My heart was racing wildly as Rich inched his way closer to me.

He was about five steps behind me when I realized I didn't have a plan. Big deal that I knew he was there; he still had a weapon, and to the best of my knowledge, both his collarbones were intact. I was a weak opponent at the moment.

I watched him inch closer as I thought quickly of something to do.

Closer.

Closer.

I could faintly hear his footsteps now. He was coming at me from my left side. There was no time to be creative. I said a quick prayer.

Closer.

I could see him raise the limb in preparation to swing.

Closer.

I could see him pull back.

It seemed as if he held the limb suspended for the longest time. Then all at once he flung it forward with so much force that if I hadn't dodged, it would have knocked my head off.

I ducked and turned, driving a punch into the bottom of his rib cage as he followed through with his swing, which hit nothing but air. His forward momentum and my lunge toward him provided for one very hard hit. I could almost feel the air being forced out of his lungs and out his mouth. I pulled back to administer another blow.

I never administered it.

I looked at Rich's face as he gasped for air and I suddenly felt awful. I didn't want to beat up Rich; I didn't want anything, except to be anyplace besides where I was at the moment. I hadn't prayed for the strength to annihilate anyone; I had prayed I would survive the night.

Rich dropped to his knees, coughing and spitting up something. I caught my breath as I stood waiting for him to get up on his feet.

"You need to come with me," I said soberly.

Rich coughed violently. "I ain't going with you anywhere."

"Don't make this harder than it needs to be, Rich."

He started to walk away from me; I followed at about the same pace.

"I can't let you walk away," I said, hoping he would give up and knowing I didn't have the strength to do much if he didn't.

"Then watch me run, fairy boy," Rich yelled, as he took off into the thickest stretch of trees nearby.

"Rich!"

I chased him for about two minutes, giving up when I realized there was no way a person in my shape was going to catch anything—except maybe pneumonia.

I was all at once aware of just how cold I was. The rain that had been mist just moments ago was gaining strength. Drops the size of strawberries began falling as the wind picked up. I had no inclination whatsoever to follow Rich any farther.

I didn't rule out the possibility of Rich turning back to come and get me. So I weaved my way through the forest in such a way he would never be able to find me.

I could see lightning shimmering all around me. I watched it strike a tree about a hundred feet away, catching a poor sapling on fire for a moment before the rain put it out. I realized for the first time that I was scared. The feeling seemed to cover me in utter despair.

I was freezing, lost, tired, getting rained on, and stuck in the wilderness with a broken collarbone. There was no way I would make it home. Even if I did know my way, there was no chance of me mustering enough strength to get there. I seemed to have enough problems at the moment to justify asking for help. I fell to my knees, halfway out of respect and halfway out of not having the strength to stand a moment more.

I prayed.

I could feel the rain increasing as my words to heaven ascended upward through the trees and into the cloudy beyond. I had no idea how God could possibly get me out of this. I was most frightened by the fact that I could feel hypothermia coming on. We were experiencing a cold snap unlike any Longwinded had ever known. The cold temperature and wet rain were a deadly duo. I needed warmth. There was no way I could build a fire with everything so wet, so I stayed on my knees beneath the trees and prayed.

The rain came harder, slicing through overhead branches and cascading like a waterfall upon me. I could feel the force of it pushing me toward the ground.

I couldn't believe it!

I had finally achieved engagement, and here I was about to die. Twenty-nine years of being single, my first glimpse of marital bliss in view, and fate had chosen to knock me off. I couldn't think straight any longer, I couldn't feel any longer. I couldn't deal any longer. I ended my prayer before I lost all train of thought.

I gave up and in.

I let the rain push me to the ground. My body fell against the earth, mud oozing up my nose and into my mouth. It was so . . .

Warm?

With the help of my knees I rubbed my body against the earth, warm mud completely covering my front side. I pushed myself onto my back and used my good arm to coat myself in the warmest mud

I had ever encountered. The rain continued to fall as I pushed myself deeper into the earth's crust, mud covering every inch of my body. I turned over on my belly and burrowed myself as deeply as I could. It was the most glorious experience! It reminded me of being young and dipping my fingers in the wax drippings of a hot candle.

My body began to warm up.

The rain became a mist again. It was such a relief to not have raindrops dancing on me any longer. In fact I was becoming so comfortable laying there in that mud I began to worry that I might be slipping into some sort of mud euphoria that ended with death. I decided if that were the case, I could live with it or die with it, whatever the result might be.

I fell asleep thinking about Charity and the high cost of quality ice cream. I blame the latter on the supposed mud euphoria. Heaven at the moment was a bowl of butter pecan ice cream and a heaping helping of Charity.

CHAPTER TWENTY-SEVEN

"TRAGEDY BEGETS DESTINY"

L ight.

I could see a pinpoint cutting though the darkness and calling me home. I would have thought it to be some kind of near-death experience, but I wasn't feeling any of the weightlessness or free floating so many people who had slipped beyond the veil and then made it back described. In fact, I felt like I weighed about four hundred pounds.

I could barely move.

I thought for a moment that perhaps this was hell, but I could hear no weeping and gnashing of teeth. Besides, I felt confident I would at least get a chance to be told about everything I had done wrong in my life before being sent there.

I pushed my arms out, as mud cracked and broke off of me; I remembered clearly where I was now. I rose from the earth like some sort of disoriented dirt man. I had done a very complete job of covering myself—there wasn't a single spot that was mud free. I wished there had been someone around to see me rise from my muddy niche. I could have given someone a really good scare.

The substance that had quite possibly saved me was now

itching like mad. I lifted my left arm up to scratch, only to be reminded of my broken collarbone.

"Ahhh!"

The sun upon the mud upon me was making things too hot. I scraped and chipped with my right hand as I went in search of water and some way out of here. With daylight I had a much better idea of where I was; I seemed to be right where Mount Taylor and Pine Point met. If I were right, all I had to do was walk straight down, and I'd run into Longwinded. It would be much easier than having to hike back up the mountain.

I thought about Rich and what a genuine burr he had become. I didn't know now if I could ever feel completely safe with him lost in the mountains somewhere. As I saw him holding that branch above me last night, I could tell he was committed to getting rid of me. He had passed the point of no return.

I had been right about where I was. About six miles later I hit a dirt road that would take me directly into town. I walked slowly, listening for any water I might be able to bathe in. I could hear no water, but I could hear and see a speeding car off in the distance. I tried to run and wave it down, but I was too slow. The car sped by without seeing me—it was Sister Wingate. I thought about going after her, but I had no idea how far the road went or where she was headed. I continued walking toward town.

What seemed like an hour later I hit pavement. I had passed a couple of houses in the woods but felt certain if I had approached their doors, I would have been mistaken for some sort of Sasquatch and then shot.

I wasn't on the pavement for more that two minutes before a car came from behind. I turned and tried to wave it down. The moment they saw me they sped off in the direction of town. A couple of minutes later Bob came racing toward me in his patrol car, his lights flashing and siren blaring. Apparently, the car I had scared earlier had run to Bob for help.

Bob screeched to a halt about fifty feet in front of me. He threw open his car door, crouched down behind it, and pointed his gun at me. A few cars pulled up behind him.

"Stop right there!" he yelled.

I couldn't decide if I should try and have some fun with this or if I should let them know immediately who I was. Even though I had scratched and scraped a lot of the mud off, I was still wearing a pretty good coat of it. Plus, there were a lot of leaves, grass, and twigs still cemented to my being.

Bob didn't give me time to think about it. He fired his pistol into the sky.

I jumped two feet into the air. Everyone stepped back at my reaction.

I was pretty certain Bob would never shoot me, but I wasn't as sure about all the folks behind him who had pulled their shotguns down from their gun racks and were now pointing them at me.

"Bob," I yelled, mud cracking around my mouth as I spoke. "It's me, Tartan."

It was obvious they hadn't understood me. I could hear someone arguing with Bob over whether I was speaking English or not. They all kept their guns pointed at me.

"Shoot it," someone way in the back yelled.

"Wait!" I screamed, "it's Tartan!"

"What did it say?" Bob asked.

"It said it ate Tartan!" someone yelled.

I wanted to just walk a few steps closer so they could see who it was and so I could knock some sense into them. But I felt pretty sure that any movement I made would merit gunfire.

"Bob," I hollered.

I could see it finally click for Bob.

"Tartan?"

"Yes," I said with relief.

"Well, why didn't you say so," he said, waving me over. "We almost shot you. You're lucky I'm a man of restraint."

What luck I had.

I walked sheepishly over to the small cluster of cars and trucks. Willie popped up from behind everyone.

"Sorry I said shoot it," he apologized.

I waved off his apology.

"What happened?" Bob asked.

I told everyone about Rich and what had gone on the night before, and then Bob drove me over to the doctor's house.

According to the doctor, my collarbone had incurred a nice clean break. I suppose that was something to be happy about, but it brought me no joy. He gave me a stark white sling to wear for the next six weeks. My muddy clothes made the white sling so white it was almost blinding. When the doctor finished, I called Fred and told him what had happened and explained why I had been away this morning. Fred was bothered as usual.

"I guess now is as good a time as any," he said.

"For what?" I asked.

"To tell you that I'm putting in for a transfer. Four years is all I can take of this place." I couldn't blame him, so I really didn't know what to say.

Sensing I was speechless, Fred said, "Just thought you should know."

"Thanks."

"Don't mention it," he said with some sarcasm.

I called Charity and filled her in on everything I had been through. What I told her was pretty much the straight truth with just a few points of embellishment. At first she was concerned about my encounter with Rich and my brush with death. But because I kept going on and on about it, and since it was after the fact and I was all right now, her sympathy didn't run too deep for too long.

"Will you come pick me up?" I asked.

"If you promise not to whine the whole drive home," she said.

"Promise."

"Bets on whether you'll keep it?"

"No way," I said. "That's like giving my money away for free."

I was able to wash up a little at the doctor's house, so at least my arms, hands, and most of my face were cleaned up. I had told Charity that when she saw me she needed to realize I would probably never look worse. She went on and on about how I was forgetting about the fact I would probably get fat and bald as I got older. I suddenly wished I had paid more attention to the male pattern balding program the other night.

Charity came and picked me up. She made me feel better about myself by telling me I looked ruggedly handsome in mud. She also tried to tell me that arm slings were in.

"Maybe in Yuma," I said.

I whined for an appropriate amount of time and then let her tell me about her night. Her dealings paled in comparison to mine, but I tried not to one-up her too much.

"I read for a couple of hours and then helped my aunt make brownies," Charity explained.

"Did I mention I slept in mud?" I asked.

"A number of times," she laughed. "Although I could have guessed just by looking at you."

"What about the fact that a known criminal broke my collarbone?"

"You told me that, too."

"Do you want to sign my sling?" I asked.

"It's too bad your wound didn't merit a real cast," Charity joked.

"I knew you were lying when you said slings were in."

Charity slowed down as we came to the Baptist chapel. Parson Stevens was outside, a small crowd standing around him.

"Stop," I said. "I want to hear what he's saying."

Charity parked at our building and we walked over to the crowd. No one noticed, or maybe no one cared about our arrival.

"It's sad that poor Mary Longfellow is dead," Parson Stevens yelled. "Sad and tragic, but what we as Baptists must do is realize that the Mormons are now down by two." He held up two of his skinny fingers and showed them to the crowd. "And for those of you who have been too wrapped up in other things to notice, Mary was the last of the Longfellows. I tell you, my brothers and sisters, that God has parted the Red Sea, and it is up to us to walk to the other side. We must take our rightful place as the majority of Longwinded."

The crowd cheered.

Parson Stevens, sensing the mob was with him, continued. "The first thing we must do is to have those Moormoons," he said with a slur, "get rid of this monstrosity that is cluttering our street and detracting from the beauty of our mountains." Parson Stevens pointed across the street at our humble chapel. "A mobile home is bad enough, but a rickety, broken, half-there junk heap is even worse. God wouldn't be caught dead in such a place."

The crowd went wild with this. I thought they were going to walk across the street, hoist our building up on their shoulders, and march the whole thing out of town. Their adrenaline level seemed high enough for them to do so.

I saw Bob pull up and get out of his car. He had obviously come to offer a little crowd control. Charity and I walked over toward him.

"He's been like this since the moment I told him about Mary," Bob said to me, referring to Parson Stevens.

"He's been like this ever since I moved to town."

"True," said Bob.

"How are Fern and Erma?" I asked.

"Fine," Bob said. "They're shaken up but seem to be handling it all right. I wish I could say the same for the town."

"What's the deal with Rich?" I asked.

"I asked for some more help," Bob said, somewhat apologetically, "but everyone above me thinks it's useless to go looking for him. The popular opinion is that he'll eventually show up, so why waste time looking?"

"Sophisticated opinion," I said.

"Sorry, Tartan," Bob said kindly.

"I guess I'll have to start locking my doors."

"Wouldn't be a bad idea," Bob said, submitting a little bit of his expert advice.

Parson Stevens's band of renegades let out a giant whoop.

"The Baptists really feel they have the advantage now," Bob commented, keeping an eye on the parson the whole time.

"Advantage over what?" I asked, disgusted with every single thing going on in this town.

"In case you haven't heard, you Mormons are down by two."

"Big deal," I said casually.

"Indeed it is," Bob said excitedly. "The biggest advantage the Baptists ever had was two, and now with Sister Wingate, they might just break that record."

"Sister Wingate's going to join the Baptists?" Charity asked for me.

"Looks like a possibility. She took Mary's death as a personal invitation from God to switch sides. Mary and Wynona Wingate were pretty close. Anyhow, the Baptists are saying that if they can pull Sister Wingate in, then it's only a matter of time before President Wingate jumps ship to their shore."

"Unbelievable," I said.

Parson Stevens was holding up a Bible and reading applicable verses to the crowd. He yelled something about them being the whale and Jonah being our mobile chapel. "We need to spit it out."

The crowd loved his analogy.

"I can't believe Sister Wingate would become a Baptist," Charity said. "She bad-mouthed them more actively than anyone."

"I know," Bob agreed. "But at this very moment she is up on the mountain praying for an answer. She told Parson Stevens she wasn't coming back until God told her what to do."

"I saw her drive past me while I was hiking down," I said.

"Yep," Bob clucked. "She went looking for her sacred grove."

"I hope she finds it," Charity said sarcastically.

"I hope it's thorny," I added, envisioning her large, self-righteous knees poked repeatedly by grove thistles.

Parson Stevens screamed something about taking the law into their own hands. He retracted the statement shortly after making eye contact with Bob.

"Spiritual law," he corrected.

I noticed Willie in the crowd and decided to go talk to him. I left Charity with Bob and slipped up next to Willie. I tapped him on the shoulder as he was yelling something about particleboard. He turned around expecting to find a fellow Baptist.

"Hey, Willie," I said.

"Tartan," he said, suddenly embarrassed. "What are you doing here?"

"Just trying to see what's going on. Is this some kind of charity drive?" I asked. "Or is it a rally to show support for your neighbors?"

"Tartan," Willie whined, pulling me by my good arm outside the circle of Baptists. "You shouldn't be here; this has nothing to do with you."

"It doesn't?"

"Tartan, you know there is no way I can deny my religion."

"Who's asking you to deny your religion?" I asked.

"I don't know the answer to everything," Willie said in a huff.

I threw my arm up in the air and turned to walk away. Willie half-heartedly tried to get back into the mob mentality.

"I don't think things will ever change here," I said as I got back to Charity and Bob.

Bob tipped back his hat and said, "Things might change if Wynona Wingate joins up with the Baptists. She is really the only outspoken Mormon left. Once she's gone, you all will have no one to fight your battles."

"Good," I said.

"I think you're underestimating the power of Wynona," Bob said seriously.

"I think Bob's right," Charity added.

Bob nodded toward Charity as if to thank her for agreeing.

I was just about to suggest that Charity and I leave this circus of stupidity when I saw Ian's Jeep heading down the street. I stepped away from Bob and waved Ian down. It wasn't Ian, however; it was Bronwyn. She stopped and rolled down the window.

"What happened to you?" she asked, referring to the mud and my sling.

"It's a long story," I said.

"Are you all right?"

"He's fine," Charity answered for me.

"I've been trying to get hold of you all morning," Bronwyn said to me. "Don't you ever work?"

"Occasionally," I said.

"I think I called just about everyone in the branch," Bronwyn continued, "looking for someone who could go give a blessing. But the few people who are capable aren't home."

"Who needs a blessing?" I asked.

"Brother Crimsal," Bronwyn said, looking at me to see if the name rang a bell. "I don't know him, but his wife said you and Ian visited them a little while back."

"I remember them," I said.

"She called asking for Ian, but he's off fishing with his dad. We really should get over there," Bronwyn said, remembering this was a minor emergency. "Sister Crimsal sounded extremely worried. I guess her husband is pretty bad off. Can you give a blessing with one hand?"

"I can use this one a little," I said, nodding toward my left.

The crowd of Baptists started breaking up, and people were walking around looking for some way to vent their rage. I could see Pastor Stevens wiping his forehead as Charity and I got into Bronwyn's Jeep and drove off.

Bronwyn filled us in on what was happening with the Crimsals as we drove over. Apparently, Brother Crimsal had been sick for weeks with what they thought was the flu. They had taken him to the hospital once, but all they did was put him on some medication that did nothing but put him to sleep. Sarah Crimsal remembered the oil incident at their home earlier in the summer. She found Ian's number and asked if I could come over and put some oil on her husband's delirious head. Certainly, the invitation to bless could have been worded better, but according to Bronwyn she had never heard someone ask so sincerely.

Since Bronwyn had such poor luck in finding someone else to give the blessing, I figured I wouldn't even try to find a partner to help administer. Two people was the priesthood of preference for most blessings, but circumstances required I fly solo on this one.

We pulled up to the Crimsals' home and jumped out. Things didn't look quite as squared away as they had the last time I visited. The grass was a little long; I could spot weeds among the flowers and the walkway looked in need of a good sweeping. Obviously the Crimsals had other things to worry about at the moment.

Sarah Crimsal hugged me after she opened the door. She didn't seem to notice all the mud, or that the object she was squeezing was wearing a sling. I tried not to wail as she crushed my arm.

"I didn't know what to do," she said. "No one knows what is wrong. I can't sleep. I can't eat. All I can do is worry. I didn't know if I was allowed to call you."

"You did the right thing," I said.

"Well," she said nervously, "how do you do this?"

"First, I need Brother Crimsal."

I introduced Bronwyn and Charity to Sarah. She then led us to her husband, Robert, who was sleeping in their bedroom. He looked so weak I was almost afraid to put my hands on his head. Sarah said it was next to impossible to wake him up due to the medication, so we decided to just give him the blessing as he slept. Bronwyn handed me the tiny container of oil (that she had the presence of mind to bring), and I put a small drop on Brother Crimsal's head.

I was suddenly reminded of wanting to give Albert a blessing the night before. I hoped he was still alive and had found his way home. I was also reminded of Brother Hatch and his weight-loss blessing. I hadn't seen him eat anything in excess in a while—I made a mental note to see how he was doing later.

I put my hands on Brother Crimsal's head and anointed him. I then gave him a blessing. Never had I been prompted to say such great things. As each word was uttered, I was amazed. He would fully recover; he would start coming to church; he would baptize his wife; he would be sealed to her in the temple; and he would be a source of great strength to the Saints in the area. Normally, I didn't like to promise anything too great for fear that it wouldn't come true. I didn't want people to start making up things about how I must be unworthy in some way because my blessings didn't stick.

This was different; these words weren't mine.

I kept hoping Robert was hearing this somehow. I received a pretty strong impression that he was.

When I closed the blessing things seemed right. Sarah's eyes, although moist, were wide open as if in shock over what she had just seen and heard—not to mention felt. Hugs were exchanged and thank yous offered as we left Sarah and Robert alone. Sarah looked very calm as we drove away.

Bronwyn dropped Charity and me off at the chapel where we had left Charity's car. A few Baptists were still standing around their building waiting for Sister Wingate to come down from the hills with her decision. Like Moses, she would soon descend, spitting mad and looking to take her place among the Baptist greats by ridding the town of our mobile cow.

I couldn't imagine her *not* joining the Baptists. I just couldn't see her asking for forgiveness from the Saints and wanting to come back to our branch. I also couldn't imagine her being humble enough to even be listening for an answer up in her grove. I'm sure her decision was made well before she sped past me on her way there.

I didn't care either way at the moment. I had only one thing on my mind, and that was a warm bath. Sister Wingate could have come down transfigured, but unless she was toting a large pool of hot water and the prospect of a little privacy, I wouldn't have cared.

᷆   ᷆   ᷆   ᷆   ᷆

Charity helped me into my house when we arrived. She started some bath water for me and fixed me a can of chicken noodle soup. I yelled for Albert a couple of times, but there was no sign of him. I was almost positive he had died out on the mountain—one more thing I owed Rich for.

Despite the fact that I was a wreck, Charity kissed me as she left. I then locked myself in and took my long-awaited bath.

I fell asleep in the bathtub, waking up four hours later when I tried to roll over and my head slipped under the water. I got out, dried off, and slipped into bed looking every bit like the world's largest raisin.

CHAPTER TWENTY-EIGHT

"MMM"

(MANUFACTURED MORMON MOAN)

My shoulder hurt much worse the next morning, and I was so sore from my encounter with Rich I didn't know if I could pull myself out of bed. I was surprised I had slept through the entire night without waking up from pain. I had slept with my sling on and it was now a tangled mess.

I needed to stay close to my outpost for the day and try to catch up on some of the paperwork I had neglected. But first I wanted to spend a little time looking for Albert.

I went to the giant pine tree and tried to find the path I had forged the night before. Thanks to the rain, there were no footprints or traces of Albert or me anywhere. I trudged back home with a heavy heart. I was convinced that Albert was dead.

The phone was ringing as I returned to the cabin. It was Charity telling me Sister Wingate had received an answer. I had never heard Charity so excited.

"Well, what was the answer?" I asked.

"I don't know for sure," she said. "I think it's good, though. Bob told my aunt the whole town is going crazy."

Going crazy?

"Didn't Bob say what her answer was?" I asked.

"No, I guess Sister Wingate is going to give a little speech in about an hour. Clark Bender is coming over to pick up my aunt; I was wondering if my boyfriend was going to do the same for me?"

"I really should get some things done," I complained, knowing full well I wouldn't miss Wynona Wingate's announcement for the world.

"I'll be waiting," Charity said.

"All right," I consented. "Let me go tell Martin and I'll be right there."

Martin wasn't at his place. I supposed he was with Loni or Orvil somewhere. Martin's lack of a phone was really starting to wear on me. I raced back to my truck and took off toward town.

⚒ ⚒ ⚒ ⚒ ⚒

Everyone was there. Sister Wingate really drew a crowd. I had called Ian before I left my place to see if he and Bronwyn wanted to come. Bronwyn informed me that Ian and his father had encountered a few problems on their fishing trip, so he still wasn't home.

From the look on Pastor Stevens's face, you would never guess Sister Wingate's news would be anything to help out the Mormons. He was smiling smugly as he sat on a tattered lawn chair next to Wynona.

Bob had set out the orange traffic cones and given strict orders to the Smith boys to keep their hands off of them. One side of our main road was now blocked off so there was room for everyone to stand and hear the decision. I scanned the crowd in hopes of seeing Fern and Erma or Martin and Loni, but there was no sign of them.

Orvil and Sherry came up to Charity and me to say howdy.

"Where's Martin?" Orvil asked.

"I guess he's with Loni," I said. I was going to say more, but Sister Wingate was standing and ready to talk.

The crowd fell silent. I put my nonslinged arm around Charity and tried to make this event a little more fulfilling.

Sister Wingate nodded to President Wingate. He then stood up next to her and laid down a couple of ground rules.

"Wynona has a lot to say," he said soberly.

This was a piece of startling information.

"So, we should all refrain from making comments until she is done. Also," he said, looking at little Lehi's parents, "do you think for once you could keep Lehi from running around?"

Lehi's parents consented with a nod.

"Wynona," he said, turning the time over to his wife.

If the crowd had been silent before, they were dead silent now.

Sister Wingate cleared her throat and began. "I was born in Longwinded, and except for the short time I left to better myself at school—I graduated top of my class—I have always lived here. I love this town as much if not more than anyone."

Sister Wingate looked very nervous. She had both her hands clenched together and hanging down in front of her. Every couple of seconds she would lift her ear to the wind as if listening for some sort of inspiration or assurance to go on.

"I have always been a Mormon," she continued. "I have also been a strong advocate of changing the Baptists to Mormons or making them leave."

A small murmur rippled though the ranks of the Baptists. Pastor Stevens looked appropriately disturbed as well.

"Sometimes," she continued, "I wonder what this town would have been like if none of us had ever cared about everyone's religion. Mary Longfellow, bless her soul, used to tell me about a short period of time when this town got along perfectly. She always said it was the happiest time of her life." Sister Wingate paused to wipe her eyes. "And all of us know there were not many occasions when Mary was happy."

Everyone was in agreement with that.

"Then old Ralph Tilldone," Wynona continued, "wrote that short history of Longwinded and kept referring to the Baptists as the 'Children of the Underworld.' I can say now, and with conviction, that Ralph shouldn't have done that."

Baptists all over nodded in agreement.

"As many of you know, I went up into the mountains yesterday to pray about joining the Baptist church. I was on my knees for over ten hours."

Everyone ahhhhed! A ten-hour prayer was about as foreign

to these folks as passing up the macaroni and cheese at an all-you-can-eat buffet.

"I was determined not to come down until I received a firm answer."

Sister Wingate put her ear to the wind again.

"Brothers and Sisters, I have an answer."

Everyone leaned forward, as if being a couple of inches closer would help them get the news that much sooner. Bob stepped up behind Wynona and patted his gun. He wanted to make sure folks knew he was there.

"It was late in the afternoon, in fact early evening, and I was growing a little weary from lack of food. I had brought a box of chocolate covered granola bars, but I polished those off within the first two hours. I swear those things are getting smaller and smaller. But I digress," Wynona said. "I decided to ask my Maker straight out if I should remain a Mormon. Well, no sooner had I asked when all of a sudden my mind was taken over with the most unsettling noise, like a small child whistling in the gardens of heaven. It seemed," she said, "as if the mountains were humming. The mountains, my friends, were humming at me. It was very faint, but oh so piercing."

Everyone looked at their neighbors to see if they too were buying this tale.

"After my initial reaction of shock, I was confused as to what this answer meant. Were the mountains humming in approval of my changing religious shrouds?" she said, her hands dancing wildly above her head. "Or were they sort of moaning over the fact that I was even considering leaving my lifelong spiritual center?" Her hands were now clenched into a tight ball as if to symbolize her center. "I had to know. Because if there is one thing I'm not, it's driftwood."

Everyone agreed with that, thinking silently to themselves about just what Sister Wynona Wingate actually was to them.

"So I asked, 'Should I be a Mormon?' The mountains hummed their approval. I then asked, 'Should I continue to curse the Baptists?' And the mountains moaned. Brothers and Sisters," she said on the verge of tears, "I found my answer, and what makes my discovery so overwhelming, and so spiritually spectacular, is that the hum is still there. Listen!" she commanded.

Everyone (including myself) put their hands to their ears and listened.

There was a long silence as we all strained to hear the mysterious noise.

Finally Bob broke the silence.

"I think I hear it," he said, somewhat tentatively.

People began to mumble and comment amongst themselves. If Bob could hear it then certainly it must be true. If the hum of God could penetrate the heart of Bob, there must be some truth to the words Wynona was speaking. Bob was our token atheist, and unlike Fern, who could be swayed by a large piece of pie, Bob was not easily bought. And now here in front of the whole town, Bob had heard the moan.

"Does it kind of sound like, 'MMMM'?" Bob asked Wynona.

"A 'mmmmm' or an 'aaaaaaaaa,'" she said with excitement.

"I can hear it," Bob said with conviction this time and standing rod straight. It was as if he had been crippled and the hum had set him free.

Willie was the next to hear.

"It's faint, but I hear it, too," he exclaimed.

"Like an angel humming," Mrs. Benderholden shouted in awe.

I couldn't hear anything but the sound of Orvil's jaw popping as he slowly chewed gum and listened.

"It is a message straight from heaven," Sister Wingate said with conviction. "And if we don't heed the drone of God, we will all be annihilated. It's a bipartisan hum."

Parson Stevens looked as though he was going to be sick. Who could possibly doubt the drone of God.

"I can't hear it," Sister Hatch yelled.

"Me, neither," Scott complained.

"Go to the mountains," Wynona screamed. "Go to the mountains!" Sister Wingate put her left hand on her hip and lifted her right to the sky as if posing for a statue.

People started jumping in cars and taking off for the hills. It was a mad rush to hear the mountains hum.

"I'll lead the way," Sister Wingate yelled, running to her car. Pastor Stevens shook his head repeatedly. This was obviously not the outcome he had hoped for. Charity squeezed my hand.

"Let's go listen for it," she said.

"Us?" I asked. Was Charity falling for this? Did she figure me to be the kind of person who would believe such a fairy tale? A hum? Humbug. It was all right for everyone else to believe it, but us? Sure, maybe Sister Wingate had heard something, but she said herself she had run out of food hours before her answer came. Wasn't there a better chance of it being her stomach than God?

"What else have we got to do?" Charity asked.

She had a good point. We hopped in my truck and followed the parade of cars heading in the direction of Sister Wingate's not-so-secret grove.

"This is so stupid," I said to Charity as we drove.

"Oh ye of little faith," she replied.

"Well, look at this town," I said. "One person hears a noise in the woods, and the next thing you know we all think it's a divine voice speaking to us from the earth."

"Cool, huh?"

"You are such a sucker," I said.

We reached hum central and hopped out of the truck. Scott was running around telling people to shut off their motors so we could all hear the hum better. Everybody else made their way up the mountainside, trying to get away from any outside noises.

Charity dragged me by my good arm up a small path no one else was taking.

"This is so dumb," I said.

Charity stopped to let me kiss her.

"This might have some merit," I said, taking a new stance.

We reached an area where we could no longer hear or see anyone else. I sat down upon an old log and readjusted my sling.

"So what do we—" I started to say as Charity sat down next to me.

"Shhh! I want to hear it."

We sat there in complete silence.

I heard a bird.

I heard another bird.

I heard the wind blowing through the trees.

I heard a squirrel scamper up a large pine and make some sort of clicking noise.

I was about to say "This is so stupid" again when I heard someone off in the distance shout.

"I can hear it!"

The woods came alive with people "shhhhing" him.

"I can hear it, too," another voice farther away yelled.

"Be quiet!" I heard Scott demand loudly.

I was going to make a joke about all the crackpots we had out here when Charity heard the hum.

"Can you hear it?" she asked in an excited whisper.

"Hear Scott?"

"No, the hum."

"You can really hear it?" I asked.

"Yes!"

"What does it sound like?"

"Shhhh!" Charity said, still listening for it.

"This really is dumb."

The whole mountain began to come alive with people professing to hear the hum.

Charity, Scott, Orvil, Sherry, the Hatches, Sister Lynn, Mr. Benderholden, President Wingate, and even Parson Stevens.

It was incredible.

People began hugging and apologizing for ever being unkind to each other. Everyone was tripping over each other in the wild rush to say "I'm sorry" first.

"This is amazing," I said, as Charity and I walked down from our spot and joined the commotion.

"There is a hum," Charity stated.

"Do you actually think it's God?" I asked, in awe of everyone making such a big to-do about it.

"I doubt it," Charity said. "But who cares. Look at everyone. God does work in mysterious ways."

"Mysterious, not stupid."

"You're just mad because you can't hear it."

"You're acting like this is some sort of miracle," I said sarcastically.

"Well, isn't it?"

"I've seen no miracle here today. I've just seen a bunch of people desperate for something to feel—or in this case hear. It would take much more than a hum to convince me God had his hand in this."

I felt someone tap me on the shoulder. I turned around to see Sister Wingate standing there. The last time we had spoken, she ended up accosting my truck hood and I almost ran over her. I instinctively lifted my hand to my face as if to deflect a blow.

"Tartan?"

"Yes," I answered timidly.

"I just wanted to tell you I'm sorry for some of the words you and I have exchanged. I realize now that I was way out of line and I'm sorry."

"What?" I asked, dumbfounded.

"I'm sorry," she said.

I couldn't believe it! Was this the same Wynona Wingate who days before had listed all my faults on the post office bulletin board? Was it?

Could she truly be sorry for some of the things she had done to me? Things like mailing me a box containing a decomposing gopher with a note that read:

"Wince if you will, but the sin inside is no gentler to the eyes."

Could she?

Is it possible that something as simple as a mountain groaning could change the personality and purpose of a person such as she?

I was baffled.

"Will you forgive me, Tartan?" she asked sincerely.

I just stood there, my mouth hanging open and tongue drying out. This was incredible! Turning water to wine was a simple card trick compared to the magic God was now performing. I was witnessing a miracle, and whether it was a hum, moan, groan, or drone, it had miraculously changed the heart of one once-heartless human.

"Will you?" she asked again.

My head was suddenly stuffed with all kinds of legitimate reasons why I shouldn't forgive someone like Wynona Wingate. The most persuasive reason was that I felt almost confident that two days from now she would have forgotten all this and returned to her former self. True forgiveness required at least a seven-day waiting period.

Could I forgive her?

Of course I could.

Would I forgive her?

Well . . .

Charity pinched my elbow with the force of a large pair of pliers.

"He accepts your apology," Charity said for me.

"Thank you," Sister Wingate gushed.

I think accepting an apology from someone who has truly wronged you requires an awful big amount of being the bigger person. The fact that Charity had done the accepting for me did little to remove the amount of pride swallowing I had done. I also believe that the heavens shouldn't push their luck.

They pushed.

Sister Wingate opened up her good sized arms and beckoned me to hug. She did some kind of wink thing with her left eye and then tried to pull me into her forgiving bosom by opening and closing her fingers.

My initial reaction was to run. Unfortunately, Charity prevented that by holding me right where I was. This hum thing was a force beyond any of our control. Charity pushed me into Wynona's waiting embrace. I let my good arm hang to my side as she squeezed me with the force of a large mother bear. She smelled like green apples and sweat and kept whispering something about us all being eternally bound together. When she finally let go of me, she hugged Charity. It was nice to know I would have Charity's empathy and not just sympathy whenever we were forced to think back on this occasion.

CHAPTER TWENTY-NINE

A RINGING IN OUR EARS

The transformation of Longwinded was one that would have baffled even Doctor Jekyll and Mister Hyde. Everyone had been affected by the hum. Orvil and Sherry heard it tell them to get married; Fern and Erma heard it give them the okay to bring their relationship out into the open. Pastor Stevens heard it distinctly tell him it was time to move on—he put in for a transfer out of Longwinded. Bob was reading his scriptures again and had changed the piece of paper hanging on his bulletin board from a yellow piece that said "If in doubt—Don't!" to a blue piece that said "John 3:17."

Clark Bender heard the hum whisper harshly that he needed to get himself in a position to take Clara Reese to the temple. He was now anxiously engaged in trying to be a better person. President and Sister Wingate had gone to see Ian to find out how they could help him with the branch and work their way back into good fellowship.

Kathy Paul and the rest of the youth in the branch had heard the hum and been so moved by it, they were doing service projects like mad. They helped the Benderholdens paint their house and did an amazing job of cleaning up the Crimsal place, as a recovering Brother Crimsal looked on.

A couple of local TV stations came out to investigate the hum and do a human interest story on our quirky little town. But no one outside the members of our community seemed to be able to hear the benign noise.

Willie and Scott had set out looking for the hum's origin, but after two days of hiking and searching, they found nothing.

The only two people who had not heard the hum were Ian and me. Most folks couldn't decide if it was because we were too righteous or too wicked. I still found the whole thing ridiculous but subscribed to the theory because of all the good it was doing.

The funeral for Mary Longfellow came and went with little fanfare. A couple of her relatives attended, but their main interest was in who would inherit Mary's vast estate. It was a shock to everyone when Mary's lawyer announced that every penny was to go to Erma. It was an even bigger shock when the lawyer read off just how much Mary was worth. (Apparently Mary had been investing.) Erma fainted when she heard the figure. And Fern?

He fawned.

Mary's relatives threatened to fight the will in court, but Erma and Fern weren't too concerned. Mary had been of sound mind when she passed on, and there were plenty of people whom Fern and Erma could pay to vouch for them if needed.

Longwinded was becoming a friendly community. In fact, the only sorrow any of us had to gab about was the fact that Rich was still out there somewhere and that Martin was missing.

Martin had last been seen by Loni a couple of days before the hum. She had invited him over for dinner, but instead of just serving him a meal, she stuck him with a marriage proposal, asking him straight out if he would marry her. She said Martin's eyes had become glazed over and he walked out without giving her an answer. Most people figured Martin had fled in fear of another marriage, never to return.

Bob, Fred, and I had conducted a small search for Martin, but we all felt pretty confident he had run away for good. Everyone was of the opinion that Martin was just a coward who couldn't make a commitment.

Everyone was wrong.

Bob got a call early one morning from a rancher who lived on the other side of the mountain. This rancher had found Martin lying unconscious in the middle of one of his fields. Apparently the rancher was made aware of Martin's presence by Rex and Albert. They were howling like mad while watching over Martin's unconscious body.

We found out later that Albert had crawled to Martin's house after I had found him on the night Rich beat him up. After seeing how bad off Albert was and not finding me at my house, Martin took off with the dogs, looking for me. He then got himself lost for over a week. Martin probably would have died there in that rancher's field if it hadn't been for Rex and Albert barking.

Martin was taken to a clinic and treated for dehydration and minor injuries, then released after a couple of nights.

I moved another bed into my place so Martin could stay with me until he was completely back to normal. I felt responsible for what had happened to him.

The town, of course, was thrilled about Martin's reappearance. The moment he arrived at my place, everyone came over, bringing gifts, food, advice, and large amounts of curiosity.

Martin sat in one of my better lawn chairs outside, answered questions about his ordeal, and told how he had survived for over a week in the wild.

"Did you hear the hum?" Sister Hatch asked.

"No," Martin said. "But Bob and Loni have been telling me all about it."

"Well, you'll get a chance to hear it," Sister Lynn said, smiling. "It has single-handedly turned this place around."

"A gift from heaven," Sister Wingate said.

"The Lord just needed a receptacle," Mrs. Benderholden said, siding up to Wynona and putting her arm around her.

Wynona *was* that, I thought.

"Our little antenna," President Wingate chirped as he gazed affectionately at his wife.

I was about to say something about how weird everyone was acting when Martin yawned.

"Why don't we let Martin get some sleep?" I suggested.

Everyone started mumbling things about the importance of sleep and how things were always better after a good night's rest. They said their good-byes and left.

I took a few moments to kiss Charity and then sent her home as well. As she drove off, I said a really simple prayer thanking God for what I considered to be a very extravagant gift. Like a toaster with a timer, real chrome, and six-slice capability, she was so much more than average. She spoke perfectly, she thought perfectly, she ate perfectly, and even though she was somewhat flawed when it came to being a good Pictionary player, she made losing perfect, which made winning something beyond description. When I let myself think about the fact that I was going to marry her, my mind was forced to realign logic. Why fate had been so good to me I did not know.

Loni babied Martin a bit more and then she left as well.

"Are you going to marry her?" I asked, after Loni was gone.

"I think so," Martin said, folding up his lawn chair and following me inside.

"She's a great person."

"True," Martin said.

"Well," I yawned, "I think I'll go to bed so I can get up early and get something done."

Martin sat there silently.

"You all right?" I asked.

"I think so. I suppose I'm just a little tired."

I would have accepted that answer, but apparently Martin felt that more needed to be said.

"So, Loni tells me you haven't heard the hum."

"Nope," I answered.

"What do you think about it?"

"I think the whole thing is incredibly bizarre," I answered. "But that hum or buzz or whatever it is surely has penetrated some pretty stale hearts."

"What would you say if I told you I knew what that hum was?"

"Do you?" I asked seriously.

Martin sat down on his rollaway bed and began to tell his tale.

"It was the day after that big rain," he explained. "I was outside mourning a couple of my soap sculptures the rain had ruined when

Rex started barking up a storm. I turned around to find Albert crawling toward me. He looked pretty bad. I took him inside and cleaned him off and felt around for any sign of broken bones. I couldn't feel any, so I laid him down on my couch where he fell asleep." Martin said "asleep" as if it were some divine ritual he wished he were participating in at the moment.

"Then I ran over to your place to see if you knew what had happened to Albert," Martin continued. "When I got to your place, everything was open. The lights were on, the TV was on, and you were nowhere to be found. I knew you never left the doors unlocked when you were away, so I started to think of things that could have gone wrong. I should have called Bob or Charity but instead I ran back to my place to see if you had come looking for Albert.

"When I got back to my place, Albert was eating dogfood like it was going out of style."

I felt so square. I didn't remember dogfood ever being *in* style.

"Anyhow," Martin went on, "I let him eat, and the second he was finished, he looked at me as if to say, 'I'm not up to this, but it has to be done.' He walked out the door and headed in the direction he'd come from.

"Rex went after him, and I followed. I thought he was going to lead me to you. He seemed so sure about where he was going. About two hours later I had no idea where we were, and neither did Albert. I tried to turn around, but Albert wouldn't go back. Rex and I kept following him, hoping that any moment we would run into you. It was like a really bad episode of *Lassie*."

"How long did you follow him?"

"For quite some time," Martin answered. "I knew deep down that Albert had no idea where we were, but I didn't want to believe it because I had no idea where we were, either. I kept telling Rex to go home, hoping I could just follow him back. But every time I said 'go home' he would roll over, which, by the way, is a trick I've been trying to teach him for weeks."

"Impressive," I said.

"Of course, the command was supposed to be 'Roll over,' not 'Go home.'"

"Whatever works."

"Anyway, since it was dark and we were lost we decided to just spend the night out there and look for a way home the next day. Well, the next day came and went and we were still no closer to figuring our way back. We were so lost! I was beginning to see mountains I had never seen before. I tried for a whole day to just hike down, figuring that eventually the mountain would end and I would be safe. But every time I headed down, I ran into a hill or an uphill slope of some sort. Water was fairly easy to find, but I had no way to carry it. The dogs found a few squirrels and I found some grass that wasn't half bad. I also discovered some mushrooms. After eating them I started to see things. I ended up even more lost and violently ill for a couple hours. I got so hungry sometimes I contemplated eating Albert."

"Thanks," I said.

"It was his fault we were even out there," Martin stated. "I think I would have given up completely if it hadn't been for the fact that I knew you and Bob were probably combing the mountain day and night looking for me."

I tried not to look guilty, hoping Bob had lied for us. Had we known Martin was lost on the mountain, we certainly would have searched day and night. I suppose we had let the idea of him running off to avoid marriage to cloud our judgment.

"Bob said you two barely ate or slept a wink. Thanks, Tartan," Martin said.

"Don't mention it," I said, making a mental note to thank Bob later.

"I think it was the third day," Martin went on, "that I began to hear this whining noise. It sounded like a cow giving birth to rhino triplets."

I was glad Martin used a description I could relate to.

"I looked for it but could never find the source. It seemed to be coming from all over at once. Then it would stop all of a sudden, making it really difficult to track. Eventually the noise stopped altogether."

"So, you never found out what it was?" I asked impatiently.

"Hold on," Martin said.

I folded my arms across my chest in anticipation.

"The afternoon of my sixth day I came across a small rock gorge. It was situated in a basin where four large hills connected. I didn't think it was any great find, but I was curious about whether there was water in it somewhere. I climbed down and walked along the bottom when Rex and Albert—who were about to keel over from fatigue—started barking at a small hole near the side of the gorge. I probably wouldn't have even heard them barking except for an echo the gorge provided.

"It wasn't that big of a hole, but it seemed to go way down. I wouldn't have given it much more attention, but I kneeled to take a look and while pulling myself up, I knocked weak little Rex over into it."

I gasped for effect.

"I couldn't see the bottom, but I could hear Rex land. He started whining like crazy." Martin paused and looked me straight in the eye. "Let me tell you something, Tartan. That hole turned the whining into the loudest noise I've ever heard. It seemed to magnify the noise a thousand times and throw it out of there with such force that it covered the whole mountain. I stood up and covered my ears, afraid I'd rupture an eardrum. When I finally took my hands off my ears, it seemed the sound was no longer coming from just the hole but from everywhere at once. It was the most amazing thing I've ever heard."

Martin sat there quietly as he reflected.

"So, what did you do?" I asked, on the edge of my seat.

"If it had been Albert that had fallen in there, I would have just left him," Martin said.

"Thanks, Martin."

"Well, it was his fault," Martin said for the second time. "Anyway, I had no rope, and of course no ladder, so I didn't know how to retrieve him. Plus, whenever I took my hands off my ears, I almost went deaf from the noise.

"Finally I figured out if I put one leg against each side of the hole, and used my hands to help me, I could shinny down the hole. I had serious doubts about doing this, but I didn't think I would find my way off the mountain alive anyway. I decided I might as well die trying to save my dog. I couldn't help but think that God, in all his fairness, would be extra lenient with a person who died risking his life for his dog."

A positive reference to God; Martin was changing.

"I had no idea how deep the hole was, but I kept working my way down. I tore off little pieces of my shirt and shoved them into my ears, hoping they would reduce the noise. It helped a little, but the sound was still almost unbearable.

"It seemed like forever before I finally felt Rex's wet nose against my ankles. I stepped down against an odd-feeling bottom—uneven and hard. I thought at first it might be the carcass of some unfortunate animal. I was wrong. It was a person.

"I couldn't believe there was someone down there. I wanted to scream, but I was afraid I would burst my eardrums. But there it was, a dead man, cold and clammy as ground beef. I couldn't see anything, but I could feel that both his legs were bent up underneath him. One was definitely broken. I found a wallet in his pocket and slipped it into mine, hoping it would provide identification.

"I made a sort of sling out of my shirt, put Rex in it, and tied it around my neck. It took forever to climb out of that hole, and a couple of times I thought Rex was going to tumble out, but eventually we dragged ourselves out of there."

"It was Rich's wallet, wasn't it?" I asked.

"It was," Martin answered. "Rich must have moaned for days down in that hole before he actually died," Martin stated. "I was afraid I might not make it back, so I threw the wallet back into the hole in case someone else were to stumble upon him at some point. Then I faced what I thought was east and started walking again. Eventually I must have passed out on that rancher's land.

"When I woke up, Bob was there asking me questions to see if I was all right. I was going to tell him about Rich, but he started in on the hum and how it had changed everything. I knew it was Rich, but I kept quiet."

"That was smart," I said. "You can't ever tell anyone what you know. If folks found out what they thought to be divine was just Rich dying, Longwinded would be torn apart again. You can't even tell Loni."

"What about Rich?" Martin asked.

"What about him? He got a far better burial than he deserved, and he's in the hands of God now. Rich stays where he is."

"I don't know if I can lie to people," Martin said.

"Most likely no one will even bring it up."

"I hope that's the case."

"It really is an amazing story," I said. "Nothing was more important to Rich than tearing us apart and look what he ended up doing to bring us together. It's amazing!"

"I still feel sorry for him," Martin said sympathetically.

"You shouldn't waste your time thinking about it."

"That's a horrible way to die."

"I suppose," I said. "But he's in no pain now."

Martin yawned and stretched his arms toward the ceiling.

"I should go to sleep," he said.

I stood up and walked to the patio door to let the dogs out. I stopped Rex and asked him to "Go home." He rolled over, then stood as if waiting for some type of reward. I patted him half-heartedly on his head and let the two out.

I closed the door behind them both and didn't bother locking it.

"Quite a story," I said as I left the room.

Sleep had overtaken Martin.

CHAPTER THIRTY

VERY MASON

I was determined to take Martin's secret with me to the grave. There was no doubt in my mind about what the truth would do to our spiritually teetering town. People had found religion through the hum. If they were suddenly informed their faith was based on a strong echo, there was no telling what would happen. I pleaded daily with Martin in hopes that he would never let what he knew out of the bag.

I wasn't completely confident of his silence.

Despite Martin's many quirks and inconsistencies, he was painfully honest. I had once seen him hike back into town to give Sherry twenty-two cents she had undercharged him on soap. He wanted nothing to do with dirty soap.

I know there is no such thing as being too honest, but I feel there are moments when we should hold our tongues. This Rich incident was one of those times. God had moved mountains with the moanings of a moron, and who were we to mess that up?

I let the right people know I was interested in Fred's position, so I was now awaiting word on whether or not I would get the job. I figured my chances were pretty good since Fred had informed just about everyone in the system about what horrible places Mt. Taylor and Longwinded were. I was sure no one in his right mind would want to fight me for the position.

Fern and Erma sold off Mary's place and bought out Willie. Their plan was to knock down Fern's old place and build a nice new home for themselves. They also had plans for redoing Willie's old place and making it into a really sharp, up-to-date filling station.

Willie had plans to use the money from Fern and Erma to build a big restaurant with Scott. So Longwinded was busy with exciting new things to think about and productive things to watch. It was as if a new wind had entered our once tumultuous town, filling our lungs with hope and sustaining our souls.

The Church contacted Ian and informed him that for the time being we would just have to use our single-wide building.

"Humility is not a negative attribute," the Church had written.

They went on to list a number of reasons why they couldn't afford to buy us a new building at the present time. They then gave statistics on how they were constructing new buildings at the rate of one per day and how they needed to cut back as much as possible. We couldn't understand why one of those buildings, built on one of those days, couldn't be built here.

We all felt pretty confident we would be using our broken building for a long time. Oddly enough no one seemed to mind it anymore. In fact, I had caught Wynona Wingate hosing it down one afternoon and polishing it with Pledge. When I asked what she was doing, she simply responded: "All things have spirits, Brother Jones. All things have spirits."

Plans were underway to build a wall for the open side of our building to replace the large quilt before winter set in. Ian had Clark Bender and Clara Reese working on that project.

No one even talked anymore about who took the other half of our building. The mystery still existed, but all had apparently lost interest.

All except Bob.

✑ ✑ ✑ ✑ ✑

It was a couple of weeks since Martin had been found. Martin had returned to his place and accepted the marriage proposal from

Loni. The tentative plan was that Martin and Orvil would have a double wedding near the beginning of winter. Loni and Sherry were becoming better and better friends as they worked at a feverish pace to get things ready.

Charity and I had just gotten back from soaking in some hot springs above the Beaver and were discussing what we should do for the evening as I flipped through the day's mail.

"We could go to the city," Charity suggested.

"Nah, too far."

"Rent a video?"

"What a novel idea," I said sarcastically.

"Then you come up with something, Mr. Creative," Charity said, turning the task over to me.

"Well, we could . . . " I stopped in midsentence and pulled out a small blue envelope from my stack of mail. "Hey, this letter's from Bob."

"Why would Bob write you?" Charity asked.

"We're pretty close," I joked.

I opened up the envelope to find an invitation to come to the police shed the following afternoon.

Tartan, Please come to the police station at 1:00 P.M. this Thursday. There is a matter of utmost importance that I must speak to you about. You must tell no one about this. That is an order. Please bring Charity with you.

                    Officer Bob Evans

"What the heck?" I asked, handing the card to Charity.

"Do you have any idea what it could be about?" she asked.

"No idea."

"None whatsoever?"

"I got out of a speeding ticket a little while back. Maybe he'll issue it now."

"With an invitation?"

"I don't know," I said.

"And why would he want me to come along?"

"Maybe he wants you to help me keep my speeding down."

"Very odd," Charity commented.

"Very," I agreed, "even for Bob."

Charity and I spent the rest of the night watching one of my two channels and speculating on what Bob could possibly want from us.

≈ ≈ ≈ ≈ ≈

The next day as we drove to the police shed, we discussed our ideas. Charity thought the most logical explanation was that Bob was going to retire and thought perhaps I might want to take his place. True, it wasn't actually logical, but Charity figured Bob might consider me simply because my line of work also required a uniform. Of course my uniform was just a green polo shirt with the Forest Service emblem on it and tan shorts. But Bob probably figured I could slide from one uniform to the next without any problem. It was a stupid theory, but I had to admit I wouldn't have been totally surprised had Charity been right.

On the other hand, I felt the reason Bob wanted to see us was far more complicated.

There was an inactive Mormon woman by the name of Betty Potipar who lived at the edge of town. She had at one time been very active in the Church. In fact, she had been the branch Relief Society president for the couple of years right before she stopped attending church. The cause of her inactivity was a ward activity one of her counselors had put together.

It seems that some years back, the Saints of Longwinded worked and scraped up enough money to attend the annual Pioneer Trek which took place near Salt Lake City. It was a five-day trip where everyone pulled handcarts and did without all the creature comforts of home.

All the Saints from Longwinded thought it was just going to be a leisurely stroll down the paths their beloved ancestors had once made. Instead, it turned out to be one of the sweatiest ordeals any of them had ever been through.

Everyone started out happy—positive they could mimic the footsteps of their forefathers with minimum effort on their part. But they all quickly realized they were involved in something much more challenging than imagined. Sister Potipar patiently prodded every-one to "keep their chins up."

"Think of the pioneers," she would challenge.

But after the first two days of the hike, everyone lost all empa-thy for the pioneers, whom they now blamed for their discomfort. Tempers became shorter and shorter, patience thinner and thinner.

"Think of the pioneers," Betty Potipar would repeatedly encourage.

"Think of your own stinking pioneers," the others would yell back as they tried to pull their bulky handcarts over rocks and other obstacles in a mad dash to get back to comforts such as porcelain potties and TV dinners.

On day four of the trek, Brother Hatch got his handcart stuck between two trees while trying to take a shortcut. No one could get it out. After everyone had tried unsuccessfully, Sister Potipar gave it a go. Well, the combination of the sweltering sun, her heavy wool dress (similar to one Eliza R. Snow had once worn), and everyone giving her flak for trying to help throughout the week caused her to crack.

As she tried to loosen that wedged handcart, she broke. She began kicking and beating the immovable handcart. Then as she defeatedly walked away from it, someone (by accident I hope) stepped on the hem of her dress, causing her to fall to the ground. She got up, wiped her sweating forehead, and screamed in utter frustration:

"Whose #$!@ idea was this Pioneer Trek, anyway?"

Everyone stood there dumfounded (which wasn't difficult for any of them to do). Sister Potipar had never used profanity before. Not even when the Smith boys had stolen her cat and sent it back to her through the mail had she succumbed to the ugly use of profanity. She prided herself on having a mouth so clean you could eat out of it.

But she blew it on the Pioneer Trek.

Sister Potipar was so embarrassed she refused to go back to church when she got home. Finally, the branch president at the time talked her into coming back and giving it just one more try. Well, she was so nervous about what everyone thought of her that she mistakenly took the sacrament with her left hand (a spiritual faux pas the Saints just couldn't overlook). Sister Potipar never came back.

Last week, out of the blue, however, Bob had been told by Betty Potipar that she too had heard the hum, and she would like to come back into the fold. She didn't want everyone to make a big deal about her coming back, so she had asked Bob to explain the situation to Ian before she gave it a go.

I was pretty sure this was what Bob wanted to talk to Charity and me about. He probably wanted us to begin fellowshipping her.

We pulled up to the shed and got out. Bob's patrol car was the only other vehicle there. I was actually nervous as Charity and I walked in.

Bob had set up as many chairs as the shed could hold (six) and was now sitting silently behind his desk.

"Hi, Bob," I said, waving my good hand.

"Tartan."

"Hi, Bob."

"Charity," he responded.

I could tell Bob was trying to appear calm and collected for some reason.

"What's up?" I asked.

"If you two will have a seat, I'll be with you in a minute. We're waiting for a couple more people."

"Who?" I asked out of curiosity.

"You'll see," was all Bob said.

A couple of seconds later, the door opened and Fern and Erma stepped in. They sat down next to Charity and me, trying hard not to look nervous.

"What's the deal, Bob?" Fern asked.

"Fern, you need to be quiet until we're ready," Bob said harshly.

Fern sank down into his seat.

The shed was suddenly hot and uncomfortable.

The door opened again as Ian and Bronwyn entered. They sat down next to Fern and Erma without saying anything.

Bob stood and removed his reading glasses. He looked over the eclectic group of people gathered in his shed and then shook his head sadly. I suddenly felt guilty for something I didn't know I had done. What could Bob possibly want from all of us? I now felt certain this had nothing to do with Betty Potipar, and Bob certainly didn't look like he wanted to announce his retirement. Ian looked at me and shrugged his shoulders.

"Let's get started," Bob said.

I watched Erma squeeze Fern's hand tightly. I wanted to ask Charity what she thought this was all about, but I was certain Bob would reprimand me if I did.

"I trust none of you told anyone else about this meeting," Bob said.

We all shook our heads, no.

"Good." Bob marked something down on a piece of paper. "It seems that somehow with the hum, Rich burning down the barn, Mary dying, and everything else that has been going on, we have forgotten about one of Longwinded's most pressing problems. Any idea what that problem might be, Fern?" Bob asked.

"Ticks?" Fern guessed.

"No," Bob said, "although they *are* unusually heavy this year. It takes me a good five minutes in the shower to completely check for them. You find those things—"

Ian, thankfully, cleared his throat, bringing Bob back to the present.

"Oh, yes, the real problem. The real problem Longwinded is facing is that the greatest crime ever committed here has gone unsolved. Someone stole half of the Mormon chapel." Bob paused to let his last words sink in. He then paced back and forth in front of his desk tapping his chin.

I had no idea what this had to do with any of us. Luckily, Bob was here to clear things up.

"Fern, where were you on the night the chapel was stolen?" Bob asked suddenly.

All eyes turned to Fern.

"I can't remember that far back, Bob," Fern said nervously.

"Come now, Fern, it wasn't that long ago."

"I suppose I was sleeping," Fern answered weakly.

"Oh, really," Bob said snidely. "What about you, Erma? Do you believe what Fern is saying?"

Erma looked at her aging fingers for a few moments and then spoke. "Fern was with me," she confessed.

Fern looked sharply at Erma.

"Well," she said, "it's no secret anymore. Fern was with me until at least two in the morning. I remember because we watched back-to-back episodes of *Murder, She Wrote* until two. Fern went home and called to let me know he made it all right and to say a few other things." Erma blushed with embarrassment.

The rest of us blushed with her.

"So, after two A.M. you really have no idea where Fern was?" Bob asked.

"He was at home. I could hear the hum of his giant freezer the whole time we talked."

"And how long did you talk?"

"This is ridiculous," Fern said, standing. "Just what are you trying to say?"

"Sit down, Fern," Bob said calmly.

Fern sat.

"We talked at least an hour," Erma answered.

"An hour, you say?" Bob asked.

"An hour," Erma responded.

"Thank you," Bob said, scribbling something on his paper.

"So, Tartan," Bob turned to address me. "Wouldn't you say it's perfectly clear that Fern and Erma had romantic interests in one another well before the chapel was stolen?"

"It looks that way," I answered.

"What did Mary think of you and Erma?" Bob asked Fern.

"Mary had no idea about our relationship," Fern said defensively.

"Oh really," Bob snickered. "How, may I ask, did you keep it a secret from Mary?"

"We broke no laws," Erma said. "I just administered her medication at a time most beneficial to us."

"And Mary never found out?" Bob asked incredulously.

Fern and Erma shook their heads together.

"Then why did Mary send me this?" Bob asked accusingly,

holding up a brown envelope with Mary's handwriting on it and pushing it toward them as if it were a flaming sword.

Fern started to sweat; Erma turned tipsy.

"Do you want me to read what it says?" Bob asked, "or do you two want to change your last answer?"

Fern and Erma exchanged worried glances.

"Mary knew," Erma finally whispered.

"That's what I thought," Bob replied. "And how did she feel about your relationship with Fern?"

"She was disgusted by it," Erma answered. "She thought Fern was too old for me and that our seeing each other somehow soiled her reputation."

"But you continued seeing one another?"

"We did," Erma said.

"I'm surprised Mary didn't fire you," Bob commented. "Or at least take you out of her will."

"She threatened to fire me," Erma said.

"And you, Fern," Bob scoffed. "Ever since you accused Mary of stealing her recipe for hot berry pie, she has loathed you. I'm surprised Mary even let you into her house. You know," Bob said addressing all of us, "I can't think of anyone she liked less than Fern, except for maybe the Baptists. Too bad Mary's not around to hear the hum; it might have done her some good."

Bob would get no argument over that. Although I alone knew that at this moment Mary was probably having to listen to Rich whine about the heat of their present state.

"It seems to me you would have had to do something extraordinary to win Mary's good graces," Bob said to Fern. "But for the life of me I can't think what. Can you?" Bob asked Fern and Erma in a condescending tone of voice.

Without giving them time to answer, Bob turned to Ian. "Did you bring the note?" he asked.

"I did," Ian said, reaching into his backpack and pulling out a folded piece of paper. Bob took it from him and read it aloud.

False President Smith,
     I hereby resign my membership in the Church. The

reason for this is because I cannot associate with a ward that meets in a camper. Tea is tea, and coffee is coffee.

May you all burn as the Lord sees fit,

Mary Longfellow

"In talking with Ian earlier this week," Bob said, "I discovered Mary's name had been removed from the rolls about a week before she passed away." Bob waved the note around for effect. "You Mormons really are down by three, not two." Bob stuck up three pudgy fingers and thrust them toward Ian.

"I wonder," Bob said dramatically, "what difference this would have made had everyone known before the hum. I have no idea why Mary didn't tell Wynona she left the Church. The best I can figure is that Mary still believed and was just doing what she felt she had to do. Mary probably wanted to keep it quiet, and if she had told Wynona Wingate, quiet is the last thing it would have been."

Bob looked at all of us sharply.

"Are things starting to fall into place, people?" Bob asked frantically. "Are pieces starting to gel?"

I had no idea what Bob was talking about. He was acting like Matlock on model glue. I couldn't imagine Bob having a theory any more believable than Martians stealing the trailer or that he had discovered large mirrors behind Scott's bar which created an illusion that half our building was missing.

After all, this was Bob. Certainly, if there had been a way to solve this mystery, someone of a higher intellect would have figured it out already. There was no trace of our building and, as far as I knew, no clues as to who had done it.

Bob was about to start up again when two Mormon missionaries came through the door. We all just stared at them for a minute. I had never seen any full-time missionaries in Longwinded. They looked so out of place. Finally one of them spoke.

"We're missionaries from The Church of Jesus Christ of Latter-day Saints, and we can't seem to find a certain address."

"Where'd you come from?" Bob asked, as if they had originated from another planet.

"We're assigned to the city, but our mission president sent us here to teach a family who is interested in the Church."

"Who are you looking for?" Bob asked, somewhat annoyed they were interrupting his secret meeting.

The shorter missionary read a name off a piece of paper he held. "The Benderholdens," he said.

We all gulped in air.

"What do you want with them?" Bob asked suspiciously.

"They called the mission home and said they would like the missionaries to come and visit them."

We all just sat there staring at the poor missionaries.

"The Benderholdens did?" I finally asked.

"I guess so," the tall elder said sheepishly. "Is there something wrong with that?"

Ian introduced himself and gave the elders directions on how to locate the Benderholdens. They left quickly.

"No one mentions a word about this," Bob demanded. "If Bruce Benderholden and his family want to have the Mormons over, so be it. But let others hear it from them, not from us."

These were odd words coming from someone with such a big mouth. Fern and Erma got up, hoping this distraction would enable them to leave.

"Sit!" Bob barked.

They sat.

"Fern," Bob continued, "where were you that night, before you found Erma tied up?"

"You know where I was," Fern responded. "I was at my place until I went up and discovered Erma."

"Had you been at your place all night?" Bob asked.

"To the best of my recollection, yes."

"To the best of your recollection, huh?" Bob asked, scratching his floppy ears. "What about *your* recollection, Erma?" Bob drilled. "Do you recall seeing Fern any other time during the night?" Bob clasped his hands behind his back as he asked.

Erma paused nervously, giving Bob reason to drill harder.

"Do you? Had you seen Fern earlier in the evening? Tell me, Erma," Bob demanded.

"Yes," Erma shouted. "Fern came up around six to get his early evening kiss."

"Was this something he did regularly?" Bob asked.

"Yes," Erma said confidently.

"Hmmm," Bob said, writing down more on his paper.

"What are you getting at, Bob?" Ian asked, voicing our confusion.

"Yeah," I said. "Fern and Erma might have been sneaking around to see each other, but I can't see how any of this ties them in with our missing chapel. If you ask me, it was probably Rich."

"Maybe so," Bob said, "but would it be all right if I told you what I think happened?"

"You are the law," I said.

"Thank you, Tartan," Bob commented, thinking I had just complimented him.

It was interesting to think about just what kind of law Bob was. If my cat were stuck in a tree and I had all afternoon to watch an overweight cop try to figure out how to get it down, there is a good chance I would call Bob. But if my child had been kidnapped, I would probably go out of my way not to ask Bob for help.

Sure he had a kind heart, and yes his intentions were well meaning, but truth be known, I just didn't view him as competent. Maybe I did possess some backwoods bigotry, but I'd ask for help from a crossing guard before I went to Bob with a real problem. Not that I didn't like him or appreciate when his screwball ways worked to my advantage. I just didn't consider him to be any more effective than say . . . mall security. Now he was about to explain how the greatest heist in the history of Longwinded had been pulled off. I sat back and folded my arms, confident his scenario would provide little more than a good laugh.

Bob leaned his ample behind against the desk, picked at his yellow teeth for a moment, and began.

"Somehow, Fern, you and Erma accomplished the impossible. You two had a serious relationship for months without anyone else in town knowing. What I find even more amazing is that you two somehow managed to keep Mary quiet about it. Impressive indeed. Let me tell you just for fun how I think you did it.

"True, Mary hated you, Fern. It's arguable whether she hated you or the Baptists more, but she disliked you through and through. Of course she loved you, Erma. In fact the only thing she loved more than you was Longwinded."

I watched Erma's eyes moisten and start to tear up at the thought of Mary.

"And you Mormons bringing in that mobile home was too much for her. She already had hard feelings about the Church, and that just cinched it for her. I think old Mary became a little obsessed and decided to play the one card she had been holding.

"And that card was Fern.

"I think Mary gave you and Erma an ultimatum: Get rid of the trailer or your relationship is history."

Fern and Erma slouched in their chairs like withered weeds.

"Fern, do you love Erma?" Bob asked.

"Yes, Bob."

"Is there anything you wouldn't do for her?"

"No," Fern answered.

"Even stealing someone's building?"

Fern remained silent.

Bob continued. "I think you conspired with Rich to get rid of the building. Of course, Rich was all too happy to help, but as usual did an incomplete job and ended up removing only half of the building."

"What proof do you have?" Fern asked with a mild amount of spunk.

"Fern, how much money have you donated to charity in the last year?" Bob asked.

Fern looked over at Charity, confused by the question.

"Not to her," Bob said. "Charity, Goodwill, Salvation Army?"

"Not a red cent," Fern said with fire. "I'm not interested in providing free crutches for everyone."

"When Loni got divorced and we took up a town collection, how much did you put into the pot?" Bob asked.

"Nothing," Fern answered. "It's not up to me to make the world right."

"Maybe so," Bob said, "but the morning after the building was stolen, you instantly took up a collection for the Mormons. Why?"

Fern didn't answer.

"I'll tell you why," Bob shouted. "Because of guilt. I think the only reason you acted on Mary's threat was because you had no idea what it would cost the Saints. When you found out how expensive the dirty deed was, you became guilt ridden."

"Who knew mobile homes were so expensive?" Fern wailed and started to sob.

There was a long silence as we all listened uncomfortably to Fern's crying.

"How *could* you two?" I finally questioned.

"Don't blame Erma," Fern pleaded. "She might have suspected, but she had nothing to do with it."

"Well, then how could *you*, Fern?" I asked.

"I couldn't imagine life without my Erma." Fern took Erma in his arms, and with the excitement that only breaking the law could create, he kissed her.

I had to stop myself from laughing.

"Hold on, Tartan, that's not all Fern did," Bob said. "I think after Mary blackmailed him into stealing the chapel, Rich blackmailed him into leaving Mary's windows open so he could sneak in and make off with some of her goods."

"Fern?" Erma asked.

"I knew Mary pretty well," Bob said. "She would no more allow Erma to leave one of her windows unlocked at night than embrace Parson Stevens. I think every night when you went up there to get your little early evening kiss, you were unlocking one of the windows after Erma had checked to see that they were all shut. Then when you came back later to get even more loving you locked it back up, knowing full well Rich had slipped in and pilfered items while you were absent."

"Oh, Fern, how could you?" Erma wailed.

"Rich was going to turn me in," Fern stuttered. "I had to do *something*."

"Then, on that fateful night Erma caught Rich, so Rich tied her up," Bob explained. "I believe that the only reason you came to me for help was to appease poor Erma and because Mary had been shocked to death."

I was amazed; it seemed Bob had actually figured it out.

"So, Fern," Ian asked sternly. "Where is the other half of our building?"

"I have no idea," Fern sobbed.

"Come now, Fern," Bob said. "Certainly you must know where it is."

"I don't," Fern whined. "Rich was supposed to haul the whole thing over the state line and sell it. I told him he could keep all the profits. That was his main incentive for doing it. Rich had such a tough time taking the first half he decided to forget about the rest of it. He was just going to leave all the wires hanging out and the water turned off, but I started to feel sorry for the Mormons, so I capped the wires and water. In fact, I had just left the building when you pulled up that morning, Bob." Fern wiped his eyes and continued. "Rich took the half and dumped it somewhere, but he never told me where. Mary wasn't too happy about the incomplete job, but she enjoyed the Mormons' humiliation."

"Go on," Bob said.

"Well, because Rich wasn't able to sell the thing as he planned, he started coming to me and demanding money. I knew Mary had so much junk she would never miss a few things here and there. I told Rich not to harm Mary, but he even messed up that. I'm so sorry, Erma." Fern put his head between his hands and tried to compose himself.

Erma put her arm around Fern to comfort him.

"Fern, you should be locked up for the rest of your life," Bob said. "You've stolen, lied, cheated, and could be classified as an accessory in a number of other crimes, but I'm not certain that putting you away would be the best thing for everyone. I have an idea that might work out better." Bob walked around to the back of his desk and pulled out an envelope and two pieces of paper.

"The reason I asked you here," Bob said to Ian, Bronwyn, Charity, and me, "is not only to witness what Fern has said, and not only because you are the highest ranking Mormons in town at the moment, but because I'm going to leave it up to you as to whether or not you want to press charges. While you're thinking about it though, let me add my thoughts. For starters, Fern is an old man, and I'm not sure how well he would weather jail, or court for that matter. He also has apparently found love late in life. I'm not sure I could live with myself knowing I had torn these two apart."

Bob sighed.

"Earlier this week I received a check from someone who wishes to remain anonymous. I promised Robert Crimsal I wouldn't tell a . . . Shoot!" Bob said, reprimanding himself for giving out Robert's name. "Well, I suppose this is just one more secret we're going to keep between us. Is that understood?"

"Yes," everyone agreed.

"Robert wasn't sure how to go about donating so much money to the Mormon church, so he turned the matter over to me." Bob handed the check to Ian.

Ian and Bronwyn both gasped when they saw the amount.

"What, what is this for?" Ian stuttered.

"It's for a new building," Bob answered. "Robert said the blessing changed his life and the hum told him directly this was something he should do."

Thank you, Rich, I thought.

"I took the liberty to call the Mormon church headquarters and inquire how much one of their buildings costs. Believe it or not, Robert's check doesn't quite cover it. I propose, however, that Fern and Erma might be willing to make up the difference."

All eyes turned on the two.

"We were planning to travel with our money," Fern said weakly.

"And throw a big wedding," Erma added.

"Well, I hate to be a killjoy, but I suggest you set your travel plans aside, or Erma will be traveling to visit you in jail, Fern."

Fern and Erma stared at their feet.

"What about the wedding?" Erma asked.

"I'd be happy to hitch you two for free. Is it a deal?" Bob asked.

"Yes," they whispered.

"What about you, Ian?" Bob asked. "As branch president of the building that was stolen, do you want to press charges?"

"No, I think this will work out fine."

"Good," Bob said. "Now the most important thing is that none of us ever whisper a word of this to anyone. This will only work if it is kept among ourselves. There are probably some serious repercussions for all of us if word ever does get out. I'm sure we're breaking some law somewhere, but for now we'll just adhere to the spirit of the law."

"What about Rich?" Fern asked. "He could ruin everything."

"I've thought about that," Bob said. "The only solution I can think of is for us all to hope he never comes back. If he does, however, I'll have a talk with him."

"I don't know," Ian said.

"Me, either," Bronwyn added.

"There is nothing else we can do," Bob complained.

Everyone thought silently to themselves about Rich, trying to come up with a solution—I just couldn't keep quiet.

"Rich is dead," I said suddenly. I couldn't help it. All of this needed closure, and with Rich still dangling around in our minds, that seemed impossible.

"What?" Bob asked.

"He's dead," I answered. Charity stared at me like I was crazy.

"How do you know?" Bob asked incredulously.

"Martin found him when he was lost in the hills. He found Rich lying on the ground, dead. I guess he died of exhaustion or something."

"Why didn't Martin tell anyone?" Fern asked.

"He was worried it would drive people apart again," I explained.

Everyone sat there silently.

I had to get to Martin as soon as possible; I needed to help him get his story straight. I didn't enjoy lying by any means, but I could see no other way at the moment. Besides it wasn't a complete lie; it was sort of like the truth manifesting itself in another form. I took a couple of deep breaths, assuring myself I could get to Martin before Bob.

My assurance was shot as Martin suddenly walked in through the door. His timing couldn't have been worse.

"Hey, Tartan," Martin said as he came in. "I've been looking all over for you."

"Well, here I am," I said, standing up quickly and trying to push Martin outside.

"Just one minute," Bob barked. "Martin, I want to ask you a question."

I sat back down slowly as Martin closed the door.

"Yes?" Martin asked.

I started talking before Bob could get a chance. "I told them about you finding Rich dead on the ground while you were lost. I also told them how you thought he must have died from exhaustion since he was just lying there intact but dead," I rambled.

Martin and Charity both looked at me like I was nuts.

"I also told them how you didn't know if you should tell anyone about Rich because you thought it might make matters worse here in town."

"Thank you, Tartan. I'll handle this," Bob said.

"Is it true?" Bob asked Martin.

Well handled, I thought.

I pleaded with my eyes for Martin to please lie. He had no idea how much was at stake here. I had no doubt all of us would keep the Fern secret a secret. Fern's freedom depended on it. But if Bob discovered the truth about Rich and the hum, there would be no holding back his big mouth. Our town would be torn asunder.

"Well," Bob asked again, "is it true?"

I could see Martin's mind working overtime as he tried to process everything.

"Yeah, that's about it," he finally said.

Beautifully vague.

"Then that's what happened?" Bob asked.

"You can bank on it," Martin tried to say with confidence.

"So Rich is dead?" Fern asked.

"He is," Martin said firmly.

We all whewed. We had achieved closure.

Bob told Martin he would need to fill out some reports about Rich and to tell as few people as possible about it. Then Bob asked Martin to excuse us as we finished up. Martin was all too happy to leave and let us do so.

"It's not easy for me to keep a secret," Bob said. "But I feel this is the best course of action for the time being. Fern, you and Ian will have to work out a payment plan; and Tartan, you help Martin keep his part of the secret. If I ever hear any of you have leaked any of this I'll lock you up. Understood?"

Bob really had worked wonders.

We all nodded yes.

"I guess we will never really know what happened to the other half of your building. For a person who was unsuccessful at so many things, Rich sure did a good job hiding that," Bob said.

We all agreed silently.

Once again the door opened. In stepped a good-looking guy who appeared to be about my age. I thought he was lost, but I heard Charity whisper in an amazed tone.

"Howard?"

"Charity," he said.

Howard? Howard, as in once-engaged-to-my-fiancée Howard? As in the Howard who Charity had to get over before she could really like me? *That* Howard?

Charity dropped my hand and stood as if to hug Howard. I could see Bronwyn and Ian frowning as I felt my heart turn to paste and slowly spread itself all over my stomach walls.

"What are you doing here?" Charity asked, pulling back before Howard could hug her.

"I came to bring you home," Howard declared confidently.

I stood tall after he said that.

Charity's presence suddenly became stormy as she pushed Howard outside to talk. Fern and Erma used this as their chance to get out of the shed as well. I didn't know what to do. I was tempted to go out and just beat Howard up, but I was pretty sure that would only make matters worse. Besides, I still had only one usable arm.

"What's he doing here?" Ian asked me.

"I have no idea," I said, pulling aside the curtains on the front window and watching Charity have a very animated conversation with this Howard guy.

"Thanks, Bob," I said, reaching for the door.

"That letter I showed Fern and Erma was a fake," Bob said.

"What?" I asked, not really caring about anything besides Charity at the moment.

"When I told Fern and Erma Mary had let me know about their relationship, I was bluffing."

"Great," I said.

"I cracked this one wide open," Bob said, sounding more like the backwards Bob we all knew and loved.

"You sure did," I heard Bronwyn say as I stepped outside and approached Charity and Howard.

Howard was about an inch shorter than I and at least thirty pounds lighter. He had short blond hair and a smile that made me want to kick him. He stood there grinning, with his arms folded across his chest. His smugness enraged me. It was as though he were just listening to Charity rant and rave and would then help her see the light and take her home.

"Charity?" I said, as I came up next to her.

Charity stopped talking and begrudgingly introduced me to Howard.

"Tartan, this is Howard."

I was going to extend my hand and at least try to be civil, but Howard blew it.

"What kind of weird name is Tartan?"

I couldn't help myself; the male inside me had to one-up him.

"What kind of dumb name is Howard?"

For the first time, Howard's smile faded.

"Let's go, Charity," he said. "I came to take you away from this Podunk place."

"How did you even know I was here?" Charity asked, frustrated.

"In Longfellow?" Howard asked.

"No, here at the police station."

"I didn't. I just stopped to ask directions to your aunt's place. Must have been fate that you were here. Let's go."

Darn that Fate!

"What about Annie?" Charity asked with an edge.

"I'll explain everything," Howard said. "Let's go."

I was so confident Charity would never go with Howard that I felt no urge to say or do anything. I knew Charity loved me, and I knew she was one hundred percent over Howard. Tonight she would be in my arms listing in detail all of Howard's many flaws and misdoings. We would laugh, maybe share some cold decaffeinated soda, and stare into each other's eyes until we were both dizzy.

My confidence crumbled.

Charity was following Howard to his car. Charity was getting into his car. Charity was driving off with him!

I just stood there.

This strange occurrence did not seem to register with me. Ian and Bronwyn came out of the shed and sympathetically patted me on the back.

"Is there anything we can do?" Ian asked.

I ignored his question.

"Are you okay?" Bronwyn asked.

I turned toward them, my expression blank and grim.

Ian and Bronwyn got the hint. I watched them drive off while I stood there completely confused about everything. Bob came out and put on his hat.

"Quite a day," he observed. "I guess I should check out things around town. I think I'll go see if Bruce Benderholden is doing all right."

I didn't respond.

"Where's Charity?" Bob asked.

I wanted to weep. No, I wanted to scream until my throat was so raw I couldn't express myself ever again! I wanted the alphabet to be six letters shorter. I wanted the English language to do away with H-o-w-a-r-d to be more specific. Of course, I needed the *a* and *r* for my name, and Charity needed the *h*, not to mention our last names. I suppose the alphabet was fine just as it was, but the world could do with one less person—Howard.

How could Charity have just walked off? How could she have not slapped Howard silly? How could she even tolerate looking at him? What had just happened? Had she really walked away from me? There seemed to be no other explanation.

I couldn't believe it. I should have believed it. This was exactly what I had always expected right from the start. I just knew the Charity deal was too good to be true. Fate had set me up, and I had fallen for it like a fat person believing in diet shakes. And now that I had finally been forced onto the scales, the wicked needle made it perfectly clear just how overweight my hopes had been. The convenient powdered drinks of possibilities had successfully tricked me into believing I was reaching my goal.

Fat chance.

This stunk. I could feel the open spaces of Longwinded closing in to suffocate me.

"Charity's gone, Bob," I said bitterly.

"Where'd she go?"

How Bob had figured out the mystery of the missing mobile, I had no idea. I waited for Bob to leave and then leaned against the hood of my truck and moaned.

I should have beaten up on Howard when I had the chance.

CHAPTER THIRTY-ONE

BRASS TACKS

I had finally had enough. Yep, this was just about as much as I could take. This was just about as much as anyone could take. My life had never been so complicated. Life in Provo seemed calm and serene compared to all this. I would rather have been home and turning down all the dates in Provo than here in Longwinded, losing Charity and all sense of hope for the future.

I wanted to give Charity the benefit of the doubt; I wanted to believe she had no interest in Howard anymore. I drove to my place, hoping she had come to her senses and was now waiting there for me.

She wasn't.

I got to her place just in time to catch Clark and Clara embracing on the front porch swing.

Just great, I thought.

I stepped out of my truck and hollered to them. "Have you seen Charity?"

"I thought she was with you," Sister Reese said.

"Nope, I guess she's with Howard."

"Howard, Howard?" Clara asked.

"Howard, Howard," I replied.

"Those two sure were close," she smiled.

"Thanks," I complained, getting back into my truck and driving off.

I had no idea where else to go. I passed Brother Hatch jogging as I drove back into town. His wristbands and headband were the most colorful accessories I'd seen in quite some time. He gave a small wave, looking about thirty pounds thinner than when I had arrived in Longwinded. At least his life was getting lighter.

When I reached town, I could see Ian's Jeep parked outside of Fern's place. I imagined there was some heavy haggling going down at the moment. I still couldn't believe Fern had been the mastermind behind our missing mobile. Never in a million years would I have suspected him, nor would I have thought Bob capable of figuring it out.

A day of surprises.

I passed our sad-looking chapel and tried to envision our new building. Brother Crimsal had really come through for us. It was amazing how everything was falling into place for Longwinded while things were crumbling for me.

I scanned the dim horizon.

Charity was nowhere to be found.

I didn't know what to think or do. Part of me thought that I should just relax. Charity would be back in a few minutes to explain everything to me. A larger part of me, however, really believed things might be over.

I needed to talk to Charity; I needed to convince her Howard would just leave her again. I needed to remind her I was the one she was deeply in love with and that the only feelings she had for Howard were hatred.

I needed Charity; I was miserable without her.

I turned off to Flint's Peak, driving slowly home.

I would find her, I thought, a strange new hope filling my soul.

If Charity really had left me, then I would go after her. There was no way I was going to let some cocky fool ruin a relationship so incredible that even Adam and Eve could have envied it.

Weeks, months, years, whatever it took, I would take. I could feel it now more than ever that Charity and I were *supposed* to be. Like Cheerios at church, we fit.

I needed her.

She needed me.

Didn't she see that?

Hadn't the heavens made that perfectly clear to her? Our relationship was meant to be. God knew it. I knew it. Charity knew it, and if necessary I would spend the rest of my days making sure Howard knew it. Let heaven and earth pass away; let every stone upon the earth turn to dust. I was committed to this. Like Nephi as he gazed upon the world from its beginning to its end, I could see everything, and everything for me revolved around Charity.

I would pack my bags. I would give up my career. I would set aside the things of the world—heck, I would even go to Yuma if necessary. No obstacle was too great to scale or barrier too high to overcome in my quest.

Howard, be darned! I would have Charity!

I pushed on the gas and sped to my place. I had plans to carry out, things to do, wrongs to right. The cosmos needed me.

My place came into view. I was so energized over what I felt had to be done, I almost didn't notice Charity standing on my porch. She had her hands on her hips and was staring straight at me.

If this was a mirage, someone was going to pay.

The light wind blew Charity's hair across her face. It took two hands to pull it back behind both of her art-perfect ears. My legs went numb, causing my feet to slip off the pedals and stall the truck.

She was smiling?

I had seen her only moments before, but she looked different now—untouchable and yet all at once inviting. I had committed myself to searching the world over for her and now here she was. I would lose a lot of frequent flyer miles, but the wear and tear I would save on my heart couldn't be measured.

I stepped out of my truck and gave an embarrassed wave (not knowing what else to do). We were about fifty feet from each other. She put her hands back on her hips and remained standing where she was.

"Where have you been?" she asked, as if we had been apart for years, wars, and countless numbers of life-induced activities.

"That's *my* question," I said, staying right where I was.

"I've been here waiting for you," Charity explained.

"Hah," I said. "I came up here a little while back and you weren't here. Where were you then?"

"With Howard," she said plainly.

"Oh, Howard," I droned. "Is he that guy you ran off with from the police shed?" I asked sarcastically.

"Yes, *that* Howard."

"Your ex-fiancé?"

"Yep," Charity said.

"The one who walked out on you?"

"That's the one."

Expound! I wanted to scream.

"Seemed like a nice guy," I said. I couldn't believe it! Here I was, a twenty-nine-year-old playing dating word games with my fiancée.

"I sensed you liked him," Charity joked.

I didn't know what else to say. She was the one who needed to be explaining. She needed to be comforting me. Were we still an item, or had she just come to tell me good-bye? I wasn't about to start in on how I had been willing to scour the earth searching for her unless she still wanted me.

"So," Charity said, "how are you doing?"

I decided to be honest and express my feelings clearly.

"Have you ever heard Brother Hatch's three Nephites story?" I questioned.

"What?" Charity asked.

"Have you heard his three Nephites story?"

"I guess I missed that one," Charity said.

"Well, a few years back," I started to explain, "Brother Hatch was trying to restore one of his old cars when he came upon a mechanical problem he just couldn't figure out—something to do with the gearshift."

Charity looked at me as if I were crazy. "What does this have to do with anything?" she asked.

"Just wait," I continued. "No one could figure the problem out.

He wrote the manufacturer, called in experts, the whole bit. But in the end he just couldn't fix it. Then one Saturday while he was out working on the problem, three guys in white overalls approached and asked if they could help. Of course he let them, thinking right off that his mechanical problems were important enough that God had sent in the three Nephites.

"Well, they fixed his car and even helped overhaul his wife's Buick. He said they wouldn't give their names, but he swears he heard the shortest one call the tallest one a something *ite. Joeyite* or *Philipite* or something like that."

Charity laughed.

"When they were finished they left without compensation, hopping into their stark white Chevy and riding off into the sunset."

"It's a miracle," Charity joked.

"Isn't it though," I agreed.

"Yeah, but what does it have to do with us?"

"Well," I said, "three guys in white overalls giving Brother Hatch a tune-up is pretty unbelievable. But there is a small part of me that believed his story. A part that thinks what he said made sense. It's the same part of me that thinks just maybe I could win the lottery—despite the billion-to-one odds. Or that maybe there are such things as mermaids and mermen. It's the part of me that believed, despite all that I know, that you were going to leave with Howard."

"You have such a clear way of expressing your feelings," Charity said, soberly.

"You know exactly what I'm saying," I said with mild frustration.

"What? That you believe in mermaids and the Easter bunny?"

"No. I thought you were going to leave," I said clearly.

The wind picked up a bit, blowing leaves and dirt around our feet and making Charity appear further than fifty feet away.

"Then you don't know me, Tartan," Charity said seriously.

"I thought I did," I replied.

"You know," Charity said, "you are pretty much the perfect guy. Good-looking, smart, funny, kind, and all those other positive things."

"You can list them all by name if you'd like."

"No thanks," Charity smiled. "It's your flaw I'd like to talk about."

Humility started to set in. "My flaw?" I asked.

"It's that little part of you that believes in mermaids, unicorns, and that your father is going to come home someday and tell you he never really left. I think you believe one day he's going to walk through the door, kiss your mother, and explain how he has just been on some secret mission all these years and would you please forgive him.

"It's the same flaw that makes you crazy enough to believe even for a moment that I would choose Howard over you. Never have I been in love like I am with you. Howard is a ghost from the past whom I just informed I never want to see again. You, however, are a thrill of the present whom I hope always to be with. That is if you'll still have me. You just need to give up fantasy and start believing in the real thing."

I hated the fact she was so correct all the time. I hung my head for a moment and then stared straight into her eyes.

"What are you saying?"

"Let's see if I can think up some off-the-wall story to best illustrate my point," Charity joked.

"No," I pleaded, "just give it to me straight."

"I love you, Tartan Jones," she said so softly I almost couldn't hear. "I don't care how we met, where we met, or why we met. I just know we had to meet."

"It was fate?" I asked.

Charity didn't answer. She just stood there smiling, reminding me of a really appealing postcard that beckoned you to come visit and made you wish you were there. The wind made the long grass around the porch sway. From my point of view it seemed to be waving me in. I let the mood move me by stepping up to her.

"So we're still engaged?" I asked.

"Now more than ever."

"And Howard's gone?"

"Who?" Charity asked.

I answered by kissing her.

Shooting stars fell from the sky, and the mountains rumbled in approval. Longwinded had been just what fate needed to bring a beautiful girl from Yuma and a hopeless soul from Provo together forever.

Three days later, without telling anyone except Ian and Bronwyn, Charity and I were married in the Dallas temple. It was an amazing ceremony. There were fewer than ten people in attendance, but the room was crammed with angels. A couple of times I felt like pushing at the air just to make some room for me and my new wife.

Charity's parents threatened never to talk to us for doing such a sneaky selfish thing as getting married without them, and my mother complained about the Dallas temple looking so similar to Chicago and Boise.

We didn't care. Our fates had been cemented.

CHAPTER THIRTY-TWO

THE
HONEYMOON

Some things are better left unsaid.

CHAPTER THIRTY-THREE

SNOWFLAKES

The snow fell heavily onto the dirt driveway. I worried that if Charity didn't hurry out to the car, I might have to start shoveling. It was a petty worry—a little shoveling never hurt anyone. Charity looked at me through our kitchen window and indicated she would be just a couple more minutes. It appeared we would be late for the branch Christmas caroling party.

I watched the snow cover everything in white as the windshield wipers swished back and forth, fighting the falling flakes and helping the defroster keep my vision clear. What a difference the snow made. Things looked so much better covered in snow. Mt. Taylor and Longwinded became a wonderland under its white blanket.

I thought how much Longwinded had changed since I had arrived. I also contemplated the drastic metamorphosis it had undergone since Charity and I returned home from our honeymoon.

Pastor Stevens's replacement had turned any remaining Baptist hostility into guarded tolerance. He didn't openly hate us, and he was receptive to the idea of us all getting along. He stressed love toward your fellowman, and we all interpreted that to include us Mormons. Ian and he met together monthly for dinner and were working on building a friendly interfaith relationship.

Fern and Erma both were baptized into the Baptist faith. Erma had joined the Baptists because she felt there was no way she, in good conscience, could join the religion that seemed to have made Mary's life so difficult. No one tried to stop Erma. In fact, everyone was happy she had finally chosen a religion. Even the Mormons attended her baptism. They were happy for Fern and Erma—and smug about their own gain.

You see, the Benderholdens (weeks before Fern and Erma got baptized) took a plunge themselves. Ian had baptized them in the back of Sister Lynn's truck. Sister Lynn had lined the bed of her pickup, filled it with water, and then backed it up to the open half of our mobile home.

Our own font!

Sister Theo was in seventh heaven. Everyone thought it would be next to impossible to totally submerge the Benderholdens and their large children in the two feet of water the truck bed provided, but somehow Ian had managed. When I asked why they didn't just do it up in the Beaver, Sister Benderholden told me she didn't want the spirit of Wally Longfellow ruining her baptism.

I didn't blame her one bit.

Plans had already been made to begin construction on our new building. Ian found out that our single-wide would be sent somewhere in New Mexico to house a couple of full-time missionaries. I hoped they would appreciate it. That chapel had done a lot for the small community of Longwinded.

Bob and I still speculated in private about where we thought the other half of our building had ended up. Bob thought it was somewhere across the state line, and I thought it was probably at the bottom of the Beaver. Our theories changed with every new supposed sighting. In fact, more than a handful of outsiders had spent weeks on our mountain or in the Beaver, trying to solve the mystery of the missing mobile.

Charity and I were renting a small house at the top of Mt. Taylor. Fred, who left as soon as we returned from our honeymoon, had been all too happy to inform me that I had his job. I wished him well and watched him drive out of Longwinded, never to return.

Sister Crimsal was taking the discussions, and Brother Crimsal was called to be Ian's second counselor. Our branch held its weekly youth activities over at their place. Sarah Crimsal was becoming quite attached to the few youth in our branch. She had even thrown a party for Kathy Paul when she received her Young Women's medallion. (I guess the CTR ring had worked.)

Dear Sister Lynn announced to us all that she had been taking college courses through the mail and had now graduated. Longwinded threw her a huge party, complete with Baptists, Mormons, and little if any talk about the differences we might have.

No one talked about the hum much anymore. It had descended, changed our hearts, and moved on. Occasionally Sister Wingate would claim to hear it telling her to bring a meal to a soul less fortunate or to speak kindly about someone. And Scott and Willie heard it tell them to name their new restaurant "Humdinger." They expected to open up sometime in the next month.

I thought often about the real cause of the hum. Poor Rich. There were no coincidences in God's plans; things had gone just as they were supposed to. Fate was a fraud. I knew now that God played no games of chance.

I saw Charity get off the phone, and a couple of seconds later she was sitting next to me in the car. I watched her put on her seat belt and smiled. We had discovered only weeks ago that we were going to have a baby, and now her pregnancy was beginning to show. My insides almost split open over the joy this brought me. I put my right hand in hers.

"Who was it?" I asked, pulling slowly out of our drive and into the dark snowy night.

"Wendy Christianson," Charity answered.

Charity, with the help of her uncle who was a professor at BYU, had managed to get Wendy into the Y at the last minute.

"How's she doing?"

"She's engaged to some thirty-five-year-old, not-so-recently-returned missionary."

"You're kidding?"

"Nope."

"How does her mom feel?" I asked.

"She's thrilled," Charity answered, as I pulled out onto the main road.

"Amazing," I said, commenting on far more than just Wendy.

There was a good-sized crowd at our building when we arrived. We got out and listened to Ian as he gave directions.

"We were going to sing to some of our inactives," he said. "But this snow will make it almost impossible to reach any of their homes."

"Let's just have the refreshments and go home," Brother Hatch yelled through shivering teeth. "I brought bananas and dairy-free eggnog."

A couple of people "Ayed" in agreement.

"Wait," Sister Lynn said. "I don't know about the rest of you, but I came to sing."

"Me, too," I yelled.

"It's not like us to let a little snow stop us," Sister Benderholden argued.

Brother Hatch looked at his eggnog and bananas. "This stuff will hold," he declared.

"All right then," Ian said. "To whom shall we sing?"

"We could sing to Fern and Erma," Sister North suggested. "They live close enough that we could walk. They've been so interested in the construction of our new building that I think they might like us stopping by."

Ian and I exchanged glances.

Orvil pulled up and helped his wife, Sherry, get out. Martin got out of Orvil's car and helped his wife, Loni, out as well. The full-time missionaries climbed out of the back hatch of Orvil's car. They all came over and joined our merry band.

"We're going to sing to Fern," Brother Crimsal said excitedly to no one in particular as we all marched to Fern's place. I smiled, amazed that Brother Crimsal was the same person I had met last summer.

The snow fell softly while we sang as one outside of the Slush & Bait shop. Fern and Erma came to the door and stood silently watching. Bob drove by on his nightly patrol and waved and everyone waved back. Bob then flicked on his patrol lights, which added to the ambiance of the night. The red lights flashing against the white flakes created a festive atmosphere.

I couldn't stop myself from crying. For twenty-nine Christmases I had been alone, always yearning for what seemed impossible—always looking around the corner in hopes of finding heaven. Who would have known it was here in Longwinded? I wouldn't be shocked in the least if the ten tribes and Enoch all had some grand reunion here someday—I hoped to still be around when that happened.

I looked up at the snow and let it fall against my burning face. Angels accompanied the flakes as they fell, filling our voices with beautiful music. I put my arms around Charity's waist and my future child. I then kissed Charity with passion on the back of her neck. She turned and kissed me.

"Sing," she said, and I did.

> Then pealed the bells more loud and deep:
> "God is not dead, nor doth he sleep;
> The wrong shall fail, the right prevail,
> With peace on earth, good will to men."

Charity's hair blew into my face, hiding my wet eyes. We sang until our throats were sore and our souls were full.

ABOUT THE AUTHOR

Robert Smith lives in Albuquerque, New Mexico, with his wife, Krista, and daughters, Kindred Anne, Phoebe Hope, Naomi Rose, and his son Bennett Williams. Robert has written his whole life, and among his many achievements he lists his first-place paper about the American flag that he wrote while in the sixth grade. The five dollars he won for his entry still spurs him on.

OTHER BOOKS BY ROBERT FARRELL SMITH

The Trust Williams Trilogy
    Book 1: *All Is Swell: Trust in Thelma's Way*
    Book 2: *Falling for Grace: Trust at the End of
        the World*
    Book 3: *Love's Labor Tossed: Trust and the
        Final Fling*

For Time and All Absurdity

Captain Matrimony

The Miracle of Forgetness